SORCERERS ALWAYS SATISFY

A Hidden Species Novel

LOUISA MASTERS

Sorcerers Always Satisfy

Copyright © 2021 by Louisa Masters

Cover: Booksmith Design

Editor: Hot Tree Editing

SORCERERS ALWAYS SATISFY

Just because I enjoy planning and researching doesn't mean I'm not the most dangerous badass mothercracker around.

The world sees me as boring, dependable David. And I like it that way. I *know* *things* and I'm *organized.* Plus, I've seen firsthand the harm a chaotic life can inflict, and I'd rather have my lists and be called dull.

Which is what makes it all the more disconcerting when a sexy elf declares his adoration and begins to "woo" me. What am I supposed to do?

Hide, mostly. It's hard, though, because Caolan and I are supposed to be working together. And he's tough to resist: sweet, competent, and so incredibly beautiful. He sees something in me that no one else does. Would it really be such a bad thing if I gave in to temptation?

But my personal life can't be the priority right now. The bad guys are gearing up to strike, and if we don't stop them, the end of the world could be nigh. I need to focus on that, not on letting Caolan show me the benefits of spontaneity. Why don't world-ending disasters come with an instruction manual?

<hr>

CAST OF CHARACTERS

<hr>

Community of Species Government - CSG

Malia - God, Head of State of the Spiritual Plane
Percy Caraway (felid shifter) - the Lucifer: Head of
State of the Physical Plane

Senior Investigation Team:
Sam Tiller (human/felid shifter) - Gideon's boyfriend
[Demons Do It Better]
Gideon Bailey (demon) - Sam's boyfriend [Demons
Do It Better]
Elinor Martin (hellhound)
David Carew (sorcerer)
Lily Heath (succubus) – killed by Tish
Andrew Turner (vampire) – Noah's boyfriend [One
Bite With A Vampire]
Alistair Smythe (hellhound) - Aidan's boyfriend
[Hijinks With A Hellhound]

Noah Cage (human) - CSG intern, Andrew's boyfriend [One Bite With A Vampire]
Aidan Byrne (felid shifter) - Shifter Species Leader, Alistair's boyfriend [Hijinks With A Hellhound]
Kirsch (demon) - Security
Rabhya (felid shifter) - Head of PR dept.
Candice (demon) - Receptionist

Caolan of Ebenkreis (elf) - King's Delegate
Garin (elf) - warfare specialist
Eerika (elf) - historian
King Radulfr (elf) - King of the Elves
Brandt (dragon) - Dragon Wing Leader
Dustin (dragon) - Grandson of the Dragon Wing Leader
Hagen (dragon)
Gytha (dragonet)

Coalition for Community Advancement - CCA
Terrorist organization responsible for genetic manipulation experiments

Dr Francis Tish (sorcerer) - Lead scientist; Sam and Noah's childhood doctor
Éibhear of Kesmegan (elf) - Responsible for the destruction of a dimension. Plotting to take over the world.

CHAPTER ONE

David

I RUN my eye over my list one last time. It looks like we've covered everything, so I ask, "Any questions?"

The people on the team I put together to facilitate the migration of two species from one dimension to another smile and shrug and shake their heads—not that I expected anything else. These people are the best at what they do. You could put them in the middle of any natural disaster with nothing but a pencil, and within hours things would be organized. With money and resources, there's nothing they can't do. They got a single-page briefing memo last night and came to the meeting this morning with reams of research and information ready to go. Their questions have already been asked and answered. I have no doubt they'll have a solid plan and timeline ready by the time I get back.

I'm so fucking jealous.

Putting aside the fact that this project only exists because the remnants of a once-great civilization will be wiped out otherwise, it's exactly the kind of thing I love to do. Lots of things to organize, endless details, a time restriction… give it to me, baby. But I don't have time to indulge myself right now, which is why I'm handing over the heavy lifting to the four incredibly talented people in front of me.

"Great. I hope to have more information about the refugees' needs later today, and I'll get that to you as soon as I can. Or, if we're lucky, I'll be able to bring you a species representative. In the meantime, I'm going to be away from my devices, so direct any questions to Sam and prepare to be patient."

There's a wave of nods and a chorus of agreement, and then the meeting breaks up and they head off to find homes, jobs, and everything else that's needed for two hundred thousand immigrants that we need to hide from the humans.

I follow them out of the meeting room and set off at a brisk pace for my team's office. I need to check in with Sam and Noah before my meeting with Percy, and then I'm going through a portal to another dimension to meet the king of the elves. Because that's just my life now.

Shaking my head, I wonder if there's time to grab something to eat. I missed breakfast this morning—entirely my own fault. I've been so busy lately that the commute back to my place—a whole thirty minutes—isn't time I'm willing to give up, so I've been sleeping on the really comfortable couch in Percy's office. Unfortunately, that means I can't just grab food on my way to and from work, and sometimes I get caught up in what I'm doing and forget to eat.

"David!"

Nope. No time for food.

Holding back a sigh, I stop and let Kirsch from security catch up.

"Got a sec?" he asks.

"Sure. Just one, though."

He launches into a hurried rundown on the latest attempts to infiltrate our security. It's only been thirty-something hours since we realized what the bad guys' evil plan is, but in that time, they've made several strikes. Our guess is they're trying to stop us before we can begin the migration, because once we have the elves and dragons (yeah, that's right) here, we'll have a huge advantage, even if we don't know the details of what they're up to.

"We're holding steady," he concludes. "Having the elves' help is making a big difference. We didn't even know we had to defend against elf spellcasting before—or that it existed. That's where our system was failing, trying to defend against stuff we didn't know about. Now, it's working perfectly."

"Great news," I tell him. It really is. I've been low-level uneasy about security breaches for almost a year, ever since we realized there was a leak in our office. No matter what we did since then, it kept recurring. Now, though, we know it was the result of an elf spellcaster modifying a sorcerer's weaves—some very clever espionage work that I'd like to examine more closely when I get the time. It took our new elf allies a very short time to identify the rogue spells.

"You're going to… uh, go over there today, right?" he asks, glancing around. This hallway should be secure, but we're trying to keep the whole other-dimension thing on a need-to-know basis for now. Ultimately it's going to be kind of moot, because once we bring the elves and dragons over, nobody's going there ever again. We don't know exactly how long it will be until the whole dimension collapses, although the elves seem to think less than a year.

"Yeah, in about an hour," I confirm, trying to sound confident and secure and not like a kid who's going to Disney World. Can you blame me for being a bit excited? It's another fucking dimension. How often am I likely to get an opportunity to see another dimension?

Probably never again.

The science nerd in me can't wait.

"I don't like it," Kirsch admits. "I wish you'd take a team with you."

"What?" I blink, surprised. "Why would I need a team?"

"For protection." The *duh* is heavily implied.

"I'm a combat sorcerer," I remind him. "I'm the one who does the protecting." Not that anyone will need to be protected. I'm going to meet the elf king so we can make plans to save his people. It's a peaceful diplomatic meeting—the worst that will happen is my pen running out of ink because I'm taking too many notes.

I'll have a backup pen, of course.

"Huh, you are. I always forget that. I'll get a report written up," he promises and strides away, leaving me feeling vaguely frustrated. Just because I enjoy planning and researching doesn't mean I'm not the most dangerous badass motherfucker around. If anything, it makes me *more* dangerous, because I *know things* and I'm organized. For instance, I'm one of only a handful of combat sorcerers in the world who know about the weaves of the Camaranth Assassins, a long-extinct society of—you guessed it—assassins. Most people didn't know they existed even when they did exist. Nearly three thousand years later, they're all but forgotten, except by people who like to research. Like me. That makes me deadly and dangerous.

And also a whiny baby, if my thoughts are anything to go by.

I make myself let it go and continue toward my office. If people want to forget that I'm a physical threat, well, that plays in my favor.

"…important to check there isn't some bizarre mating ritual. What if they're like giraffes, who smell each other's urine to know if they're ready to mate?"

Again? I stop in the office doorway. This happens way too often. For a while, I even wondered if there was a camera in the hallway and they were deliberately baiting me with these weird conversations. Then I realized that's just the type of people they are. My closest friends and colleagues, the ones who have my back and who I rely on in the direst of situations, are the type of people who sit around discussing giraffe mating rituals, degrees of best-friendship, and anal beads.

It doesn't make sense to me either. But I wouldn't change it.

"Alistair, you're not allowed to adopt a giraffe," I say, channeling as much authority as I can. "No giraffes." I'm not sure why they were discussing giraffe sex, but it's best to cut these things off before they turn into full-fledged plots. I learned that the hard way.

Surprisingly, my colleagues all jump away from their huddle around Sam's desk, looking varying degrees of guilty.

Uh-oh.

"What's going on?" I ask, crossing to my desk and waking up my computer.

"Nothing's going on," Sam sputters. "Why would you think there's something going on? Nothing!"

Uh-huh.

I look over at him, and he must guess that I'm suspicious—who wouldn't be—because he lifts a takeout cup from his desk and holds it out to me. "Coffee? Still hot. And look, fruit toast! Also still warm." He gestures with his free hand to a paper bag stamped with the name of the coffee place down the street. Their fruit toast is my favorite, and now that I'm thinking about it, I can smell it… along with the melted butter smeared on top.

My stomach growls.

"Thanks," I say, trying not to sound desperate and pitifully grateful as I go over to take it. I don't want any of them guessing that I've been sleeping in Percy's office. "What's the occasion?"

"What do you mean?" Sam asks innocently—*fake* innocently—as I take a sip of the coffee and try not to moan.

"Well, you don't normally bring in breakfast." I glance around at the staring eyes of my friends. Yeah, this isn't suspicious at all. "Has everyone else had theirs already? How is mine still hot?" Are they trying to soften me up so they can breed giraffes or something? Because as weird as that sounds, I wouldn't put it past Alistair and Andrew.

"Is it good?" Andrew asks, strangely intent. If I didn't know they'd never do such a thing, I'd wonder if they'd drugged my coffee.

Although, just because they'd never drug it doesn't

mean they haven't put something else in it. I draw back for a second and examine the cup.

Meh. Who cares? It still tastes good.

"Yeah, sure. It's good. What's going on?"

"And the toast?" Ellie pushes, a gleam of laughter in her gaze. "You haven't had the toast."

Yeah, okay, I can't keep ignoring this. I put the cup down on Sam's desk, and—I kid you not—they all *groan*. Even Gideon!

"What have you done to my food?" I demand. "Don't screw with me."

"We didn't do anything," Alistair protests, giving me puppy eyes. You'd think it would look ridiculous coming from a six-foot-five tank of a man, but he always pulls it off. Must be the hellhound in him.

"Then why are you all watching me like I'm about to ingest the formula for eternal life? And nobody answered me before—what's the occasion?"

Suddenly, all gazes are averted as an awkward silence falls.

I sigh.

"Fine," Noah says abruptly. "Sam didn't buy you breakfast. Caolan brought it for you. He left a note too. I had to write it for him because the translation spell doesn't work with written language." He holds up a folded piece of paper. It doesn't escape me that Alistair and Andrew both watch that paper like it's made of pure gold. "I didn't let any of these idiots see it, though."

I take the folded paper and stare at it for a long second before shoving it in my pants pocket. How is this my life?

Really. Is the magic testing me? Did I offend it somehow? I've always considered myself to be a good person. Hardworking. Dedicated to protecting and caring for the community. But I must have done something to piss off the magic for it to be putting me through this now.

It can't be something I did in a past life—I've had a past life regression, and I know they say it's the soul that's eternal, not the personality, but my soul must be pretty damn stubborn, because I wasn't that different in any of my past lives. Dependable. Sensible. Or as some would put it, boring.

I'm okay with that. Boring people live longer and are less likely to have knife-wielding one-night stands burst into their place of work shrieking about being done wrong (*cough* Alistair *cough*). I have my home, my interesting and hectic job, and a small group of people I know I can trust to be there, whether I need them or not. My life was perfectly ordered, just the way I like it.

Until recently. Until portals between dimensions were opened for the first time in nine thousand years and the elves came through.

Well… one elf. Only one elf makes me want to hide under my desk and hope to go unnoticed.

Caolan of Ebenkreis.

It's ridiculous. I'm a 463-year-old lauded combat sorcerer with a wide range of subspecialties, and a member of the most senior team in the Community of Species Government. I answer only to the lucifer. People defer to me as a matter of course. Some of them are even *afraid* of me—mostly the ones who've pissed me off in the past. Calm and dependable doesn't mean I can't wreak havoc when I want to.

But this one elf makes me want to flee in terror.

He claims to be *in love with me.*

Don't get me wrong. It's not that I don't consider myself a loveable person. I am. I've been in loving relationships before. There's no reason why someone shouldn't fall in love with me. But Caolan claims to have fallen in love the moment he saw me. That just doesn't happen. People who "fall in love" that quickly fall right back out just as quickly when the shine wears off—believe me, I have experience being a no-longer-shiny subject of "love." But in the meantime, Caolan declared in front of my boss and colleagues—some of whom will *never* let me forget it—that I'm the most beautiful creature he's ever seen. He stares at me *all the time*, and even though I've known him less than two days, on three separate occasions he's dropped to one knee to tell me he worships at the altar of my glory.

What the fuck does that even mean?

And I guess now he's bringing me gifts.

The whole situation is made tougher because my friends are delighted by it all and are actively encouraging him. Just to put that in context, we have Alistair and Elinor, who are hellhounds—need I say more?—Andrew, a vampire born in the middle ages who would fit right in at a college frat party, Sam, a hopeless romantic whose intimidating boyfriend, Gideon, tries to make sure he gets everything he wants, and Noah, a twenty-year-old human who wants to learn more about elven dating rituals and is sacrificing me to further his education. Oh, and did I forget to mention my boss and longtime friend, Percy, the lucifer? Officially, he told Caolan there could be no relationship between us because we're ambassadors for our respective peoples, but he seems to be constantly coming up with reasons for me to meet with Caolan, or for

Caolan to be invited to meetings he really doesn't need to be at.

It's all a bit suspicious.

But the worst part? The absolute worst part?

At first glance, Caolan ticks all my boxes. Even the ones I didn't know I had.

So you can see why this is a disaster, right? How am I supposed to organize and oversee the migration of his people to Earth *and* do my bit to prevent Tish and Éibhear (our supervillains du jour) from taking over the world *and* keep the whole thing secret from the humans if I'm all distracted by my hormones?

It can't be done.

Wait, wait… I was wrong. That wasn't the worst part. The worst part?

Elves don't keep time.

I'm the kind of guy whose daily planner is neatly filled out in fifteen-minute blocks. I keep a regular schedule for all things in my life. If you're organized, it's easier to deal with emergencies when they crop up.

Elves, on the other hand, break the day up into six parts: morning, midday, afternoon, early night, midnight, and late night. How can anyone keep a reasonable schedule when you can't set appointment times? In less than two days, Caolan and the two other elves who are already here have been late for meetings nearly a dozen times. It's doing my head in. In fact, on my to-do list for later today is a trip to a department store so I can buy them all watches. That might be the only way to save my sanity.

"David?"

I snap back to the present and meet Noah's questioning gaze.

"Why did Caolan bring me coffee and toast?" If you were suddenly living in another dimension that you had very little familiarity with, would you know that coffee (or its interdimensional equivalent) is the perfect gift?

Wait, that doesn't make sense.

I pick up the cup and sip. I need more coffee.

"Because he wanted you to have a hearty breakfast?" Andrew suggests with that wicked gleam in his eye that he gets when he's causing trouble.

"Because he's courting you!" Alistair sounds far too delighted by that fact.

"Uh-huh. But why specifically coffee—a double-shot latte, my favorite—and fruit toast, which I also love? How did he know to get those items? And where to get them from? And where did he get the money to buy them?"

The treacherous bastards say nothing. Andrew looks up at the ceiling. Ellie looks at her nails. Alistair widens his eyes as much as he can, looking not so much inno-cent as deranged.

"Don't be so suspicious, David," Sam says, sounding so guilty that I'm surprised he's not shrieking a confes-sion. "Maybe he cast a spell or something."

"A spell that creates money?" I challenge.

"That'd be a neat trick," Gideon mutters, and it's such a ridiculous thing to hear from a scion of one of the wealthiest families in the community that we all turn to look at him.

"Is having so much money that you could literally use it as toilet paper and still never run out not enough for you?" Andrew asks. Gideon flips him the bird.

"Don't try to distract David," he says. "He asked you some questions."

"Traitor!" Alistair gasps. "How could you throw us under the bus like that?"

"That was kind of a douche thing to do," Sam tells his boyfriend. "I mean, I still love you, but I'm seriously reconsidering what secrets to tell you."

"You've already told me all your secrets. And David's smart enough to already know the answers to those questions. All I did was skip us past the part where we pretend to be innocent and deny everything." He straightens Sam's stapler.

"Okay," I interject, because this could go on for a long time. "Let's pretend I spent fifteen minutes—which none of us has to spare today—wheedling the truth out of you." Giving in to the demands of my stomach, I rip open the paper bag containing the fruit toast and take a huge bite from one piece. Fuck me, nothing's better than that. I close my eyes to savor the taste and hold back a moan.

"Did we stay strong until the end?" Alistair asks. "What finally broke us?"

"And more importantly, do you want some time alone with that toast? Fuck, David, we need to get you laid."

I open my eyes and glare at Andrew. He smirks back.

"Isn't that what we're doing?" Noah demands impatiently. "Stop being an asshat, Andrew, so we can convince David this is a good thing."

"Yeah, Andrew, stop being an asshat," Alistair chimes in, switching sides instantly. "You're David's best friend forever. That means you have to be nice to him while you're manipulating his life for his own good."

Sam swivels in his chair and squints at Alistair. "It

concerns me greatly that you think it's the job of a BFF to manipulate lives."

Alistair rolls his eyes. "And yet you had no problem suggesting that Caolan buy David breakfast," he counters.

I switch my focus to Sam. "Oh, Sam." I shake my head. Truthfully, I'm enjoying this toast too much to be truly upset. I mean, convincing Caolan that I'm not his one true love or whatever will be harder if my friends are encouraging him, but it's tough to be mad at them for telling him to bring me toast and coffee.

"At least this way you get to eat," Sam counters. "It's not good for you to be skipping breakfast."

Uh-oh.

"I don't skip breakfast." I shove the rest of the piece of toast in my mouth, just in case he takes that as a challenge and confiscates my food.

Elinor laughs outright. "Do you seriously think we don't know you've been sleeping in Percy's office?"

Crap. Do they actually know, or are they guessing?

"Don't be ridiculous." I wave my hand as though the very thought is absurd. "I have a very comfortable bed at home. Why would I sleep in Percy's office?"

Six disbelieving gazes fix on me.

"We could have a very lively debate about this," Andrew says, "and I'd enjoy that very much, but as you pointed out before, none of us has the time today, so here's our trump card: we set up a spy cam to catch you in the act."

That sound you hear is my head exploding.

"You set up a spy cam in Percy's office? Are you *insane*?" My brain scrambles through the many issues this could cause. "Did you at least clear it with Percy and security first?"

Gideon holds out his hand, palm up, and wiggles his fingers. "Pay up." Andrew and Ellie hand over cash, grumbling all the while.

I look over at a chuckling Noah in stunned horror. "Do I even want to know?"

"They thought you'd freak over us recording you sleeping. Gideon said you'd care more about the security side."

"I don't even know where to start," I mutter, shaking my head. "Wait, yes I do. Get that camera out of Percy's office right now. How long has it been there? Do you not understand how much classified information gets talked about in there?"

"Relax," Ellie chides. "It was only there for one night. Percy knew all about it and switched it off when he got in yesterday morning." She sniffs. "We'd never risk a security breach." Somehow, she manages to sound offended, like she wasn't just part of the most stupid, hare-brained scheme—

Wait, that's not true. They've done dumber shit before.

I throw back the last of my coffee. Thankfully, it's not too hot anymore.

"Okay, fine. The last few days, I've slept on Percy's couch to save time on the commute."

"You could crash at our place," Sam points out. "It's a lot closer than yours, and the guest suite is more comfortable than Percy's office."

"You have a guest at the moment," I point out. I'm *not* crawling into bed with Caolan—he doesn't need that kind of encouragement. Which reminds me…

"Let's get back to the whole thing where you told Caolan to bring me breakfast."

Alistair claps his hands. "We're helping him woo you! He wanted to know the best way to show you how much you mean to him, since the declarations of love seem to send you fleeing in terror."

I want to bang my head against the wall, but it's too far away. "I don't mean anything to him. We met two days ago. We've barely spoken, and none of it's been personal." Declarations of adoration aside. "He shouldn't be *wooing* me, and you sure as fuck shouldn't be helping him." I stop and take a breath. That got a little heated.

My friends are staring at me. Alistair's eyes are wide, and there's a delighted grin on Andrew's stupid face.

"Did you just raise your voice?" he asks. "You did! Something got under your skin enough for you to raise your voice. *Caolan* got under your skin. The wooage is working!"

Seriously, *how is this my life?*

"Wooage is not a word." It's the only thing I can think to say. Noah groans.

"Oh my god, that's not going to discourage them, David. They're sharks, and you just went swimming with an open wound."

What?

"What?" Sam asks him. He shrugs.

"It seemed like a good analogy at the time."

My phone chimes discreetly. It's the five-minute alert for my meeting with Percy. "This has taken up way too much time," I say. Fuck it, I needed to review with Noah and Sam. I look at them. "Have you both got things under control? Do you need anything from me?"

Sam nods, and Noah shakes his head.

"We're good," he assures me. "Eerika is coming back in today, so you can tell the migration management team that they can call me with questions about what the elves might need. I know it's not a perfect solution, but until you get an elf liaison, it's something."

"Yes. Thank you. That's a great idea. I'll call—"

"I'll call and let them know," Sam cuts in. "We'll hold down the office. You go to your meeting. I'm stealing half an hour this evening, though, for us all to debrief. I think it's important we have the chance to talk and bounce theories. We can do it over food at Gideon's and my place."

"We can?" Gideon asks. Sam gives him a look, and he nods. "We can." This time, he sounds glum. I almost smile, but part of me is worried they're somehow going to turn that meeting against me. Still, Sam's right—we work best as a team, and we need to be together for that.

"Fine. Add it to my calendar. I better not get there to find you've all fucked off and left me with Caolan and a romantic dinner for two."

"Oooh," Alistair says, and Sam throws a pen at him.

"Cross my heart," he promises me. "Although if I'd thought of that first, I probably would have done it. But we really do need to catch up, so that will have to wait."

I'm not entirely sure I can trust him, but I don't have time to continue this conversation right now. "Okay. I'll be out of range for most of the day, so I'm routing my calls to you."

He nods. "I'm on it. Between me and Noah, we can handle the office. Relax. Go."

Andrew laughs. "Like David could ever relax. It's one of the things we love about him."

I don't bother to tell him he doesn't make sense, just drop the empty coffee cup in Sam's wastebasket, flip Andrew the bird, and head for the hallway. Gideon and Alistair, who are both part of this meeting, follow me out.

"You mad?" Gideon asks in a low voice, shocking me. It's not that he doesn't care—he does. He's actually a great friend. But he's a silent, stoic friend who'd rather we all went away. He doesn't usually ask that sort of thing.

"Why would he be mad?" Alistair demands. "He's living the plot of an epic movie. A brave hero fighting to save the world and win the love of an elf. All the *Lord of the Rings* fans would be going nuts if they knew about this. You have your very own Legolas!"

A sharp pain stabs behind my right eye.

"Shut up, Alistair," Gideon growls, then mutters, "Want me to run interference with Caolan?"

I stop dead in the hallway, my jaw dropping as I turn to face him. He shrugs uncomfortably.

"You'd still have to handle all the official stuff, but I could try to head off the declarations of love. Maybe I could stop the poetry too."

"Noooo! Not the poetry!" Alistair wails.

Poetry? There's going to be poetry?

Shaking my head to clear that thought, I manage a smile—for Gideon, not Alistair. He's still blathering on about "the unique ingenuity of elvish poetry."

"Leave it for now. As you say, I still need to be on good terms with him for the official stuff. If it starts to get out of hand, I might take you up on that."

"Anytime," he says firmly. "I don't want you to think we don't have your back."

"Of course we have your back," Alistair says, suddenly dead serious. "If you really, truly want Caolan to back off, I can have a word with him. He and I are bros now. We just also want you to be happy. You deserve to have a nice man lavishing attention on you and licking your toes."

I honestly don't know what to make of that. Is it something Caolan has said to him, or is Alistair just making shit up in his offbeat way? Or maybe it's something he and his significant other, Aidan, like to do. With Alistair, it's hard to tell.

So I just nod. "Thanks. I'll, uh, think about it and let you know."

"So I think that's everything," I say half an hour later, rechecking my list. Aside from a quick update for Percy, this meeting's been about my upcoming trip through a portal. Percy wanted to go himself, but we all vetoed that idea. No way were we letting the lucifer enter an unstable dimension that's ripping itself apart. Which means I got nominated to be our ambassador to the king of the elves—not that he's likely to be anything but thrilled to meet me. After all, I'm literally going to be there so we can plan the best way to save his people from extinction. But it's the first time there's been official contact between our dimensions for nine thousand years, so it's important I don't fuck it up. Especially since we all forgot that the elves actually exist and aren't just myth. A lot of what Noah and Eerika talked about yesterday was the etiquette stuff I'm going to need today.

But we've covered that. Percy's also given me a shortlist of things he wants me to tell the king, and another shortlist of things he wants me to try to suss out for future discussions. Gideon and Alistair had their own lists for me, which were less about diplomacy and more about military and intelligence. They're both keen to get as many fighters across as possible before Tish and Éibhear strike again.

So we should be done here, just waiting for Caolan to arrive and open the portal. Except Gideon and Percy are exchanging a look. You know, one of *those* looks. The one that means they've discussed something behind my back and feel that now is the time to unleash whatever it is that's going to piss me off. I'm a little surprised— usually I'm the one exchanging that look with Percy. I don't think he's kept anything secret from me since I first joined the team.

"Just one more thing," he says in his calm, soothing way. Part of that comes from him being the lucifer, but not many people know he always had this gift for making people feel better. I've known him since before the magic chose him to be the lucifer, and he's always been better than any drug on the market. "Gideon's coming with you."

I say nothing while I process that. "Okay. Why?" Don't get me wrong, I'm thrilled to have Gideon as a teammate—I was the one who suggested recruiting him. He's insightful, intelligent, and dependable, as long as you don't want him to represent the team at a community outreach night. But I don't need his help with this. And more to the point, he's needed here today.

They exchange glances again. Alistair looks studiously at the table.

"For your safety," Gideon says bluntly. "We vetoed Percy going because we can't guarantee his safety, and the same applies to you. We'd all be a lot happier if someone else could go instead, but there's nobody who has the necessary skills *and* enough seniority to negotiate in Percy's stead."

This day has just been a complete clusterfuck, and it's not even ten o'clock yet. I try to get my head around what they're telling me.

"I appreciate your concern for my well-being," I begin carefully, then toss aside the idea of being diplomatic. It's Gideon, after all, and we don't have time to pussyfoot around the issue. "I can take care of myself."

"We know," Percy says. "None of us doubts that. But if something bad happens, you'll be outnumbered. Having Gideon there gives you someone to watch your back, at the very least."

"What's going on here?" I demand. "We need Gideon *here* today, not following me around like an overqualified bodyguard. If you're really that concerned about me being there alone, I'll take someone from security, or an enforcer. We can't spare Gideon—or Alistair, or anyone else from the team," I add, just in case they get that bright idea. I'm a little miffed that they've been discussing this but deliberately left me out.

Percy hesitates. "It has to be Gideon. If things go truly bad, he can teleport you out of there. We don't have any other demon with as much strength and the right security clearance."

Teleport me from another dimension? It's been done, of course, but it nearly killed Noah. Plus, he's human. We don't know if demons could replicate it or if they're limited to same-dimensional teleportation. And it's really not something you want to experiment with under pressure, what with the whole risk of death and all.

I pinch the bridge of my nose. "Do you really think that would be a good idea? Really," I repeat. "Someone tell me what's going on. Has the magic given you a hint that there might be a problem? Because I don't understand why you'd waste Gideon's time like this *and* risk potentially losing both of us if something does go wrong."

Percy and Gideon exchange glances again, and it's enough to make me want to yell.

"You guys are doing this wrong," Alistair says, leaning forward. "I'm taking over."

Alarm flashes across their faces, but before they can say anything, he continues.

"It's like this, David. You're Percy's second-in-command, and a lot of things would go to shit if something happened to you. That makes you a valuable resource, which means your safety is worth taking Gideon's time and risking him. Although we all hope that doesn't become an issue, because Sam likes him and we need Sam to be happy, not all mopey and shit."

Fucking Alistair and his jokes. "I'm not Percy's second-in-command," I begin, but Percy makes a face, and I stop. "What?"

He shrugs. "I was going to get you to sign the papers to make it official last year," he admits. "But when we were at the CCA compound to rescue Sam, that one enforcer said you were in charge when I wasn't around —do you remember? And you went ballistic at him."

"In your own way," Alistair chips in. "Because ballistic for you is mildly irritated for everyone else."

Would anyone really care if I smacked him?

My phone chimes with the reminder that it's time to meet Caolan for the trip to his world. I stand.

"I don't have time for this right now. Nothing's going to happen, and—"

"Sit down," Percy orders, and it's so unusual to hear that tone from him that I find myself planting my ass back in the chair without even thinking about it.

"Look," Gideon begins, "believe it or not, we're not trying to make all the shit you're doing harder for you. You've been unofficially Percy's second-in-command for a long time, probably close on ten years." He holds up a hand when I open my mouth to argue. "You want to say that we're a team, that we're all equals, but that's bull-shit. You're our go-to guy. You know more about CSG than anyone. Everyone comes to you when they have something they're not sure if they should bring to Percy. And you're the first person people look for when there's a major issue. The thing is, it was fine for all that to be unofficial before. None of us wanted the additional responsibility, and everyone at CSG knows the way things work. None of us cared all that much about what your title was." He stops. "If we were better people, we probably would have said something to you so you could negotiate a higher salary."

Now there's a thought. Although, my current salary is more than sufficient for my needs. It's not like I have expensive hobbies—I don't have time for hobbies.

"But now we're in the middle of the fuckup to end all fuckups," he continues. "Things that we could let slide before now need to be addressed. If the situation gets out of control and something happens to Percy, or we need to put him in secure lockdown, there needs to be a clear chain of command. We can't have people wondering who they should take orders from, you or their species leader or whoever they see as an authority figure. It needs to be you, and it needs to be official."

He has a point. We've never needed to think about it before, because things have been smooth sailing for centuries—and nobody's ever before tried to upset the order of our reality. That's a new crisis.

"Why can't it be you?" Or anyone else.

For a second, I think he's going to leap across the table and rip my throat out. Gideon doesn't have a lot of patience. Great guy, though. Exactly who you want backing you up when you take on the forces of evil. His glare alone could make them reconsider.

Alistair saves me from death by demon when he bravely—foolishly?—puts a restraining hand on Gideon's arm. "We need him alive, remember? Or it really might end up being you." As Gideon sucks in a (calming?) breath, Alistair turns to me.

"You're not listening, David. It can't be Gideon because it already *is* you. You're doing the job, just without the title and the paycheck."

The practical side of me has to concede that what they're saying is true. The stubborn side, though, doesn't want to accept it. Too bad I pride myself on being practical.

Sighing, I nod. "What do you want from me?"

Percy pushes over his tablet. The document on the screen is the standard addendum to employment contracts that we use when someone gets promoted or changes departments at CSG. It shows the new job title, a brief job description, and the updated salary and benefits. I skim over the first page, trying not to wince when I notice that the job description is a pretty accurate summary of my workday, then flip to the next page and can't hold in the low whistle when I see the dollar figure.

"Are you sure that's not overpaying me?"

Alistair rolls his eyes. "Are you seriously arguing about being paid *too much*?"

"It's not too much," Percy says before I can reply. "It's actually at the lower end of the scale for the role and your experience, but I figured you'd prefer the extra money be used for one of the outreach programs."

He really does know me too well.

"Why don't you put the rest into programs as well?" I suggest. "Everything above my current salary."

"No" is his firm reply. "If you decide you want to donate, that's your call, but CSG is paying you at least somewhat close to what you're worth. Use the extra to find a place closer to the office so you don't end up crashing here all the time." The level look he aims my way tells me we'll be discussing that in more detail later. And here I was thinking I'd been so sneaky.

Huffing, I grab the stylus he's holding out, sign the doc, date it, and enter my employee ID and password when the little box pops up. There. It's official. I'm now continuing to do my job.

"Are we good? The king is expecting us."

"The king is expecting you sometime in the morning," Percy counters dryly. "And we'll all be surprised if Caolan is actually here and waiting already."

"You're feeling sassy today," I point out, and he laughs.

"I'm enjoying this. It's not often I get to turn the tables on you. Now, about Gideon coming with you."

"It's really not necessary," I protest. Percy just grins, somewhat evilly. It's Gideon who speaks.

"That's no longer your decision to make. Being Percy's second puts you in the command hierarchy, which means that determining the danger level of any given situation and deciding whether it merits additional protection or force is my and Alistair's job. And Andrew's, Ellie's—even Sam's."

I blink. "I'm a member of the team myself. That doesn't apply to me." The act of law he's referring to gives us seniority over pretty much everyone, including Percy, when decisions need to be made to ensure their protection.

"It applies," Alistair tells me cheerfully. "We checked. In a situation where the lucifer is under threat, all members of the hierarchy are immediately put under increased guard and are subject to protection orders." He smirks. "And we decided after Noah was kidnapped that there was a direct threat to Percy. Remember? We all agreed, and you were the one who sent out the directive to increase protection for him and the species leaders."

I remember, of course. And I stand by our decision. I just didn't think it would be biting me in the ass like this.

"Funny how you didn't mention this until after I'd signed the paperwork accepting the job title."

Gideon holds up his hands, palms out. "To be fair, we did tell you what we wanted from the beginning. Making it your legal obligation was our fallback."

I can't hold back a chuckle, even though I hate that they've manipulated me like this. "Fine," I concede. "Gideon comes with me. But teleportation is an absolutely last resort," I warn him. "I'm not risking you unless we're both facing imminent death, okay?"

"Fine by me," he agrees.

Percy smiles and nods. "Thank you, David. That will set my mind at ease."

Yep, now I feel like a pile of cat crap for making him worry. Pushing the guilt aside to deal with later—probably when he's piling on more over the whole sleeping at the office thing—I stand again. "Then we'd better get going."

"You should read the note first," Alistair suggests.

"What note?" I wish I could tell you I mean that, but I don't. I'm just trying to throw him off the scent. I know *exactly* what note he's talking about. It's been burning a hole in my pocket since I put it there.

Because it could cause diplomatic problems if I don't deal with it properly, of course. Not because I want to read it.

"The note Caolan left with your breakfast."

I should try to remember that Alistair cannot be thrown off the scent. Stubbornness, thy name is hellhound.

"What's this?" There's a note of delighted intrigue in Percy's voice as he leans forward. Then he clears his throat. "I mean, David, if you're engaging in overnight visits with—"

"Oh, stop. You know I slept here last night—I've heard all about your little spy camera."

The lucifer of all species looks crestfallen before he hides it. "Good. We need to be, uh, professional. So what's this about breakfast?"

"I mentioned to Aidan that poor David is so overworked that he's been sleeping at the office," Alistair said. "Aidan must have said something to Caolan about it, because this morning he came to the office and said he was worried about David not looking after himself properly and wanting to know if there was anything he could do. Sam suggested he could bring David breakfast."

"And he did? Oh, what a lovely gesture." Percy lays a hand over his heart and sighs.

Kill. Me. Now.

"Did you say there was a note?" The wide brown eyes of one of my oldest friends fix on me. I briefly wish I'd hit him with the cricket bat that one time I almost did when we were children. "Have you read it yet?"

"No. And I'm not planning to. Caolan and I need to remain on a professional footing. If his gift hadn't been perishable, I would have returned it." That's almost true. I'd return most gifts, but if he gave me something like an elven spell book, I might waver. Over the last few days, I've learned that elven magic is a unique combination of my type of sorcery—drawing power from an inner well and weaving it into what we need—and human-style wielding of existential magic. So while I could never perform an elven spell myself, I might be able to take elements of it and adapt them for pure sorcery. Honestly, I'm itching to try—if we weren't dealing with a disaster, I would have cornered one of the elves and begged for help already.

Alistair gasps, and Percy draws back like I've slapped him. Even Gideon frowns.

"You have to read it!" Alistair declares. "You can't do this to me. I'm too invested in this story now for you to ruin it for me."

I don't even...

"Stop talking," Gideon tells him, then turns to me. "You need to read it. We're meeting him now. What if he's said something in the note that you need to know prior to the meeting?"

Welp, can't argue with that. Guess I'll have to read it after all. But…

"You do know that I'm not telling any of you what it says? Because even if I feel that his behavior is inappropriate, it's still a private message and would be a betrayal of his trust for me to share."

Gideon manages to hide his disappointment—just. Alistair and Percy don't even bother trying. In fact, Alistair begins whining immediately. I tune him out—it gets easy after a while—dig the note out of my pocket, and unfold it. Noah's neat handwriting covers the paper, but there's no way Noah would ever say these words.

Life would be poorer without your glory. Please allow me to take care of you so I never have to live without the wonder of you in the world.

It's completely over the top, much more suited for people who are actually dating, and I've never been one to go for such sappiness—practicality is my game—but I can't help the flutter of tiny butterfly wings in my stomach as I read it. Maybe it makes me selfish, but there's a part of me that really likes knowing somebody thinks of me this way. That somebody, however misguided they might be, looks at me and sees more than just practical, dependable David. He sees someone worthy of wild passions and flowery declarations.

Which is ridiculous, because I've spent most of my life working hard to be practical, dependable David. I love having an organized life, and I love knowing that my friends and coworkers know they can rely on me, that I'll never let them down. This is who I am, and more importantly, it's who I want to be.

But I guess that doesn't mean I don't also want to be the person who fills someone else's every thought.

Look at me, learning something new about myself.

"Okay, let's go," I declare, pushing all self-realization to one side. It's just another thing that has to wait until later.

Gideon obliges me by standing and following me to the door. I can still hear Alistair whining to Percy about how I've deprived him of an important element of the story arc in this "living romance" as it closes behind us.

CHAPTER TWO

Caolan

I STROLL alongside Garin toward the office where our new allies work. Once our operations were moved from Sam and Gideon's house back to the CSG building, we were allocated a room in which to work. It's just down the hall from their office and a nice size, with actual windows, which some other rooms don't have. Sam told me it was used as a meeting room, but it's ours for as long as we need it.

Eerika, Garin, and I have found it useful to retreat there and exchange notes on what we've learned. I thought we had a decent understanding of the Earth species, but apparently they've changed a lot since the last time we had any meaningful interaction with them, nearly eleven thousand cycles ago.

That's another thing I need to get used to—thinking of things in terms of Earth time. Their cycle—or year, as they call it—is longer than ours. For them, our last contact was nine thousand *years* ago. And they break the day up into tiny pieces. It's going to take a lot of effort to schedule myself so rigidly, but I'm definitely going to try. It will make David happy.

My pace quickens. David. I think I'm on time to meet him, but we've been notoriously bad at timekeeping so far. It's just so difficult to keep track of all the… mintees? No, minutes! That's the word. Minutes. We don't have an equivalent for it in any of our languages, so the translator spell uses the original English word. It sounds clumsy and is difficult to get my mouth around. But eventually, I will need to learn the native languages. There's no point relying on a translator spell for the rest of my life.

The usual pang of fear and sorrow stabs at me as I'm reminded once again that my beautiful home will be no more. Not that it's truly beautiful any longer— Éibhear's selfishness has rendered it unrecognizable. Still, it hurts on a cell-deep level to know it will be destroyed and I'll never be able to go back there. Earth seems nice enough, and I'm definitely grateful to have somewhere to come to—all who survive are—but it's not my home.

Not yet, anyway. Maybe one day I'll be able to think of it as such. When the ache of loss has faded to a dull throb and I'm comfortable in these new surroundings. Perhaps I'll even have someone special to call my own.

Which brings my thoughts back to David.

Beautiful David.

I can't help but smile when I think of him. These Earth species look a lot like us, but there are enough differences to bone structure and facial features that it's easy to see them as alien. I never thought I could so easily find one of them attractive, but David truly is, both outside and in. His soul shines from him, a little dented in parts by his life, but pure and good. I just want to bask in his presence and heal his past hurts.

There are other things I want to do with him, too, but it would be an adventure in and of itself: sex with a sorcerer. It's not something I've ever done before—how would I have, with travel between our dimensions banned?—and I'm not sure if things have changed since all the old stories.

Still, licking every inch of his skin should be safe enough.

"Why are you smiling like that?" Garin asks me, then groans. "You're thinking about your sorcerer again, aren't you?"

"He's not mine," I remind him with a wistful sigh. Even if Lucifer Percy hadn't requested we not become intimately involved until diplomatic matters are settled, David himself seems reluctant to do so—at all. I would be discouraged, except his friends have been very supportive and reassuring. They say he's just so dedicated to his work that the idea of having more than that in his life is a strange one for him. It's easy to believe, since he's sleeping in the office instead of at his home.

Besides, his soul calls to mine in a way that can't be an accident. I can't technically see if they're paired, not being able to see my own soul, but I can't imagine that they're not. I've never experienced this kind of intrinsic connection with anyone before, not even Ailíse, and we *were* paired souls.

As always, I feel a twinge of loss for Ailíse. It's been a long time, but part of me will always miss her. That same part is also excited to start something new with David.

"He's yours," Garin scoffs. "I can't see soul bonds

like you, but even I can tell there's something between you. These Earth people are just slow. He'll realize soon enough. Did you talk to his friends this morning?"

I nod. "Yes. Aidan was right; he *is* sleeping in the office. Sam said he wasn't eating properly because of it and suggested I bring him his favorite breakfast."

"Excellent idea. Every time I drink a decent ale, I fondly remember the barmaid from the tavern in my hometown when I was young. She always brought me the perfect ale."

It takes me a moment to process that and make the connection. "You think if I keep bringing him his favorite foods, he'll associate the pleasure he gets from them with me?"

He nods. "Yes."

I suppose it can't hurt to try. If nothing else, it will ensure David has some good meals. Anything that keeps him fed and healthy can't be bad. "Thank you. That's a good idea."

"And while we're visiting with the king, you should ask him whether David's soul pairs with yours. You've been desperate to find out."

"I have not," I declare, somewhat indignantly. Yes, I'd like to know, but whether our souls pair or not doesn't change how I feel about David. I am *not* desperate to find out.

"If Eerika or I could have told you, we would, just to keep you from fretting," Garin continues blithely, as though I hadn't spoken.

"I wasn't fretting," I protest. "David and I will have a beautiful relationship even if our souls aren't paired."

He claps me on the shoulder as we reach the door to David and his friends' office. "That's the right attitude."

He pushes open the door and goes in. I stare after him and wonder whether maintaining a lifelong friendship is really something I want to do.

I can think about that another time. I don't want to be late for David.

But when I follow Garin into the office, David's not there. Could I be early? Or am I so late that he gave up waiting?

"Are we late?" I ask, somewhat fearfully. That's not the kind of thing that will impress David with how much I care about his feelings.

Sam smiles. "No, you're right on time. The others are running a bit behind—Percy had some last-minute instructions to give them."

Excellent! When David arrives, he'll see me waiting and know my timekeeping has improved. Although, if he's meeting with the lucifer now, has he had any time to eat?

"Did David get his breakfast?" I ask Sam, eyeing his desk where I left the food and trying not to sound anxious.

"Oh, he did," Noah assures me. "He was very appreciative. Tell me, is gifting food a traditional part of elven courtship?"

I eye him warily. He looks innocent, but something about that question makes me feel as though there's a trap right in front of me. "When the situation warrants it," I answer cautiously. "There are few 'traditional' elements to elven courtship. We're not that formal when it comes to forming relationships." I pause for a beat, waiting to see if I used the contraction correctly. My translator spell is learning and adapting, but I'm still hesitant about many of the more casual and informal aspects of their language. After all, I don't want to inadvertently offend the people who are giving us sanctuary.

Nobody looks confused or amused, so I must have said it right. I mentally congratulate myself.

"Well, David really enjoyed his coffee and toast," Sam assures me.

"If you don't mind me asking," Andrew says, getting out of his chair and coming around the desk to perch on the front of it, "what are your plans to progress this courtship?"

"I told him to keep bringing David his favorite foods," Garin volunteers.

"That's an excellent idea," Elinor says, smiling approvingly. But then, she's a shifter, and while I haven't known these people long, I already know that shifters are very committed to food and eating.

"Food's good," Andrew agrees. "Fuck knows, someone needs to make sure David's eating properly. But what else?" He leans forward. "David's my best friend. It's my job to have his back."

The translator spell fumbles a little with "have his back" but finally suggests "protect his back" as the best alternative. Which means Andrew is looking out for his friend, and I like that. David should have friends who want to take care of him. "The first step is to show David I am serious in my admiration and that he can trust me not to use any feelings between us to impact the diplomatic situation we're both part of," I say seriously. "That means respecting Lucifer Percy's directive and David's wish not to progress to an intimate relationship just yet." I shrug. "I will continue to express my adoration of him through words and small gifts, and by the time the situation settles, he will be confident in my esteem and ready to progress."

"Oh my god, I don't know if that's adorable or creepy," Noah mutters, and panic stabs at me.

"Creepy? I don't want to be creepy. Creepy is bad, correct?"

"Creepy is bad," Andrew agrees, "but I don't think you're being creepy. Just to be on the safe side, I'm going to talk to David, and if he feels at all creeped out, I'll let you know that you need to back off."

I nod. "That would be a most excellent solution. David should feel comforted and… and fancied by my attention, not threatened. If I need to slow the pace of our courtship and solidify our friendship first, I will. I have time."

Elinor tilts her head and squints. "When you say you have time, you're talking about the fact that you won't die until you're ready to, aren't you?"

It seems odd to have it put so bluntly, but… "Yes."

"David doesn't have quite that much time," Noah says gently. "I mean, he's still got more than me, but not near as much as you."

Andrew straightens abruptly and crosses his arms over his chest, his face set. He often seems displeased when Noah refers to his own lifespan, and I make a mental note to find a way to delicately discuss this with someone.

"I don't plan to need centuries," I assure Noah. "A few decades should be more than enough."

He makes a choking sound and mutters something about "slow burn," but Sam smiles. "That's great. We're all very much in favor of David having a life outside of his work, and we don't know you well, but we think the way you adore him is probably a good start."

Relief sweeps over me. Having the support and approval of David's friends is important. Few relationships are successful when family and friends hate your partner.

"If you have suggestions on the best way for me to proceed, I would be happy to hear them." I'm eager to know more about David, and any assistance they can give would be helpful.

"Well," Sam begins, but then falls silent and looks toward the doorway. I look also. There's nobody there, but a moment later, David appears, followed by Gideon. Sam must have heard them coming. I have to say, I'm quite envious of some of these shifter abilities—enhanced hearing, sight, and smell would be nice to have.

I smile at David, feeling my insides warm a little at the sight of him. He looks tired, but we're all a little tired right now, given the catastrophe we're trying to avoid. The glow of his beautiful soul still shines through. He's pretty from a physical perspective, too, with his thick black hair and dark blue eyes—contrast between hair and eye color is commonly held as a standard of beauty amongst my people. We like contrasts. I wonder how he'd look with his hair long, framing his face?

I hold back a shiver of desire.

"Good morning, David," I say, eager for him to see that I'm here waiting for him, not late. "And you, Gideon," I add. "I hope you're well."

Gideon doesn't smile back, but his habitual scowl lightens a little. I've reconciled the fact that his expression doesn't always match what he's saying and feeling.

Which is just as well, or I'd be constantly on guard against attack when around him. "Good morning," he says, going over to Sam. I smile again, this time automatically, because it's so nice to see how their souls resonate together. They complement each other perfectly.

A paired soul relationship is a thing of joy.

David musters up a smile, but it's entirely professional and not at all natural, sending a little pang through me. One day, he'll smile like seeing me is the only thing he needs to be happy. My soul sings with the certainty of it.

"Good morning, Caolan, Garin. I apologize for being tardy—Percy had some unexpected additions to our meeting agenda." He casts a slightly sour look at Gideon and then turns it on the rest of his friends. Andrew laughs outright, while Elinor whistles and looks up at the ceiling.

Noah's reaction is the most interesting. "I told them to stop wussing out. Jesus fucking Christ, imagine taking years to offer someone a promotion because you don't want to have to talk him into it."

The translator spell takes a moment to put "promotion" in the right context, but then joy bursts in me.

"Oh! Congratulations," I tell David. How wonderful that others are recognizing his worth!

Andrew laughs again, and this time Sam snickers a little too. David narrows his eyes at them but gives me another of those hideous polite smiles.

"Thank you. It's more for political expediency rather than anything else."

Elinor makes a harsh, drawn-out sound, which the translator spell tells me is an indication of displeasure.

Or the sound a spiritual entity might shout, which makes no sense at all.

David ignores her, keeping his attention on me. I like that.

"Thank you also for being on time. I appreciate how difficult that is for you, and I want you to know that we all value the effort you're making. Later today, I hope to get you all some watches—timekeeping devices—that will hopefully make things easier for you."

A timekeeping device sounds like a particularly cruel and twisted form of torture, but now that we're living on Earth, conforming to at least some local customs will help us fit in. So Garin and I exchange glances, then smile and nod.

"That would be most helpful," my childhood friend says.

"I can take care of that while you're out," Sam offers helpfully. "Although, rather than watches, should we think about phones? They're going to need them eventually anyway, and this way we'll be able to maintain contact more easily."

"Yes," I burst out. "Phones. An excellent idea." I've seen them using these phones they speak of. They're not all the same, but the general principle applies to them all —the ability to communicate over distances. It's also an information repository and can create images of people and places. I would very much like one.

Sam bites his lip, smiling. "I'll arrange for them, then."

"Wonderful," Garin says, nodding. "I would like one with the kitten bubble exercise, if that's possible."

I frown at him. "What kitten bubble exercise?" And how did he learn about it?

"Same question," Sam says. "And also, what even is a kitten bubble exercise?"

"Alistair showed it to me. His phone has it. There are kittens in bubbles, and the purpose of the exercise is to return them to their parent cat. It requires strategic thinking."

"Ohhhh." Sam nods while Gideon mutters something about Alistair that seems quite uncomplimentary. "That's fine. You can add that after—ask Alistair to show you how."

Garin seems satisfied by that, but I'm still rather miffed that I haven't seen this exercise. I am generally considered to be the better strategist of the two of us.

"Okay." David's voice interrupts my plan to corner Alistair and convince him to show me the exercise. "We're already running a little behind—that's our fault —so maybe we should get a move on. Is there anything we need to discuss before we go? Or anything you need?"

I shake my head. My hair slides forward over my shoulder, and David's gaze goes to it. He's difficult to read, but I'm sure that's admiration—perhaps lust?—in his gaze, so I give my head another small shake. I do have lovely hair, and I'm not against using it to secure his attention.

"There is nothing," I reply with my most alluring smile. "We are ready to go."

David swallows, then says, "Okay then. Uh, Percy has requested that Gideon come too. Is that okay?" There's a faintly hopeful note in his voice that confuses me. Does he think we will deny Gideon the right to join us? Why would we antagonize our allies over so small a thing? Further, why would I risk displeasing David for no real reason?

"Of course it's okay," I confirm, turning to smile at Gideon. He smiles back, shocking me.

"Thanks, Caolan," he says. "I appreciate it, even if David doesn't."

David… doesn't? I look back at him, but his face is back in that polite, neutral mask. Did I say the wrong thing? Should I have forbidden Gideon from joining us?

"Don't be a douche," David tells Gideon, then turns his pretty eyes on me. "He's teasing," he assures me. "Sometimes he does that just to confuse us all. Of course I appreciate your willingness to accede to Percy's whims."

The words are mostly right, but there's an underlying bite to his tone that concerns me. It's going to take quite a lot of time to fully understand how these Earth species communicate. For now, I will accept his words at their apparent value. "Shall we go, then?"

Gideon kisses Sam, making my soul sing, and leads the way from the office. Garin and I follow, but as I pass David, he lays a hand on my arm, making my whole body tingle.

"Could I have a word?" he murmurs, and after a brief moment of confusion—which word? How do I give it to him?—the translator spell advises that he wishes to speak with me.

"Of course." I try not to sound too eager. I've noticed that he doesn't seem to appreciate public displays of my fervor. But I do inject as much restrained enthusiasm as I can manage into my voice. *Anything you want, you have only to ask of me.*

He removes his hand from my arm, which is disappointing, but falls into step beside me as we leave the office. The hallways are not so narrow, but neither of us is small, so our shoulders brush occasionally as we walk, and it's wonderful.

"I'd like to thank you for your thoughtful gift this morning," he begins, speaking softly—although after only two days amongst his people, I already know it's not soft enough to prevent others from hearing. "It was most kind of you. But I would be wrong if I didn't remind you that things must remain professional between us."

"It was a professional gift," I blurt. Did he read my note? Did Noah transcribe it correctly? I'm sure he did; he questioned me closely about the intended meaning so there wouldn't be an inadvertent mistranslation. "An offering between diplomatic envoys." I wish I could take it back as soon as the words leave my mouth. What a completely stupid thing to say.

David clears his throat, and I sneak a sideways glance at him. There's a tiny smile on his lips, and my heart leaps with joy. I made him smile! Even if it was because of my foolishness.

"I truly appreciated it," he assures me. "But gifts are not necessary between us. On a diplomatic level. Or any level."

Ahead of us, Gideon half turns and shoots David an incredulous look, one eyebrow raised. I knew he could hear us.

"I disagree," I reply, lowering my voice even more as we approach the busy reception area, forcing David to lean in close to hear me. "Gifts are very necessary between us. But in future, I will reconsider how I deliver them." I quicken my step, entering the reception and approaching Gideon and Garin. Behind me, David says "What?" but he's too late and I'm able to avoid answering. I'm not one of King Raðulfr's top strategists for nothing.

The wards on the CSG offices prevent us from opening a portal inside, but the reception area is outside the wards. Gideon gestures to the guard—enforcer—standing by the door to the stairwell, and he nods and turns his attention to the door. His job is to ensure no humans enter while the portal is open. It's unlikely, since very few humans come to these offices, and even fewer of those are unaware of the existence of nonhuman species, but the community of species has survived for nine thousand years by keeping their presence a secret from humanity, and none of us want to be the ones to ruin that.

Gideon glances at the panels above the elevators, which shows the numbers of the floors the elevators are currently on, then gives me a nod. "You're good to go."

I take a breath and reach inward and outward. My inner power bubbles up as the life force flows over me, through me. I envisage the void and the portal room at the main barracks and then channel the power into the correct form.

A portal opens before me, glowing with the green of my soul essence.

I've done this literally millions of times in my life, but it never fails to fill me with awe. There is something about creation in any form that is beautiful beyond belief.

And this portal is a very nice one, if I do say so myself. It's a shame David doesn't know enough about portals to understand what a great specimen it is.

Perhaps I can invite him to watch some of the trainees practicing and give him a basis for comparison.

"What an excellent portal, Caolan! I don't think I've seen one so stable and powerful. You're a true craftsman."

Or I could just let Garin point it out. This must be why we've been friends since childhood.

"Thank you," I say, trying to sound modest as I step back and motion to him. While I *can* maintain the gateways after passing through them, it's easier to do so from this side. And while I haven't had a portal collapse since the very first days of my training, I'd rather not take any risks with our alliance still in the early days—and especially not any that might impact David's safety.

Garin salutes me cheekily, then steps through the portal. I feel the light static of his presence brushing against my power.

David takes a step forward, but Gideon pushes past him. It makes me frown, because Gideon, though reserved and sometimes brusque, is not rude. David, though, just sighs and rolls his eyes, so it must be okay.

"What can I expect to see on the other side?" Gideon asks me. "Your king won't be standing there waiting, will he?"

I shake my head. "Unlikely. It's a portal room, and we don't allow people to be in them if they're not using an active portal. That makes it easier for those of us creating portals. The room itself is empty. Only Garin should be there—maybe he will have called in whichever guard was outside the door."

"Thank you." Gideon nods, then walks through the portal. I shiver—his energy is different from anything I've felt before. Aidan's and Alistair's weren't, when they used my portal to come here from the place we met—not really. They felt a lot like dragon shifters. Gideon's is different again. Perhaps it's a species variation? This is yet another piece of information that has fallen by the wayside since our peoples stopped interacting.

David moves closer to me and eyes the portal.

"It's safe," I assure him, and he smiles at me. It's such a lovely smile. I'll have to make sure to do things to draw it out more often.

"I know. It's just such a huge thing. I'm so honored to be able to take this step and help build the alliance between our peoples."

He says it seriously, and it strikes me once more how amazing he is. I suck in a deep breath, on the verge of darting forward and kissing his pretty mouth, but before I can move, he walks through the portal.

Just as well.

I close my eyes and savor the feeling of his energy brushing up against mine. It's different again from anything I've ever felt, which lends credence to the theory that it's a species variation. It's also imbued with the basic essence of David, and I would gladly hold this portal open all day just for this feeling.

Sadly, though, he reaches the other side all too soon. Sighing, I open my eyes and follow him through.

In the portal room on the other side, Garin is explaining why it's best to stand at least six feet away from the gateway and not within a direct line from it. Most of the reason is a hangover from our military training, where we were told it's not wise to stand in front of an open doorway without knowing what's on the other side. Some of it, though, is related to the fact that portals can very easily become unstable. I haven't had that happen to me in millennia, but I'm not going to be the only one operating portals for them in the future, so it's best they learn safety protocols.

I turn back toward the portal and visually check it before closing it down. It winks out, and as always, I feel a tiny pang of sorrow and need to cheer myself by thinking of the next portal I can create.

"That was incredible," David says. "I've seen you open them before, but it just didn't prepare me for the experience of walking through it."

I bask in his admiration. Garin snickers.

"Thank you. I don't often get to introduce someone to a portal for the first time. I'm honored to have been your first."

Gideon coughs, then sucks in a breath and chokes on it. David smacks him on the back, saying, "Really? I expected that reaction from one of the others, but not you."

Wheezing, Gideon waves his hand and shakes his head, and David turns toward me.

"As much as I appreciate that sentiment, you should be aware that it's an expression that doesn't translate well." He purses his lips. "Well… it does, but it has a certain connotation in our society that… I mean… uh…"

My confusion is mounting. I glance over at Garin, who shrugs, seeming equally stymied, then run back over my words, trying to see where the problem is.

Gideon gets his breathing back to normal and says —rather hoarsely—"What David's struggling to say is that being someone's first in our society often refers to being their first sexual experience." He pauses, glances sideways at David, whose cheeks have gone an adorable shade of pink, and adds, "I regret to inform you that you wouldn't be David's first."

David's arm swings out and thwacks Gideon solidly in the chest. "I'm taking down your privacy wards," he threatens. "Alistair is going to be able to just walk into your house whenever he wants."

Gideon's eyes widen, and I decide it's time to intervene before he harms my beloved. I like Alistair, but he has a lot of energy, and I can understand why Gideon might want a method of keeping him out sometimes.

"The king is waiting," I say hastily. "Shall we go?"

Closing his mouth on whatever he was about to say, Gideon glares at David one last time, then follows Garin toward the door.

Outside, a single guard is standing watch. Her job is to keep people out of the room unless they need to create a portal, and to call for an escort for any newcomers. Well—that's traditionally a duty of a portal room guard. Since time began collapsing, there aren't any newcomers. Every survivor we could find is now here, in one location. Except for Éibhear and his people, of course, but since they're responsible for the whole drama, they're not welcome to visit.

The guard, Ingrid, smiles when she sees Garin and opens her mouth—presumably to greet him. Then her gaze falls on Gideon and David, and her jaw drops. Perhaps I should have warned her when last I was here that I planned to bring visitors.

To her credit, she recovers quickly and inclines her head formally in greeting. "Welcome. It is a pleasure to have visitors from your dimension again." It's very elegantly said, but unfortunately, in elvish. David smiles at her and glances toward me. Gideon just stands there expressionlessly.

"She bids you welcome and is glad for the renewed contact between our homes," I explain quickly, then turn to Ingrid, who already looks chagrined. "Do you know a translator spell?" I ask her, and she shakes her head.

"I've never needed one."

I make a mental note to talk to someone about that. Everyone will need to know a translator spell when we migrate to Earth, at least until we can learn the native languages.

"I will translate, then." I look over to David and Gideon and repeat it in their language.

David nods, then smiles again at Ingrid and says, "Thank you for your welcome. We are honored to be here and to meet you. I'm David Carew, and this is Gideon Bailey."

I quickly translate, then tell them her name.

"The king is waiting," Garin reminds us, then repeats it in elvish for Ingrid's benefit. She nods and inclines her head again. David and Gideon follow suit, and then I lead them down the corridor.

"I know we've already spoken about how we should greet your king," David says quietly, "but is there anything else I should know?"

Mentally, I run through the official protocol for anything I might have forgotten to tell him. "I don't think so. Incline your head in greeting but wait for him to make the first verbal greeting. Address him as Your Majesty unless he requests otherwise. Do not draw any weapon in his presence unless it is in his defense."

"That won't be a problem," David assures me. "We

don't have any weapons." He stops walking suddenly and turns on Gideon. "Right? No weapons, yeah?"

"No weapons," Gideon repeats. "I'm not an idiot, David."

For some reason, my beloved does not look convinced, and for a moment, I think he might demand to search Gideon's person. Finally, though, he lets out a breath and turns back to recommence walking.

"The king will likely not stand on formality," I say, wanting to reassure him. "Nor will the wing leader. We are all so grateful for your offer to take us in and for all the assistance you are giving."

He seems about to respond, but from up ahead, there's a shout.

CHAPTER THREE

Caolan

A BLUR of movement races down the hallway toward us, skidding to a stop only feet away in the form of blond-haired, hazel-eyed, innocent-faced trouble. I press my lips firmly together to hold in my groan. Garin is not so circumspect, audibly sighing.

"Are these the Earthlings? They *are*, aren't they? They're so exotic!" Dustin reaches out as though to touch, and Gideon moves forward in front of David, suddenly seeming much bigger—and scarier.

Dustin's eyes widen, and for one hopeful moment, I think he's going to withdraw instead of embarrassing us.

It's a moment of delusion.

"*Look at you!* Are those horns real? Are you a shifter too? How did you get so big? Can I touch your muscles? Are you that big *all over*?"

David makes a sound, but when I look over at him, his face is calm and untroubled. That doesn't stop me from wishing that Dustin didn't have a translator spell. I could save this situation if only they couldn't understand him.

Well… maybe.

"I bet you *are* big all over. You can show me, if you like. I love big men." He bats his eyelashes in a way that makes me wish the roof would collapse just to provide a distraction from this agonizing moment. How will our guests ever take us seriously after this? "And big men love me. I have skills, and I'm very bendy."

Gideon, to his credit, remains stone-faced as he says, "I'm in a committed relationship."

Dustin leans in and licks his lips. "How committed?"

Garin slaps a hand over Dustin's mouth before he can say anything else. Technically, touching him like that is a breach of protocol, but it's probably the only thing that's going to stop Gideon from harming him, and since protection from harm is one of the few reasons permitted for breaching protocol, there shouldn't be consequences.

"Very committed," Gideon growls, looming in an extremely intimidating manner. If I were Dustin, I'd be terrified. Unfortunately, he just looks more excited.

"They're paired souls," I hiss before he can wriggle away from Garin's hand and make this even worse. Then I turn back to scary Gideon and trying-not-to-laugh David—I can see the twinkle in his eyes—and say, "Please forgive Dustin for his forward and outlandish behavior. He's young still and very… excited by the prospect of meeting new people. Perhaps a formal intro-duction?" I shoot a sideways glare at Dustin, who looks rather chastened now. Possibly because I pointed out how young he is. He likes to pretend he's a sophisti-cate… although his habit of behaving like a spoiled adolescent usually gives him away.

Garin gingerly removes his hand from Dustin's

mouth, hesitating for a second before taking it away, just in case the young one decides to say something else.

"Prince Dustin, grandson of the dragon wing leader, I have the pleasure of introducing you to David Carew and Gideon Bailey, ambassadors for Lucifer Percy of Earth."

David and Gideon both incline their heads just as I showed them to.

"It's very good to meet you," Dustin says, sounding more subdued than before. I know him well enough to know that won't last, so I don't allow any time for the conversation to restart.

"King Raðulfr is waiting for us. Your grandfather is there also?" I ask, gesturing for us all to begin walking again.

"Yes," Dustin says. "Uh… could you tell them that you requested my presence when you arrived?"

David coughs. I resist the urge to close my eyes. This is not how I wanted him to see me, having to manage and pander to a spoiled prince.

"Why would we do that?"

"No reason. Just because I want them to know I have friends. And that you value me as an ambassador of dragonkind. Yes, that's a good reason. Tell them you thought I'd give our guests a strongly positive impression of dragons and invited me to meet them before the formalities began." He beams at me, clearly not registering any irony in this situation.

Garin chuckles, shaking his head and leaving the mess to me.

"Do you really think I can tell a lie like that with a straight face?" I could, but… "And do you really think I should lie to my king without good reason?"

He pouts. "You're so mean. I made a good impression. Right?" He turns to look at Gideon but continues before anyone can answer. "And there is too a good reason."

"You haven't told it to me yet," I remind him.

He doesn't reply. We're getting closer to the king's sitting room. Twenty feet. Fifteen. Ten—

"They treat me like a baby," he blurts in elvish, his face flushing as he darts a glance over his shoulder at our guests.

"Maybe you shouldn't behave like one," I reply, then feel bad. "They're very protective of you," I add. "It's only natural that they want to make sure you're safe." We have so very few dragons left, and we've lost thousands of fledglings in recent times, most of them not yet even old enough to fly. It was a devastating day.

"It's not that," he says miserably, and I almost feel sorry for him. "I understand them wanting to protect me. But they won't let me *help*. Anytime I ask to be assigned a job, they tell me not to worry about it. And this morning, they banished me from this meeting. As though I can't be trusted to contribute something useful!"

I glance at the door to the king's sitting room, just feet away, and wonder how I can possibly handle this— and why it got dumped on me. The life force has a wicked sense of humor.

"Have you considered," I begin, trying not to sound impatient and bring on a tantrum, "that the best way to show your grandfather and the king that you can contribute something useful is to not cause problems?"

"I don't cause problems!" he declares indignantly.

"Yes, you do. The very first thing you did upon

encountering ambassadors from another dimension—a dimension that is our *only* hope of survival—was to make embarrassing sexual innuendoes to someone who clearly indicated he was not receptive to them. We can only hope that they're not so offended that they withdraw their offer of sanctuary." I know them well enough by now to know they wouldn't do that for so minor an offense, but Dustin needs to understand that his actions have consequences. Young dragons are by nature very capricious and excitable, but if Dustin wants to be given responsibility, he needs to learn when that kind of behavior is acceptable and when it's not.

His eyes widen, and he looks over my shoulder to where our guests are standing a polite few feet away. "They wouldn't, would they?" he whispers.

"I don't believe so," I concede. "But you had no way of knowing that. And whether they would or wouldn't, your greeting to them was inappropriate."

Heaving a sigh, he scowls. "You can't lecture me like you're my family," he mutters.

I fold my arms over my chest and wait. Technically, he's right—he outranks me by a lot. But we both know his grandfather holds me in high esteem and would trust me to correct his behavior in this situation.

"Well, fine, *you* can," he grumbles. "But don't do it in public or other people will get the idea they can too."

Garin snorts, proving that he's been listening even while speaking to our guests.

"Apologize to Gideon and then go," I tell Dustin. "If the subject happens to come up, I'll say we ran into you in the hallway, but I won't mention what an ass you made of yourself."

He glares indignantly but doesn't object to being

called an ass. Instead, he sniffs, then plasters on a charming smile and turns toward the Earthlings, switching back to English.

"Please accept my apologies for my untoward actions. I respect your commitment to your partner and regret if I have made your visit uncomfortable. We are all most grateful to you for your offers of assistance in our time of need, and so pleased and excited to resurrect contact between our peoples." He finishes with a polite bow.

This Dustin is going to be an excellent statesman and leader someday. He just needs to grow up first. If he modeled this behavior more frequently, instead of only showing his grandfather and the king his immaturity, they would gladly accept his offers of assistance.

Gideon doesn't say anything, but the lines of his perpetual scowl soften slightly. David smiles and returns the bow. "Thank you, Your Highness. Your apology is most gracious, and we accept."

Dustin opens his mouth—probably to say that dragons don't use formal modes of address—but the door to the king's sitting room begins to open, and he yelps and takes off down the hall.

His grandfather, Wing Leader Brandt—tall, with silvering dark hair and an austere-looking face but mischievously twinkling eyes—appears in the doorway. "Caolan," he says warmly, thankfully not seeming to notice that his only remaining grandson just fled the scene, "welcome back. Why are you standing here in the hall?" His translator spell is absolutely flawless—I can't tell the difference between his English and that of the native speakers I've spent the last few days talking to. Admittedly, he's somewhere in the vicinity of thirty thousand years old and has had a lot of time to work on such things, but still… the only exposure he's had to English was when he asked me to speak it to him for a short time yesterday. For the spell to not need more adjustment time is just… astounding.

I hold back my inner desire to gush over his magnificence and incline my head in greeting. "We stopped to talk to Dustin," I say truthfully.

Immediately, his expression darkens, but it's underlaid with the fond exasperation we all feel when dealing with Dustin. He's a nuisance, but a loveable one. "Did he accost you?"

"He ran into us." That's not a lie, but it also won't stand up to inspection. "Allow me to make introductions," I add hastily. David comes forward and inclines his head as I introduce him to Brandt.

"Welcome," Brandt says, taking both his hands in his. "I am so happy to meet a sorcerer again. It's been far too long."

David's head jerks slightly as he realizes he's meeting someone who actually visited Earth before their species wars. I wonder how Brandt recognizes David's species so easily—experience, or a dragon thing? Probably a combination.

"I am so honored to meet you," David says, regaining his composure. That's one of the things I love about him—he's so difficult to upset. "And may I say, your grandson has such beautiful manners."

Brandt blinks in shock, but I fall even more in love with David. How can I not? He wouldn't even have understood what Dustin and I were talking about, so his kindness comes from an instinctive knowledge that Dustin is insecure and needy for approval.

I want to kiss him right here in the middle of the hallway while Brandt looks on.

"*My* grandson? Are you certain? Dustin?" Brandt asks, completely discombobulated and glancing at me for confirmation.

David's smile is warm and slightly amused. "Yes. Oh, he was enthusiastic, but young people often are, and he made us feel most welcome." He looks over his shoulder at the hulking demon. "Right, Gideon?"

Gideon steps forward and inclines his head, then answers, "I've never had such a warm greeting from a stranger before."

Garin squeaks, but Brandt is too bewildered to notice.

"That's… wonderful. I'm so pleased he… Yes." He seems to gather his wits and lets go of David's hands to reach out to Gideon, but then changes his mind, presses his fists to the middle of his chest, one on top of the other, and bows shallowly. David draws in a surprised breath, and Gideon's jaw drops, but he returns the gesture.

"Did I do it correctly?" Brandt asks. "It's been such a very long time, and I know things change quite quickly on Earth."

"Perfectly," Gideon assures him. "We don't use it commonly anymore, only in ceremonial rites. Were you acquainted with many demons before the travel ban?"

Brandt's laugh has a wicked edge. "Oh, my boy, I was acquainted with every species at one time or another. We dragons only become sensible once we reach ten or so thousand years. Before that, I was partying on Earth every chance I got. I lived for nearly a hundred years with a demon couple. They were both so beautiful… and so *inventive*." He leers.

How did this day go so far awry? It was supposed to be simple. Important, but simple. I was going to impress David with my proximity to the king and the importance of my place here at court. Not have to act as authority figure to an overgrown child and then have one of our most senior leaders brag about his wild days.

Damn dragons.

"Is the king waiting?" I ask hastily as Garin makes a gagging gesture and David and Gideon seem at a loss for words.

"Of course he's waiting. We've been standing here in the hallway chatting. What else would he be doing?"

So much for hoping the dragons would use their company manners. It seems we've reached the "just old friends" phase of dragon-Earth relations.

I hustle everyone into the king's sitting room in the hopes that getting this encounter back onto a more official footing will repair the impression we've made so far.

"Caolan!" King Raðulfr booms, standing from his favorite armchair by the window. He likes to look out over what's left of the world, the enclave within the shield. He told me once that seeing how little remains bolsters him to keep fighting until the end. That was the night before he sent me to Earth with orders to do anything I could to derail Éibhear's plans and warn the Earth species. At the time, I thought it was a fool's errand. I thought he was misguided to care about thwarting Éibhear when our own end was so close.

I have never been so glad to be wrong. Because if he hadn't insisted on pushing forward, if he hadn't given me those orders, our people would not be saved.

Pushing down the emotion that wants to flood me at how very close we came to total extinction, I walk over to him and incline my head. "Good morning, Your Majesty. You look well today."

He does—there's a glow of barely contained excitement to him.

"I feel five thousand years younger," he declares. "Introduce me to our most honored guests."

I do so somewhat cautiously, afraid my usually proper king will reminisce about some long-forgotten indiscretion on Earth, but thankfully, he doesn't. Within minutes, we're all seated comfortably and being served refreshments. The talk is friendly and inconsequential— décor, the view from the window, portal travel, and then a moment of consternation when the refreshments arrive and we all realize we aren't sure if any of them are unsafe for our guests to eat. Fortunately, the life force confirms to King Raðulfr and Brandt that all is well.

"This is a concern I hadn't considered," Brandt says, frowning. "When we move to Earth, what will happen? I used to eat freely of your foods, but that was long ago."

"We're already working on it," David assures him. "The sorcerer species leader is working with a team, using DNA samples donated by your ambassadors. That allows them to work on it from a scientific perspective and also gain verification from the magic—I mean, life force. One of the things I need to ask you for today is DNA samples from dragons so we can perform the same due diligence there. I do feel foolish for not having considered that it would apply in reverse for us here, though."

"You can take my DNA," Brandt says immediately.

"And I'll ask for a few more volunteers. Is it likely to be a problem?"

"It doesn't look like it," David says confidently. "The magic was able to confirm that fresh foods, particularly those grown or farmed organically, are fine for elves. Caolan, Garin, and Eerika have been eating those and haven't advised us of any distress." He glances over to me for confirmation, and I nod.

"The usual reaction to a change in diet, but no pain, no sickness, no major symptoms." In fact, their fresh produce seems remarkably similar to ours in many ways. It makes sense, of course, since our planets have such a similar atmosphere and evolutionary history.

"What they're doing now," David explains, "is working through the different types of processed foods, additives, and fertilizers and pesticides we use. Organic fresh produce can be difficult or expensive—or both—to source in remote locations and during winter in some places. A wider range of options would be better, even if you choose not to eat them."

Brandt asks a question about what "processed foods" means, and David begins to explain. He seems quite happy discussing the technical details, and Brandt has been a sponge for information as long as I've known him —which is a long time—so I nab one of the little treats from the refreshment tray and settle back.

A slight movement from King Raðulfr catches my eye, and I look over. He's staring at me, wiggling his fingers slightly—clearly trying to get my attention. When he has it, he slowly pans his gaze across to David, then back to me, and then winks.

What...?

Does he know? About my feelings? But *how*? I've

come back twice to provide updates since meeting my beloved, but I definitely didn't tell King Raðulfr that I had fallen hopelessly in love with my counterpart from Earth. I certainly didn't mention that I was overwhelmed by my emotions, that I want to spend my days catering to David's every whim, that merely being in his presence is enough to make my life better.

So how could he possibly know?

The conversation shifts then, with Brandt asking King Raðulfr's opinion, and our unsettling stare is broken. As David explains how they hope to establish temporary encampments for our people while more permanent settlements and housing are arranged—all things I've already been made aware of—I lean toward Garin's chair.

"I think His Majesty may have attached a spy spell to me," I whisper. "Could you scan for it?" It seems incredible—the king has always trusted me in the past. Why would he utilize a spy spell now? Especially given how unreliable they are.

Garin lifts his eyebrows, just as surprised as I am. "Why do you think so?" he whispers back, glancing over at the king—who seems blissfully unaware of what we're saying. Shouldn't the spy spell alert him? Or does he not care that I've found him out?

"He knows about me and David." I quickly explain what just happened.

Garin smirks.

My stomach sinks.

"There's no spy spell," he informs me. "I told the king about your budding romance when I came back yesterday."

"It's not just a romance," I hiss, then realize what he just said. "*You* told him? Why?"

He shrugs. "You need someone who can see paired souls to tell you if you and David are. I can't help you with that, but the king can. Also, it was going to come out eventually, so I thought it would be a good idea to get in early and tell him how special the connection between you is."

I close my mouth. It's hard to be angry when a friend is thinking of your best interests. Although I do wish I'd been able to tell the king myself.

"What are you whispering about?" Brandt asks suddenly. "Come now, you know I can't stand not knowing secrets."

Well, damn. This is *not* what I had planned for today. Will David be upset if I mention my ardor for him?

"I imagine it's to do with that matter we were discussing earlier," King Raðulfr says easily, and Brandt's face lights up with a grin even as my gut clenches in dread.

"Oh! I've been waiting to ask about that—did it turn out as hoped?" he asks, just as gossipy as any courtier.

The king nods, smiling.

Brandt puts a hand to his chest and sighs.

I try to unclench my teeth as I ask, "How many people did you discuss the matter with?" The worst thing that could happen right now, with David still so uncertain about our relationship, would be for someone to talk to him about it. I should be able to get him back to Earth without running into anyone else, but with the migration plans proceeding, he's going to have contact with many elves and dragons, and if they know, they won't hold back.

Oversharing is a cultural failing.

It seems to have missed me, though. I'm very discreet and private about my feelings.

The king waves a hand dismissively. "Just Brandt."

Finally, some good news. "It might be best if we keep it that way."

"But—" Brandt begins to protest.

Firmly, I repeat, "It would be best. When the time comes, I'm sure you can be the first to spread the news." I sneak a sideways glance at David, mostly to see if he's guessed what we're talking about, but also partly because I like looking at him.

There's a tiny quirk to his lips and a curious gleam in his eyes. I'm going to assume that means he doesn't know we're talking about him, but he finds the antics of my leaders to be charming rather than ridiculous. I can be glad for that much, at least.

Then he looks at me, and for the first time ever, there's a softness to his gaze. It's warm. It's… dare I say, fond?

"I think we're all going to get on well together," he declares. Hope perks up inside me.

Maybe this day turned out well after all.

LATER, while David, a silent Gideon—I'm still not entirely sure why he came. He hasn't said a single word since he greeted the king—and Brandt discuss the specific needs of dragons, the king takes Garin and me next door to his office.

"Your Majesty," I begin as soon as he closes the

door, but I don't get the chance to say more before he pounces, wrapping me in a tight hug.

This has never happened before.

Literally never.

I've worked for King Raðulfr in some form or other for thousands of years, and never has he embraced me, much less with such fervor and enthusiasm.

I meet Garin's gaze over the king's shoulder. He's as wide-eyed with shock as I imagine I am.

"Ah… Your Majesty?" I manage. Am I supposed to hug him back? We don't generally lay hands on the royal person, but it seems rude not to hug him back. I compromise by giving him a genial pat on the back.

"I'm just so thrilled for you!" he exclaims, finally letting go. I take a few quick steps back in case he decides to get grabby again. I wonder if there's a way to put Garin between us without seeming odd. "You've fallen in love, *and* it's with a paired soul"—my heart jumps, joy filling me—"*and* it will cement relations between species and help pave the way for our acceptance on Earth!"

The bottom falls out of my world. I hadn't thought of that. Why didn't I think of that? It's even been discussed that David and I are representatives of different peoples coming together after not having contact for millennia. How did I miss the fact that our relationship would be held up as an example of cooperation between species—between worlds?

Garin seems completely unfazed by the king's comments, so clearly he thought of it. David likely has too—that might even be the reason he's so reluctant.

The king's not done yet. "I can think of no greater reward for someone who has served so tirelessly for so long than for the life force to grace you with a loving partner, but even in love, you find a way to aid your people."

Er…

How do I diplomatically tell him that my people were the last thing on my mind when I met David?

Garin shakes his head slightly, so I dredge up a weak smile and say, "You're too kind, sir."

"Sit, sit. Tell me all about your David. Garin says he's reluctant to enter a relationship before our alliance has been solidified?" He strides around his desk and sits in the large thronelike chair.

I perch on the very edge of one of what I privately think of as the supplicants' chairs and say, "Yes. He's also a very practical man and not used to the concept of paired souls." I hesitate. "You did say our souls are—"

"Beautifully, wonderfully, unmistakably paired," he assures me. I'm still not sure what to make of this more effusive, almost casual version of my king. Could it possibly be that some heretofore unknown alien being, desperate to escape the forthcoming destruction of our dimension, has taken over the body of our leader and plans to flee to Earth with no one the wiser?

Or maybe the king slipped and hit his head? Though surely somebody would have noticed that. He's very rarely entirely alone.

Just as I'm trying to think of a way to ask that won't earn me a reprimand and a demotion, King Raðulfr makes a sound of pure pleasure, raises his arms to the ceiling and tips back his head, and says, "I feel giddy today. Giddy, I tell you! It's like a weight has been lifted from me and I can finally breathe again. I haven't failed my people. They're not all going to die. They're going to live, and be safe, and our numbers will grow again, and everything will be okay." He lowers his arms and looks at us both. "I shouldn't burden you with my worries, but it's been a tough road, especially these last few centuries, when everything really started to look hopeless. All I had to hold on to was my faith in the life force and my thirst for vengeance." He tips his head and gives me a wry little smile. "I know you thought I was crazy when I told you to go to Earth and do whatever you could to thwart Éibhear. Maybe I was. Certainly, we could have used you here, helping to maintain the settlement. But I have been vindicated! There is hope, and there is love, and we will enact our revenge upon Éibhear so we can all live happily ever after."

Garin clears his throat. "Forgive me for asking, sire, but have you been drinking?"

My sentiments exactly.

He laughs. "No, but I feel almost as though I have. I was so worried. I've been so worried. Even after you came back and told me the lucifer had offered sanctuary and asked for Garin and Eerika to go with you and begin work on the plans, I was worried. I thought it could not be true. I thought perhaps their offer was too good to be true. Or that it would have conditions attached that I could not in good conscience agree to. It wasn't until I saw your David and his pure, beautiful soul that I knew all would be well. A soul like that would never knowingly subject thousands to death or misery if it could act to prevent it."

Ahhh... I understand now. He feels the way I did when Lucifer Percy first made his offer and I wanted to weep and shout my joy all at once. I had to restrain myself, not wanting to make a bad impression and cause him to change his mind, but the king is free to express himself.

But I didn't realize that he also could see David's soul so clearly. That's not a gift we have—even those of us who can see paired souls only see the direction of soul growth, not the essence of the soul itself. I thought I could see David's glowing soul beauty because of what he means to me, but if the king can see it also…

I turn to Garin. "Can you see David's soul?"

"Of course not. You know I can't see… wait. Do you mean his *actual* soul, not just the pair bond? I didn't even know it was possible."

"Neither did I," I admit. "I thought it was because I'm in love with him."

We both look to the king. He's got a distant, thoughtful look in his eye.

"Your Majesty?" Garin prompts.

"Yes… No, I've never been able to see a soul before either. But the life force is being very calm and reassuring right now, so I have to assume it had something to do with it. Perhaps a way of showing us that migrating to Earth is a wise choice?"

Considering that the alternative would result in our extinction, I really don't see how the migration could *not* be considered wise, but it's already decided, so there's no value in further discussion.

"That's probably it," I agree. "I'm sure if others also see it, they'll mention it, and then we'll know it's something else."

"Excellent point. Now. Tell me, how do you plan to convince your David that he should cleave unto you forever?"

I resist the urge to squirm. While I appreciate his

support, I'm not certain I want to discuss courtship plans with my king.

He watches me expectantly.

On the other hand, I don't seem to have a choice.

I sigh. "As I mentioned, he's extremely practical and committed to work. His primary focus right now seems to be the current situation with Éibhear and now our migration. Attempting to distract him from that may cause him to think I don't respect his work ethic—or take the current crisis seriously. Now that I've established my feelings for him, I believe the best move would be to step into a supportive colleague role. Show that I can be a valuable part of his life. And then once all is settled, I can test the waters again for more."

King Raðulfr purses his lips, appearing to consider my words. "I like it," he decides finally. I don't mention that I hadn't asked for his opinion. "It shows your commitment and at the same time respects his boundaries. And in the meantime, we'll have plenty of opportunities to show you in the best light. In just a short time, I can already tell you both have so much in common."

It seems King Raðulfr has decided to help me woo David, and I'm honestly terrified by the very thought. He has innumerable resources at hand. And that "we"… did he mean the royal we? He doesn't often use it, especially not in informal situations like this one, but the alternative is that he plans to rope others into whatever cockamamie scheme he has planned to "show me in the best light."

But, once again, I really can't refuse.

"Thank you," I say weakly, and Garin shoots me a sympathetic grimace. I'm not going to forget that this is all his fault.

The king nods in satisfaction, then thankfully moves on to working out the minutiae of our next steps. David believes that with sufficient input for his team of organizers, we'll be able to begin the migration in as little as a week and potentially be finished within just a few months. The actual travel time is inconsequential, of course, since a portal takes only a few steps to cross, but there is the detail of opening and maintaining portals large enough to allow big groups to cross quickly. We considered using smaller portals and keeping them open for longer stretches of time, but ultimately that is a larger energy drain, and we don't have so many elves left capable of opening portals that we can afford to exhaust them. Lingering at the back of all our minds is the knowledge that at any time, the collapse of our dimension could speed up, and at that point, we'd need to be able to move as many people as possible as quickly as possible.

The first group to travel to Earth will be a tactical response team, accompanied by several officials with the requisite knowledge of what a settlement of elves and dragons will need. The tactical team will assist to locate and neutralize Éibhear while also assessing the safety of the proposed settlement locations. As soon as they judge it appropriate, we'll begin migrating civilians—a group of young and able-bodied first, so we can put them to work assisting with the setup and maintenance of the settlement and then have them help the elderly and young families to acclimate when we start to bring them over. Small groups of soldiers—not that we have many left—will accompany each migration group, until all that's left behind is a rearguard to ensure nobody's been missed and nothing of value has been forgotten.

Still up for debate is when the king and Brandt will move to Earth. Garin and I would like it to be with one of the early civilian groups, but he seems to think he should be one of the last.

"We don't need to decide this right now," Garin finally says tactfully. "It's past time for lunch—why don't we see if our guests are hungry?"

The king narrows his eyes. "Are you trying to manage me?"

"Absolutely," Garin assures him. "We're determined that you won't be the last one to leave, but we don't want to argue with you about it."

I nod. "A lunch break is a tactical decision," I add. "A temporary cease-fire that will allow us all to regroup."

He stares at us, then throws back his head with laughter. "People ask me sometimes why I rely on you two so much when there are others with more experience," he chortles. "This. This is why." He heaves himself out of his chair. "Come on, then. Let's have lunch."

CHAPTER FOUR

David

I've RUN out of room in my notebook. I had about forty pages left this morning, and I thought that would be enough.

I hadn't fully anticipated dragons.

Mind you, I don't think anyone could have fully anticipated dragons. I thought I was prepared, based on what Caolan and the others had said. I thought they'd be oversized hellhounds. And as exhausting as hellhounds are, I've been dealing with them for centuries.

Having met only two dragons but with close to seventy pages of notes (I borrowed some kind of parchment-y writing material from the king), I'm now convinced we might need to make some contingency plans for dealing with dragons.

It's not so much that they need special food or living conditions, although we will need to make sure they have decent-sized outdoor spaces to shift in. It's that they're… quirky. Yeah, let's go with that. Hellhounds are quirky too, but they don't weigh upwards of a hundred thousand pounds (how do they even fly?)

and have the ability to breathe fire. Stuff like that can easily lead to "pranks" getting out of hand, Wing Leader Brandt informed me, which is why we need to ensure any settlement with dragons is as close to fire retardant as possible—or invest in a lot of fire extinguishers.

How the hell do you make an entire settlement fire retardant? The cost of doing that for just one house would be astronomical… and maybe impossible. I mean, there's always something around that can burn, right?

So… yeah. Most of my notes are a warning list about dragons. On the plus side, Brandt has promised that there will be at least three mature, sensible dragons among the tac team and officials who'll be coming back to Earth with us today. They'll be able to advise us more specifically on what will and won't work to prevent dragons from exposing us to humanity and possibly also setting the world on fire. (Note to self: no dragons in drought-affected areas.)

Of course, Brandt's definition of "mature and sensible" might be somewhat different from mine. We'll just have to wait and see… and keep all our fingers and toes crossed.

We're reaching the end of our visit, and I'm both mentally exhausted and revved up to get stuck into work. This has been very productive, and I'll be able to get a lot done with the information we've obtained.

In case you were wondering, Gideon has been somewhat helpful. Not very helpful, because he spent most of the day with his mouth closed and his expression set to resting bitch. But he did occasionally chip in with information I didn't know offhand, and he had a few suggestions for the best way to lay out settlements to allow for dragons.

"Everyone should be ready to go," King Raðulfr is saying, "but if you'd like a tour first, I'm sure there's time. We'd be so sad if you didn't get to see at least a little of our world… before it's too late."

Tour? I try not to sound too chipper as I agree, because it really is devastatingly sad that their world will cease to exist. On the flip side, when the fuck else am I ever going to be able to explore a different dimension? This is my only chance to see the elf homeworld.

"Caolan can show you around," Garin declares. "I'll go and check on how things are going with the tactical team."

"Of course," Caolan replies, smiling at me in that way that seems just a little bit too intimate and always makes me think about what he'd be like in bed. *Bad David.* "Also check how soon the equerry thinks we can migrate His Majesty to Earth."

The king's brows shoot up. "I thought we were in a cease-fire about this? I'm not going early, Caolan." He sets his jaw stubbornly.

I hesitate, because this isn't something I should be getting into the middle of, but it's also an item on my to-do list that I was eventually going to ask about, so…

"Actually, I was hoping that at some stage fairly early on we could have a ceremonial meeting between you and Percy," I venture. "Maybe sign an accord or something to make it seem official, and we'd livestream it throughout our community. I'm sure we could come up with a weave or spell to share it here, with your people, too. A show of unity and commitment to a peaceful integration."

Caolan and Garin are smiling. The king looks slightly disgruntled, which concerns me, and Brandt just seems thoughtful.

"Is this the outcome of a conspiracy?" the king grumbles. Fuck. Have I offended him?

"Of course, it's not necessary," I hasten to add, but he just waves a hand.

"It's necessary to set a good example for all our people. I just don't like having my preferences thwarted." He sighs. "Please go ahead and arrange it, and I'll make certain I'm there."

"Thank you, I will." I mentally move it from one part of my to-do list to another.

"Before we go," Caolan says, "I think it would be a good idea to involve Dustin in the migration."

Brandt's jaw drops, and the king begins to sputter. My heart melts.

"Hear me out," Caolan rushes on. "He's a widely known member of the court, very well liked, and he'll talk to anyone. Assigning him as a sort of spokesperson visiting back and forth from Earth over the course of the migration will allow a transfer of information to civilians from someone they know and trust without having to pull officials away from their work."

This is a big problem. Huge. Mammoth, even.

I mentioned earlier that Caolan ticks a lot of boxes for me, physically and in terms of work ethic and dedication. Well, today, watching him interact with his king and seeing how competent and trusted he is, he ticked a few more, and now, listening to him give that bored young man—dragon—a purpose, he fulfilled the entire fucking list. Because I might not have kids, but I used to work for the Community Integration Agency, and I've dealt with enough young people who are trying to find their place in the world to recognize one when I see him. Is there anything hotter than a man with a social conscience?

"He's flighty," Brandt protests. "And not in the good way."

There's a good way to be flighty?

"He's bored," Caolan counters. "He needs something to focus on besides getting into trouble."

"That's what concerns me," King Raðulfr begins. "What if he plays some of his pranks on Earth? This is a very delicate situation. The last thing we need is for him to give a poor impression."

Caolan spreads his hands. "I believe if we give him a task and impress upon him how important it is, he won't fail us. But if he does, I will take full responsibility. And I'll take responsibility for him while he's on Earth, since I'll be there anyway."

Fuck, he just keeps getting better. This is bad. Very, very bad.

I make myself relax. Percy said no fraternization while we're working everything out. So, there we have it —it doesn't matter if my self-control is faltering, because I've never acted in any way that would cause problems for CSG, and I'm not about to start now.

It's all good. Really. It is.

The king and Brandt are still umming and ahhing, but Caolan seems to be talking them around. Garin is just standing there smirking like he knows a secret.

"Sam would help keep an eye on him," Gideon says suddenly, and what? Sam has enough to worry about without babysitting a hyperactive dragon who hit on his man. Although, if Sam hears about that whole episode, there's a good chance Dustin will be too cowed to even think about causing trouble. Sam might seem affable and adorable, but he can be very scary.

Not to me, because I'm normal. But he did successfully wrangle a team of hellhounds for five years and is living with Gideon. So, yeah. Scary.

"He will?" Garin asks, sounding surprised. Possibly he's also thinking back to what happened this morning.

"Yes. Sam's a big believer in helping young people get on track," Gideon says firmly. "And he's a great person to ask for guidance when you're unsure of something."

That's true.

Brandt looks at me. "What do you think?"

"I'm in favor of having a civilian liaison," I admit. "I think it will ease a lot of the concerns your people are going to have. And it does need to be someone they know and trust. A young person who seems somewhat unofficial might have a better impact."

He still looks doubtful, but asks, "You said he was well-behaved when you met him?"

Tricky, tricky, tricky. How to get around this without outright lying to our new allies. "I was very impressed by his manners," I say. "Gideon?"

"Yes. And he was very… warm and friendly."

I concentrate on not laughing. That's certainly one way to put it.

Finally, they concede. "I'll find him and tell him to get his things organized while you're on your tour," Brandt says. From the determined set of his mouth, I expect he plans to lecture his grandson into submission as well.

"Thank you," Caolan says. "I think he'll surprise you."

THE TOUR IS… unbelievable. Even stoic Gideon seems impressed. If this is what their planet is like with a tiny portion protected by a bubble and the rest mostly ravaged, I'm devastated to have missed out on seeing it in its full glory. I can't even begin to imagine how the elves and dragons must be feeling right now.

Of course, given that the deterioration has been going on for thousands of years, they might also just be relieved at the thought of getting to safety.

We stroll across the almost feathery orange grass back toward the king's residence. Caolan kept the tour pretty concise, avoiding the areas that cater mostly to civilians. The official announcement about the migration won't be made until after we've left, so he didn't want to freak too many people out by turning up with a sorcerer and a demon, even if some—most?—of them wouldn't recognize us due to the travel ban. It's somewhat surreal—as a sorcerer, I've always blended seamlessly with humans. No human could look at me and tell I'm not one of them. But here… here, I stand out like a sore thumb.

I glance back over my shoulder at the tree with leaves made up of softly glowing lights. It's hard to see the glow properly in the daytime, but it must be spectacular at night—like a tree of fairy lights. Part of me really wants to see if we can transplant it or at least bring some cuttings to Earth, but it's going to be hard enough hiding two new sentient species and the few domesticated animal species they've managed to keep alive thus far. Plants, with their propensity to cross-pollinate, would be almost impossible. Even if they're thought to be a previously unknown or new species, there are bound to be enough DNA differences to attract attention.

Right now, attention is the last thing we need. So… the trees and other flora stay behind and die with the dimension.

We reach the building, and Garin is waiting for us. "Everyone's ready," he announces. "Including Dustin, who's vacillating between being excited and self-important and terrified. I'm not sure what Brandt threatened him with, but he's promised me six times already that he's going to make his people proud."

"That's a good beginning," Caolan mutters. "I hope he remembers it."

The courtyard they lead us to would have been lovely once upon a time, but with conditions being as they are, has been allowed to fade away. The ornately bordered garden beds are being used for vegetables—I can tell because Caolan pointed out the main kitchen garden as we passed it, and the foliage was all the same. I guess given the limited land area they have, it's wasteful to have a decorative garden instead of a practical one, but I wish I'd been able to see it as it once was. Even the fountain, which is still running, has been commandeered for practical purposes, with irrigation lines leading off it.

Two clusters of people are gathered near the far wall, and without being introduced, I can identify which is the tac team and which are the officials, even though they're dressed similarly. Trust me on this—when you spend enough time around enforcement and government, you learn how to tell. I guess some things are universal… interdimensional?

Standing apart from both groups is Dustin. He's trying very hard to look unconcerned and cool but also practically trembling with excitement. Just seeing how happy he is would be enough for me to give Caolan a big kiss for making it happen… you know, if I was doing that kind of thing. Which I'm not. Because Percy said I can't.

Percy said I can't. Percy said I can't. Percy said I can't.

My new mantra sucks.

Dustin spots us just then, takes a step toward us, stops, hesitates, then comes over. It's sweet.

"Good afternoon," he says formally. "Garin told me you helped to convince my grandfather that I would be good for this job. Thank you for that. I will do the best job I can." His stilted little speech comes to an end.

I incline my head. "You're welcome. I'm sure you'll be excellent." Gideon says nothing, so I add, "You'll be spending some time with Gideon's boyfriend, Sam. It might be a good idea not to mention all the details of our first meeting. Sam is mostly easygoing, but he would get mad about that."

Dustin's eyes widen, and he sneaks a sideways glance at Gideon, then nods fervently. "It never happened," he vows. "It will never happen again." He winces a little on that last bit, as though making such a promise pains him. I bite my lip to hold in a smile.

Caolan, who slipped away to talk to the more official-looking members of the party, comes back then with two of them in tow. "David, Gideon, meet Even and Rae. They're leading the teams coming with us to Earth today."

We exchange greetings. It's difficult to tell for sure if they're elves or dragons, because visually the differences between elves and dragons in biped form are very few—or, at least, that's my assumption after having met four elves and two dragons. But there's a depth and richness to the color of dragon eyes that hasn't been there in any of the elves I've met, and a very slight difference in the sense I have of them. They're very similar, much like how I perceive hellhounds and felid shifters. The first impression is just shifter, and then the other differences make themselves known. Although, honestly, usually the easiest way to tell whether a shifter is a hellhound or a felid is size. Hellhounds are just bigger as a rule. There's no such trick with elves and dragons—they seem quite closely related, and the main sense I get is "other."

But there does seem to be a dragon*ish* vibe coming from the head of the tac team. I don't want to ask, for fear of being rude, so it will have to wait until I can take Caolan or Garin aside and find out discreetly. I also want to remind them that until we can neutralize Tish and Éibhear, we need to be absolutely certain that the dragons are fully aware of Éibhear's plan to kill the magic. I've been assured it's impossible that any dragon could be manipulated into inadvertently assisting or be a spy for the other side, but I'm a bit paranoid, what with the whole plan to kill the magic and take over the world.

Wait… has that not come up yet? Sorry. So, in a nutshell, nine thousand-ish years ago, the species wars broke out on Earth. It started with some petty tribal leader getting pissed off because the lucifer wouldn't let him wipe out a neighboring tribe, and somehow escalated into widescale attempted genocide, with the much more populous humans trying to kill the rest of us. The elves and dragons, who until then had apparently been frequent visitors through the portals, retreated home, and King Raðulfr instituted a travel ban until things were safer on Earth. Unfortunately, that never really happened. While the magic finally noticed that it wasn't just the usual pestilences etcetera killing us off in droves and stepped in to end the wars, it did so by making all of humanity forget the existence of other species and forcing us to live under the radar. King Raðulfr decided that allowing travel to Earth under those circumstances was too risky, both for his people and ours, and the travel ban remained in place. That wiped out an entire section of their tourism industry, and elves who were making their living from opening portals to Earth had to find something else to do. Éibhear was one of those. He began experimenting with opening portals in time and created a new travel industry—one he had complete control of, since he didn't share his method. It made him very rich, but apparently time wasn't designed to have people jumping back and forth, and anomalies began. When it was discovered that his time portals were causing the destruction of the dimension, the king asked him to stop. He agreed—for a fee—but while the main part of the population was hoping their dimension would be able to heal, he secretly continued his now-illicit business for those wealthy and immoral enough to still want to hire him. The result is the pending collapse of the entire dimension.

When the magic—or as the elves and dragons call it, the life force—made King Raðulfr aware of what was happening, Éibhear was stripped of his ability to open portals and of the right to be reborn. The next time he dies, it's forever—his soul will never again reincarnate.

It's a heavy punishment, but the destruction of millions of worlds and millions of lives is no small crime. However, Éibhear was still not remorseful. Determined to survive the apocalypse, he and the small group of followers he'd amassed—mostly those who'd used his services with the full knowledge of what the outcome would be—reached across dimensions to make contact with Tish and the CCA. The new plan: take over Earth. Tish, once the leader of an insignificant anti-human cult, was assured of elfin support in overthrowing Percy as lucifer and taking control of the community while Éibhear forces humans to bend knee to him. And how do they plan to prevent the magic from stepping in this time?

By killing it.

Lost to the mists of time, unknown to most and thought only to be a folktale to others, there is a method by which existential magic—the essence of life itself—can be made corporeal. An elfin spell, read over the lucifer's seal of office, willingly witnessed by representatives of every species, and sealed by dragon flame. And once the force that binds all of existence is bound to a body, that body can be slain.

We don't know what would happen then—we just don't know. But one of the few things the magic itself has communicated to us is that it would be bad.

So the lucifer's seal is under guard, as is the king's spell. And I've been told that every living dragon is accounted for, all of them on our side. But I can't help being wary. Any dragon who's part of the advance party needs to be kept absolutely safe.

"Let's go, shall we, before we attract too much attention? We can talk more once we're through the portal,"

Garin suggests. Part of me wants to protest about leaving this place—there's still so much I could see and do—but that would be beyond selfish, since this is their home and they're going to have to leave it forever. Not to mention, the reason we're leaving now is to make the arrangements to ensure they don't die with it. Saying "I want to look at your pretty trees some more" seems a little tactless in that context.

We make our way back inside the building and through a few hallways. Gideon sticks even closer to my side now that we're surrounded by strangers, and oddly, so does Dustin. He's quiet at first, then he takes a deep breath and turns on his charm.

"Have you enjoyed your visit, David? I know most of it was taken up by business, but I hope your impression of our home hasn't been overshadowed by our recent troubles."

Recent troubles? That's a very genteel way of putting it.

"It's been lovely. Your world is truly amazing. I'm only sorry my visit couldn't have been different," I say, choosing my words carefully.

He nods, somehow looking sad and impossibly young even while smiling. "Yes. I was born after the travel ban went into effect, of course, and I'm so excited to see Earth, but these aren't the circumstances I'd always hoped for." The smile turns wistful. "I haven't even been able to see my own world in its real glory. The time blips had already begun when I was born. It wasn't so bad at first, and I believe my childhood was comparable to those of my parents and other elders, but there are so many things I wanted to do and see as an adult that never happened."

"I can never hope to understand," I begin, then my

brain snags on what he said about the blips not being so bad when he was born. Didn't those begin thousands of years ago? Do dragons develop more slowly than we do? Our lives are much longer than human ones, but most of our brain development is complete by the age of twenty-five. I would put Dustin as being in his late teens, early twenties at most, but he's talking as though he's been alive for millennia.

Something else to add to my list of questions to discreetly ask. Maybe Noah will have learned something about this from Eerika.

"Uh," I stumble a little, having lost my train of thought. "I wish this hadn't happened, but I'm so very glad that our people have been able to reconnect—and of course, we're happy to welcome you to Earth."

"Thank you, David. We're so grateful. When my grandfather told me, I… it… We're so grateful." He clears his throat. "I have a liking for adventure, and I spent some time reading about Earth, hoping the travel ban would be revoked at some stage and I could visit. Garin said it's very different from how it used to be."

"Yes. Our species have remained the same, more or less, but even without the societal shift, things have changed a lot. The most important thing for you to remember is that you can never let humans know we other species exist. Not ever," I emphasize, remembering Caolan's warning that dragons liked to play fast and loose with rules. "The magic caused them to forget us because they were trying to wipe us out of existence. Nothing that we've ever learned has indicated their stance might be different now, so secrecy is the only thing keeping us alive."

He swallows hard. "We have to live in hiding?"

There's a slight tremor to his voice that makes me feel like an ass. *Good one, David. Traumatize the kid.*

"Not entirely," I say, while Gideon huffs slightly at my other side. "We live openly, but we keep parts of ourselves secret. Gideon, for example, uses a glamor to hide his horns when he's amongst humans, and he would never teleport if he knew one might be able to see. Other than that…." I shrug. It's a bit of a simplistic explanation, but hopefully will give him the idea.

"Oh. That should be okay. Will we be able to shift?" The tremor is fainter, but still there.

"Yes." I make it sound as firm as I can. "We're still working out some of the details, because dragons are bigger than the shifters we already have, but we will absolutely make sure there are places you can safely shift —and fly. Caolan said you were able to hide yourself from sight?" I hope he was right. We're kind of counting on that.

"A distortion shield?" Dustin sounds intrigued all of a sudden. "Sure. I've only ever used it for short periods, to… uh… while playing games with friends and stuff." He avoids my gaze, and I guess that a distortion shield is the tool of choice for anonymous pranks. "But there's no reason why I couldn't maintain one for longer. I wonder if it would be possible to…" He trails off, clearly considering all the angles of adapting a spell. I know the feeling—sometimes I get lost in thought for hours when I'm designing new weaves.

Which reminds me, I keep meaning to ask someone about the similarities and differences between sorcery and elfin magic. That's something Dustin can help with and fits right into his new job description as liaison between our people.

But a glance at his face shows he's completely wrapped up in whatever he's thinking, and anyway, I recognize this corridor—the portal room is just up ahead. Vacation time is almost over; time to start preparing for the mountain of work ahead.

And oh, fuck. I still need to knock it into my team's heads to stop encouraging Caolan. Mostly because I don't know how much longer I can hold out now that I've seen him on his home ground, orders from Percy notwithstanding.

An evil little voice in the back of my head begins to whisper. *You saw how excited Percy was about Caolan bringing you breakfast. And things are pretty solid now between the elves and us. The king agreed to a ceremony and everything. I bet if you told Percy you wanted to give things a shot with Caolan, he'd be okay with it.*

"Talk to me," I beg Gideon desperately. He startles and immediately scans the vicinity.

"What?" he asks, his eyes asking questions that have nothing to do with my current problem.

"Talk. Distract me from my thoughts."

He relaxes slightly and smirks—well, it's what passes for a smirk for Gideon. On anyone else, it might be called a twitch of the lips.

"Sure. Your birthday's coming up, isn't it?" It's just a tiny bit louder than it really needs to be, causing heads to turn.

"Not for a week," I mutter, still trying to keep my brain off the thought of tangling my hands in Caolan's beautiful, silky hair.

"It's your birth day?" Dustin comes out of his reverie to ask, sounding both confused and curious. "I think my translator spell is not working correctly."

"Not my actual day of birth," I explain. "The anniversary of that day."

His face lights up. "This is something you commemorate? How?"

Well, it's a distraction. "We note it," I correct. "Commemoration is mostly for young children or special landmark ages. Though it's not uncommon to spend part of the day with friends or family—a meal or drinks." Or, if you're Elinor, a week of movie nights that match snacks and drinks to the theme of the movie. Alistair hasn't had a birthday since joining the team, but it's coming up soon, and that's causing low-level dread.

"What do you do for young children? This could be something to excite them about leaving their home."

I'm taken aback, but he's right. Caolan was totally justified to suggest he act as liaison—he's already planning to have a positive impact.

"A birthday party is the most common celebration, although they can take many forms depending on the child's preferences and the family's budget. Usually there is a cake. At some point during the event, small candles are put on top and lit, and then everyone sings 'Happy Birthday'—uh, a song specific to that purpose. The birthday person blows the candles out and makes a wish, then cuts the cake and everyone has a piece."

"What kind of wish?" he wants to know. "Is there a criteria? Who is responsible for the fulfilment of the wish?"

I wince. "It doesn't work that way. There's no guarantee that the wish will come true. In fact, it's bad luck to say out loud what you've wished for. It's just something we use to teach children it's okay to dream, I suppose." I stop, because I've never really thought about it before. How many times have kids made wishes that could never possibly come true, but done it anyway?

Hope is a powerful thing.

"There's also usually gifts," I race on, not wanting to get sidetracked—or worse, have him decide that we should develop some kind of standard for wish-making and a committee responsible for fulfilling them.

"What kind of gifts?" He seems fascinated by the idea. In fact, we seem to be getting a lot of attention from those around us. Wishes and gifts are the kind of things people want to be part of, I guess. How much farther is the portal room?

"That depends on the person, the age, and the givers. There's not really a standard. Small children often receive toys or books or clothes. As specific interests begin to develop, their close family and friends would tailor gift choices to suit those."

"This is very exciting. I think I need to learn more about children's birthday parties. Would that be possible?"

"Absolutely," I assure him. "I'm sure Noah and Sam can show you how to access the information you need." They can set him up on YouTube or google "kids party ideas" and leave him to read through the millions of results. "Just be sure to check with one of us before you begin planning an actual party," I caution. The last thing we need is for him to get carried away and try to recreate a live-action fairy-tale party complete with fake snow and bejeweled costumes—and hire an island to host it on.

"Of course," he promises. "For now, just understanding how these parties work will be enough. Then I can tell the children about them next time I'm here, and they can start thinking about how they would like to celebrate their birthdays on Earth." He smiles at me. "How are you going to celebrate your birthday?"

"Oh, I won't do anything special. My sister, Jane, will call, and probably my niblings as well. I'm sure Sam will organize a cake at the office. Alistair and Andrew will likely have some kind of gag gift—uh, joke present. And I might spoil myself and buy a new TV," I add impulsively. I'm going to have some extra cash with this promotion, and my current TV isn't even a flatscreen. I'm hardly home with free time to watch it, and it still works, so it just never seemed necessary to get a new one —especially since I can access streaming services on my laptop, tablet, *and* phone. But maybe it's time to update to a smart TV.

I could even use it as a monitor when I bring work home. That would be a huge help.

"TV?" he asks, and the full weight of what we're doing strikes me.

Luckily, Caolan steps in. "You'll see in a little while," he says. "You'll like it—it's an entertainment format." He looks around the group, and I realize we've stopped outside the portal room, crowding the hallway. Who knew thinking about the latest in smart TVs could be so absorbing? "The room won't hold us all, so we're going inside in groups of five—not including me. I'll be operating the portals today. I'm aware that some of you are capable, but I'm the only one who knows exactly where we're going. Also, until our new allies have had time to acclimate their people to this ability, let's not flaunt it."

There's a general murmur of consensus as I try not to notice how attractive he is when he takes charge. He looks at me and Gideon. "Would you like to be in the first group?"

"I think that's best," Gideon agrees. "They're expecting us, but familiar faces would be safer initially." The security team at CSG is still nervy about portals after what happened with Noah.

It's quickly decided that the first group will consist of me and Gideon, Garin, and the two team leaders. Dustin pouts, clearly disappointed that he has to wait a few extra moments, but it makes sense to have senior people and those familiar with the environment be the first. We—they—will be able to direct the others on what to do when they arrive.

Walking through the portal is an experience that's so mundane and yet the most profound thing I've ever done. I mean… it's a portal between dimensions. When I took those steps this morning, the metaphorical weight of that was pressing down on me. But at the same time, it's just a few steps. There's the light tingle of Caolan's magic, but if it weren't for the glowing green color, the portal could almost be any other doorway.

And then I'm back at CSG, in the top-floor reception area. Caolan has assured us many times that he can sense how many people are present at the other end before he opens a portal, and even if humans did make a habit of visiting our offices (they don't), the guards have been told to be extra vigilant now. So I'm confident that stepping through a glowing green gateway isn't going to traumatize anyone who sees and expose our existence to humankind.

Sure enough, the only people there are the guard on the stairwell door, the executive receptionist, and Garin, who went ahead of me. They both manage to look bored—I guess they've seen portals enough times in the past few days to no longer find them exciting.

The receptionist, Candice, sees me, smiles, then picks up her phone and says, "David's back," just as Gideon comes out of the portal.

"Is someone looking for me?" I ask, going over to her desk, and she laughs.

"Please. Someone's always looking for you. But in this case, Percy just asked to be told when you got back. I don't think it was anything specific—he didn't ask that you go see him or anything."

"Thanks, Candice." Her gaze goes over my shoulder as more of the elves and dragons begin to arrive. "Could you ask Sam to come out here, please?" He's the one who made the accommodation arrangements for this advance group.

"Sure." She picks up her phone, eyes not shifting from the newcomers, and I turn back to help Garin and Gideon direct them toward the executive conference room. It's not big enough to hold all of us, but the reception area is going to get crowded, and I've been told it's essential to keep bodies away from the opening to the gateway.

Sam comes into reception, followed by Noah and Andrew. Noah, I can tell you one hundred percent is here because he's curious. Andrew… well, he might be curious, or he might just be hovering over Noah, who's still not back to top form after nearly dying.

Dodging bodies, they begin to make their way over.

"Is that one a human?" one of the elves—or maybe it's a dragon?—whispers to another just a little too loudly. Noah just rolls his eyes and keeps going, but

Andrew stops and hisses, his fangs and claws coming out.

In response, the dragon—definitely a dragon— growls, the sound raising every hair on my body.

Fuck.

Before I can step in, Noah pivots, takes two steps back, grabs Andrew's arm, and yanks. "Stop being asses, both of you. We have more important things to worry about than interspecies pissing matches."

"But—" Andrew begins.

"Either go help David or go back to your desk. If you cause any trouble, you're sleeping on the terrace tonight."

I bite my lip to hold in a laugh. On the terrace? He won't even let him have the guest room or the couch? Noah's a vicious thing.

Muttering, Andrew stomps toward me. Behind him, Noah turns his gaze on the dragon. "Yes, I'm a human. That doesn't mean I won't set you on fire if you don't stop being a douche."

The dragon smirks. "I like fire. I like *you*. Maybe we can roast meat together." The words are weird, but the innuendo in his voice is unmistakable, and Gideon lunges forward to grab Andrew in a headlock just in the nick of time.

Fuck. My. Life.

It's been literally minutes. The advance team is still coming through the portal. How did things already get out of hand?

Noah laughs. "Dude, no. I'm taken. Also, not sure if it's a translation problem or not, but that pickup line won't work here." And he turns his back and continues toward us. If you weren't watching for it, you'd never see he's just a little shaky and slower than usual. "Did you see the orange grass?" he asks when he reaches us.

"We *walked* on it. And saw the tréghel trees," I brag.

"What are—" he begins, but Sam interrupts.

"You can talk about all that another time. Don't give me that look, Noah; I don't have the time or patience for it today."

Noah clearly sees that Sam is one wrong word away from a killing spree, because he prudently closes his mouth.

"What's up?" I ask Sam.

"I have a call list for you," he starts, "and at some stage in the next little while, we're going to sit down and I'm going to yell at you for babying everyone, because the calls you need to return are less than *half* of what you received. All those others were for things people can do their own damn selves."

I try not to wince. "And you told them that, didn't you?"

"You bet your ass," he mutters.

"I like *him* too," the dragon who flirted with Noah says, and instantly Gideon seems to swell to twice his size, growling in that bone-chilling way demons do before they attack.

"Taken!" Sam shouts, launching himself at Gideon and wrapping his arms around him. "I'm taken!"

"He's taken," I reiterate firmly. I thought we'd avoided battle, but clearly that was optimistic of me. "Tell you what, you all refrain from flirting with anyone for now, and I'll organize cocktails or something with a bunch of single people."

The dragon, whose name I should probably learn, frowns. "Single? No, we need more than one."

Fucking translator spells. "Available. Unattached. Potentially open to your attentions."

"Ahhh." He nods. "Yes. Okay. Let's do that." There's a murmur of agreement among the elves and dragons just as the portal winks closed.

"Let's do what?" Caolan asks, pushing through the crowd to join us.

"David's matchmaking," Garin says brightly. "He's hoping to begin relations between our people with… *relations*." He wiggles his brows.

"Was there anything else?" I ask Sam somewhat desperately.

"Aside from the hookup event we now need to organize?" he snarks, but then adds, "Yes. Many things. So… call list. It's on your desk. So is a stack of updates, phones for Caolan and Garin, and a printout of your updated schedule for the day. You have two new meetings in addition to dinner at our place. Percy wants a few minutes of your time when you have it, but he said to stress that it's not urgent. And I booked out a few floors at that executive short-stay hotel two blocks over for the advance team. It took some fast talking, and we paid more than the going rate because they had to find other places for some other guests, but I made a big deal about it being a foreign delegation who are really unfamiliar with America and how we wanted to keep them together." He turns to face our guests. "Did you hear that? If anyone at the hotel asks, mention how glad you are to all be staying together. And how strange you find this place."

I can't see his face, but from the widening eyes and fast nods, I'm guessing it's somewhat manic.

"How much coffee has he had today?" I murmur to Noah, who shakes his head vehemently.

"We don't ask those sorts of questions," he hisses.

Gideon and I exchange a glance.

"Sam, why don't we go over to the hotel and get everyone checked in?" he suggests. "It's a great day. We can walk."

"Great idea," Andrew agrees as Sam spins back to look at us. "We'll work out assignments and get everyone sorted with their phones and show them how things work, and you and Gideon can update each other on what's happened today, then report to the rest of us when you get back."

"Is this the room list?" Noah asks, taking a sheet of paper from Sam. "Great! By the time you're back with the keys, we'll have allocated everyone to rooms."

"I do *not* like being managed," Sam announces, and for a moment I think we might all need to duck for cover. "But I do want to go for a walk. Come on, Gideon." He turns toward the elevator, then calls over his shoulder, "I'll be back in thirty minutes. There had better not be chaos waiting for me."

As if on cue, the elevator doors open, and Gideon obediently follows him inside.

"That was close," Andrew says when they're gone. "I love Sam, but since he stabbed Alistair with that pencil, I've been afraid to turn my back to him."

Since he...

"I'm sorry, what?"

"It was beautiful," Andrew tells me, his expression going dreamy. "Alistair was being Alistair, sticking his hands in everywhere while we were trying to get work done, and Sam finally snapped, grabbed a pencil, and stabbed it right through his hand."

How long was I gone? I've left them alone for longer than this before. And for it to be *Sam* who snapped…

"What was Alistair *doing*?" Sam loves Alistair. They're best friends, have been for years. What could he have done that was so much worse than everything else he's done over the years?

"Just being Alistair," Noah says dismissively. "I think Sam was just really on edge. He was sorry after, especially when Al got back from the infirmary with his hand bandaged and started acting all pathetic."

I pinch the bridge of my nose, because fuck me, now we're all going to have to deal with Alistair nursing an injury. Nobody is whinier than an injured hellhound. "Was there any significant damage?"

"According to Alistair, he's maimed for life," Andrew says dryly. "But Noah called the medic, and she said the pencil didn't hit anything important. With his natural shifter healing, it should be fine within a week."

"Did someone tell Percy?"

Noah rolls his eyes. "Percy knows. Believe me, everyone knows. They all heard Alistair howling like a big baby."

I leave that alone. I mean, just this once, Alistair might have been justified in being dramatic, but I don't want to encourage him.

"Has Al gone home?" That might explain why he hasn't come out to see the newcomers. I expected him and his enthusiastic curiosity to be the first in line.

"No, he's being brave and determined at his desk. The guilt was killing Sam."

I sigh. "Okay. Okay. Can you two do those room

allocations—use the exec conference room. And, Andrew, did you say something about phones?"

"Yeah, Sam figured everyone would need to be able to communicate, so he got a bunch. The guy at the store loves him now—gave him a pretty good discount and chucked in some accessories too."

"Great. So allocate rooms, hand out phones, and demonstrate how they work?"

"We got it," Noah assures me. "Go do your things."

I look around. "Did everyone get that?" I feel crappy about abandoning them all right after they arrive—and before I even meet them properly—but I'm itching to get my own phone back in my hands and see what else has happened while I've been gone.

"I have a question." My new friend, the flirty dragon, waves a hand.

"Yes. Of course."

"Are *you* taken?"

"You seem to be overly concerned with this, Hagen," Caolan snaps, stepping forward. "Do I need to remind you why you're here and what's at stake?"

There's a general air of surprise, maybe because Caolan's not usually a snappy person, but the dragon— Hagen—inclines his head. "Of course not. My apologies."

That last is directed at me, and I stretch my mouth into a smile, murmur "No problem," and shoot a pleading look at Noah.

"Great! So we'll let David go check on things—don't worry, he'll be back later for you to perv on—and get you settled before Sam comes back and stabs more of us with pencils. I'm Noah, and yes, I'm human. This is Andrew, and he's a vampire. Why don't we go around the group, and you can introduce yourselves and tell us whether you're an elf or a dragon. Oh, and if I'm talking too fast or say something your translator spell doesn't understand, please speak up."

I back away from Noah's chipper yet somehow scary impersonation of a camp counselor and escape down the hallway toward the office.

Where I find Alistair.

I know he knows I'm standing in the doorway. He's a hellhound—he smelled *and* heard me coming down the hall. In fact, I wouldn't be surprised if he'd heard at least some of what happened in reception. But he continues to peck one-handed at his keyboard, cradling his bandaged hand against his chest and sighing pitifully.

If things weren't so ridiculously busy today, I'd find his performance amusing.

"Do you want me to have you reassigned?" I ask, heading for my desk. "Or maybe you should be on injury leave?"

His head snaps around. "What? No! How can you even contemplate that at a time like this?"

"Should I report Sam to HR, then?" I scan the call list. Sam really has done an excellent job of narrowing these down to essentials only.

"Not after I spent twenty minutes convincing the medic not to," Alistair grumbles. "I'm devastated that my bestest bestie could treat me this way, but he's under a lot of stress, and maybe he'd told me six times to get out of his way."

"Only six?" I'm only half listening by this point. The idea is to give Alistair the chance to unload his woe so he and everyone else can actually get back to work.

"Maybe it was more. Who remembers these things? Well, now I'll have a wound to remind me, but I will survive and come out stronger for it."

"Uh-huh."

"I refuse to abandon you all in this time of need, no matter how difficult and painful work is as a result of my grievous wound."

"We appreciate your sacrifice." A thought strikes. "Have you called Aidan yet?"

His expression turns sheepish. "Not exactly. I texted and told him I'd had an accident but am okay."

"That's very low-key of you. Why?"

"He'll take Sam's side, and I can wait until tonight to hear my lover say 'I told you so.'" He shrugs. "He said last night that I should try to stay out of everyone's way while people were so stressed out. I laughed, because everyone loves me, right? But I guess Sam was a little too close to the edge."

"He still loves you, though," I assure him.

"Oh, I know. And as soon as all the stress is passed, I'm going to milk this for everything I can get. Two hundred years from now, Sam will reach for the last cookie, and I'll make a sad face and mention how my hand still aches sometimes when it's cold, and he'll let me have it."

I can't help it; I laugh. "You're such an asshole, Alistair."

"And yet, I'm universally revered. Where are the others? They didn't come back with you?"

"Sam and Gideon went for a walk to prevent another stabbing incident. Andrew and Noah are—"

"Phones!" Andrew races in, looks around, then dives behind Sam's desk and comes up with a two-foot-square box that looks to be full of boxed smartphones. He then comes over to my desk and grabs the two sitting on top.

"They're handing out phones and room allocations to the elves and dragons," I finish, and Alistair leaps up, knocking his chair back.

"There are dragons here? Wait, I'll help! I need to see if my new tertiary best friend is among them."

My eye twitches, but Noah and Caolan will be there, and I'm sure between them they can keep things from getting too far out of hand.

"David's going to host a hookup party," I hear Andrew say as they leave, but I don't bother calling them back to correct him. It's not worth the effort.

Thanks to Sam's strict guidelines, the call list only takes half an hour to get through, and I manage to go through my emails at the same time. I am the master of multitasking. Then I text Noah to see if I'm needed there.

NOAH:

Phones a HUGE hit. Have gone through basic functions already, and Alistair is now introducing them to apps. Should be good for a while.

Has Alistair made any friends?

Too many

Great. When this crisis is over, Alistair is going to have a bunch of flying, fire-breathing dragons to egg him on.

Pushing the thought aside, I go to see if Percy's got a few minutes.

"He's just finishing up a call," his assistant tells me.

"Can you hang around a few minutes, or do you want me to text when he's done?"

"I can wait a few minutes," I decide, but Percy's door opens barely ten seconds later.

"I thought I smelled you," he says. "Come in."

I smile at his assistant, then follow him inside. We settle at the small table by the window, as we often do, and out of habit, I activate the privacy wards. Not that this conversation is going to really need them.

"How did it go?" Percy asks. "You seem to be fairly relaxed."

"Sam fixed it so my to-do list is only two-thirds the size I thought it would be," I tell him. "It's like a surprise vacation."

He laughs, then says, "Once this initial chaos settles, we need to talk about you taking a vacation. I can't remember the last time you did."

Distract, distract. Because I can't remember either.

"The king has agreed to a ceremony that we can livestream."

"Splendid. I'll have PR set something up—subject to approval from you and Caolan," he adds. "I trust you not to let them make me look stupid, and Caolan's the king's delegate, so presumably he feels the same way."

I concentrate very hard on being neutral, but it's useless. I must exhibit some physiological change—respiration, scent, *something*—because Percy perks up.

"What?" he asks.

"Nothing. Just thinking about all the ways PR could make you look stupid. Do you remember the time they suggested an ermine robe? Talk about insensitive."

"No. Don't try to distract me. Whatever it is, tell me now. Is it about Caolan? It *is*, isn't it? What happened?"

Here's the problem with working for a man you basically grew up with: boundaries don't exist. When we were teenagers, Percy and I told each other everything. That relationship changed when we reached adulthood, and we drifted apart a lot over the subsequent centuries, but our connection is forged in steel, and when the magic selected him to be lucifer, he sent for me immediately.

How can I possibly keep anything secret from him?

"It's really nothing," I insist. "Just… it was interesting seeing him interact with his people and his king. And… oh, I should have mentioned earlier. We brought the grandson of the dragon wing leader back with us. He's going to act as a spokesperson of sorts for their civilians—answer their questions and let them know what to expect from Earth."

"That's a clever idea. Caolan's?"

He's like a dog with a bone. Or a cat with… well, pretty much anything.

"Yes. In fact…" I sigh. "I'm pretty sure he came up with it because the kid—his name's Dustin—was feeling overlooked. He's… well, the first thing he did when we met him was make a pretty heavy pass at Gideon."

"This is perfect," Percy whispers, and I wonder if he stopped listening at some point. "Without even knowing it, Caolan hit right on your soft spot."

"No—"

"Yes. Insecure adolescents are your kryptonite, and you know it. And it seems like Caolan feels the same way, which means you have even more in common than you thought." The self-satisfied expression on his face is so very catlike that I smile. "This is what's bothering you —you're becoming more attracted to Caolan."

Because of course Percy of all people would know that I already felt attraction.

"Maybe," I admit, then, "Fine, yes. You already know he's just my type, physically, and if he was only offering a shag, I'd already have asked you to relax the rules. Finding out now that I actually like him as a person and that we might have things in common is… disconcerting."

"Why? Isn't it a good thing? He seems pretty devoted, and you've always been a monogamous relationship kind of person."

How dare he be so reasonable.

"Things are so complicated. And he can't tell time, Percy. Worse—he doesn't seem to care! What if he just never wants to learn? What if once this crisis is over, it comes out that he's happy to flitter through life without regard to schedules and commitments and responsibilities—"

I stop, because my voice is rising like it always does when I start down this path. Percy puts a hand on my arm, a solid sign of comfort and security. I've always been able to rely on him. If Percy said he would be there, he wouldn't forget or disregard that commitment because something more interesting came up.

Taking a deep breath, I loosen my muscles and force away the bad memories.

"Sorry."

"You don't ever need to apologize to me," Percy says fiercely. "And if you're genuinely worried about this, I'll enforce the no-fraternization rule until the end of days. I'll even come up with other rules to keep him away from you completely. But…"

I sigh again. "Yeah. But."

"What if you start slow? Tell him it's too soon for you to know if you feel what he's feeling, but that you're attracted to him and would be open to exploring that."

I blink. "That's the most genteel and boring way of asking for a no-strings fuck that I've ever heard. Well done."

"I've always had a gift for diplomacy," he says, deadpan. "But in all seriousness, I think you should do it. When's the last time you even had sex, anyway? All that pent-up tension can't be good for you."

If it was anyone else, I'd make a stupid joke about having had sex more recently than him, but I'm one of the few people who knows why Percy hasn't had sex for nearly a year, and the last thing I want to do is hurt him. So instead I say, "It hasn't been that long."

Has it?

Not that I'm pent-up—that's what my hand is for. A quick wank in the shower takes care of any tension with no fuss. But when was the last time I got off with more than my hand for company? Or even with a little more finesse?

"Okay," I concede. "Okay, so maybe it would do me good to hook up with someone." He gives me a look, and I sigh. "Fine, with Caolan. It would do me good to hook up with Caolan." Just saying the words out loud puts me in the mood, which is a little embarrassing. Not to mention awkward, since I'm at work, in a meeting with my boss.

"Good! So, I'm officially relaxing the rule about personal relationships between us and the elves. Feel free to tackle this however you like." He leers, which is very unlike him.

"You've been spending too much time with the hooligans who work for you."

He laughs. "They are hooligans, aren't they? Even the levelheaded ones. Did you see what Sam did to Alistair? What am I supposed to do about that? Obviously we don't want people thinking they can just stab their coworkers with pencils—or other office supplies—but on the other hand, there isn't a person on this plane or the next who hasn't felt an overwhelming urge to stab Alistair at some stage."

"I'll come up with some story to spread that makes it sound like Sam's been punished. Alistair will support it —he's planning to milk Sam's guilt all through eternity, but he'd be the first to protest if we actually tried to fire Sam."

"Good."

We talk for a few minutes more, just a general update, and then we both have other meetings.

"Dinner at Gideon and Sam's?" he asks me as I get up to leave.

"Sam put it in my schedule," I confirm. "A daily update is probably a good idea right now, anyway."

"I can't wait for this all to be over," Percy mutters.

Oh fuck yeah.

CHAPTER FIVE

Caolan

I COULD SPEND *days* just using my phone.

These devices are going to be very helpful in transitioning my people to life on Earth. It's hard to be sad when you can listen to music or play a game or read a book just at the touch of a button. Noah showed us how to make voice and video calls and send written messages, although that's still difficult for us, because the translator spell is verbal and auditory only. After that, Alistair came and showed us all kinds of apps, including the one Garin talked about with the kittens trapped in bubbles. There's also one that will help us learn to recognize written words while we work on an adaption to the translator spell.

But for now, I reluctantly put it in my pocket. Garin, Dustin, and I are expected at Sam and Gideon's home for dinner and a review. Eerika has begged off, claiming she's all talked out—which is fair, because I've never seen anyone ask questions as much as Noah. She's going to stay at the hotel and make sure there are no problems with the advance teams as they settle in. I've just checked in on all of them myself, and they're acquitting themselves as I would expect of such highly trained individuals, but this is a very strange place, and Eerika has the advantage of having been here a few extra days.

Dustin comes out of the apartment he's sharing with me and Garin (although technically, I'm still living at Sam and Gideon's house). I'm not willing to leave Dustin without direct supervision for long. He's been very well behaved so far, but all his natural exuberance has to be building up, and it's best if I'm there to deal with the fallout when he lets it free. He looks a little nervous right now, and I'm reminded that not only is he still quite young—only four thousand—he's also very sheltered. We can't really blame him for being spoiled, and he *has* been trying very hard today.

"Are you ready?" I ask, and he nods.

"Could we walk there?" he asks uncertainly. "Is it very far?"

"I'm not certain," I admit. Given the need for speed and secrecy, I've been traveling from my lodgings to the office building via portal, so I'm not familiar with the distances or how to navigate them. We walked from the office to this hotel, guided by our hosts, but nobody mentioned which way we would go to get elsewhere. "Why don't I call Sam and ask?" I suggest, because that means I get to use my phone.

It's shockingly easy, and soon I hear Sam's voice in my ear. "Hello? Caolan? Is everything okay?"

"How did you know it was me?" I ask, astounded.

"Noah programmed all your numbers in all our phones," he says, sounding amused. Certainly more relaxed than he was earlier today. "The same as he put our numbers in your phones. That means that when you call, your name shows on my screen."

These phones are amazing devices.

"Is something wrong?" he asks.

"No, nothing's wrong. We were just wondering if it would be possible to walk to your house. Is it far?"

"Not far at all—just a few blocks. When you exit your hotel, turn to the left. Uh… do you remember what we talked about today, about crossing streets?"

"We have to wait for the walking man," I say. "I remember."

"Great. So you'll need to cross three streets. When you get to the building on a corner with the big red door, turn right. There's one more street to cross. I don't think you've seen the front of the house, though, have you? I'll get someone to wait out front so you don't miss it."

"Turn left. Cross three streets. Turn right at the red door. One more street. We can do that."

"Are you all disguised to look like humans?"

"Yes. We decided to leave those spells active most of the time, so we can get used to having them."

"Then we'll see you soon. Call if you need anything."

I press the red circle to end the call, just like Noah showed us, then put my phone back in my pocket. "Easy," I declare. "Let's go."

DAVID HAS BEEN WATCHING me across the table all through the meal. At first I was worried that I'd committed a huge error, but it didn't take me long to realize that wasn't the reason. I've seen that expression on the faces of many people before.

He desires me.

Yes.

This is excellent. His attraction to me is increasing. He'll soon realize how deep the connection between us is. Of course he's been distracted by all the things that have been happening, and it's caused him to overlook his growing personal feelings for me, but clearly something happened today to change that.

Maybe he was impressed by how resourceful I was in arranging the walk from the hotel? Or perhaps he liked the forceful way I shut down Hagen when he dared to flirt with David.

Just the thought makes me angry, but I push that aside. No time for it.

I smile at David, just a little. Just enough for him to know that I'm here and worship him.

He takes a deep breath and looks away, so I turn my attention back to the conversation. We've already gone over all the important details, and now Alistair is telling everyone the story of how Sam stabbed him. I've already heard it—he told us all this afternoon—but this version seems to be embellished somewhat. Sam has his head in his hands.

Dustin is extremely enthralled by Alistair's story-telling, so I nudge him and give him a warning glare. It would be very bad for him to start stabbing people.

When I glance back up, David is watching me again. A shiver of delight runs through me. He can't look away!

He meets my gaze, holds it, and then tips his head slightly toward the door. Is that…? Is he inviting me for an assignation?

Looking away, he pushes back his chair. "Excuse me," he murmurs, then leaves the room.

My head is spinning. This is it. I was prepared to wait so much longer, but *this is it*.

I count to ten, then mutter something that comes out in a garbled combination of two languages and slip away from the table. David's hovering in the hallway, and he puts a finger to his lips, then grabs my hand and pulls me down the corridor and up the stairs. It's not until we're in the guest suite that he lets me go—and I instantly regret it. His hand in mine felt so right, warm and strong and slightly rough.

"We have to be quiet," he says in a low voice, "or they'll hear us."

I nod, not sure I trust myself to speak. Is he going to declare his feelings?

"I want to talk to you about… us. This… situation between us."

Yes. I nod again.

"You've, ah, you've made it quite clear that you're, ah, attracted to me."

That's… an understated interpretation of my feelings for him. I smile. He's so earnest and focused.

His pretty blue eyes narrow. "Are you laughing— You know what, never mind. I should get right to the point. I'm not the kind of person who can fall in love easily, but you're very attractive, and I'm open to a sexual relationship with you."

I blink. Disappointment settles over me. He just wants sex? He hasn't realized he loves me too?

I suppose I'll have to wait, after all. And in the meantime…

"Okay."

It's his turn to blink, and a cautious expression crosses his face. "Okay? You understand that I'm not committing to any kind of emotional connection—this will just be sex."

"Yes. That's fine. I like sex, and I love you, so why would I say no?"

He pinches the bridge of his nose and shakes his head, muttering something I don't quite catch, then lowering his hand with a sigh. "I should have checked— are we even sexually compatible? As species, I mean. Do you know?"

"Oh yes," I say happily, then lower my voice when he glances anxiously toward the door. I don't want to do anything to add to my beloved David's stress. "The living archive has many stories about sexual exploits between our species." Just thinking about some of them makes me hard.

"Your archives sound much more fun than ours. Okay. Well… that's good. But just to reiterate, this is just sex. Not a relationship."

"Of course," I assure him. "Just sex." For now. This will make my wait much more enjoyable, not to mention, it's much easier to make an emotional connection with someone you're having regular sex with.

Momentarily pushing aside my anticipation, I ask, "Is this going to cause trouble with the lucifer? I can be discreet, but if I understand the shifter sense of smell correctly, he'll be able to tell anyway." I really want to be with David, but not even for him will I endanger the future of my people.

He flushes that pink color I like so much. "No. Uh, he's okay with it. I mean, he said that given how well our diplomatic endeavors have gone, he's willing to relax the, uh, fraternization rule."

I might not be able to smell a lie the way shifters and vampires can, but even I can tell that David did a whole lot of prevaricating there. "I don't mind if you talk to your friend about our sex life. That's okay. Although if you're not comfortable with it, I won't talk to anyone."

He closes his eyes briefly. "Let's work that out later," he suggests. "We can't stay away too long, or they'll know without us having to tell them anything." He clears his throat, then adds, "So, maybe you could come to my house tonight? If that's okay."

If I hadn't already been in love with him, I would be now. "That sounds wonderful," I say gravely. "Just one thing." I reach out, snag the front of his shirt, and pull him into my arms. He fits perfectly, and his mouth is almost level with mine. I only have to bend a few inches to kiss him.

Fireworks explode through me, and my eyes drift closed. His lips are soft and warm and part readily, and his mouth is hot, sending burning lust coursing through me. He wraps one arm around my torso and plunges the other hand into my hair, grasping the back of my skull and tilting my head to suit him better, and I *love* that take-charge part of him. I love it even more when he grinds against me, the hardness in his pants delightful evidence of how much he wants this… wants me.

In the back of my mind, I'm barely aware of the knock.

"Caolan, are you in— Ohhhhhhhhhh."

David leaps out of my arms, opens his mouth, then closes it again. A flurry of emotions crosses his face— shock, horror, resignation.

I will make this better for him.

Turning to Alistair, I'm somewhat taken aback by the naked delight in his expression.

"I was going to ask if you knew where David went, but now I don't have to." He clasps his hands under his chin. "This is wonderful!"

"You can't tell anyone," I order. "This is private between me and David."

Alistair seems shocked and dismayed, but David smiles gratefully at me. I would do anything for that smile.

"Why?" Alistair whines. "Why would you hide the beautiful shining light of your love? Your relationship should be celebrated. By me. With karaoke."

The translator spell struggles with that last word, but it doesn't really matter right now. The important part is making Alistair understand.

"We're not in a relationship. David and I are going to use each other for sex."

Alistair's jaw drops. David moans.

Did I say something wrong?

Based on the slow grin spreading across Alistair's face, I think maybe I did.

"Ohhhhh," he says. "Well, in that case, there's no point trying to keep it a secret. Unless you take crazy precautions, half the team will be able to smell it on you, you dirty birdy." That last is directed at David, who sucks in a deep breath.

"You should have been spanked more as a child," he

says, but it's with that exasperated, hopeless fondness most people use when talking to Alistair. I've heard the same tone in my own voice when speaking with certain dragons.

Most dragons.

"People say that to me all the time." Alistair shakes his head, mischief in his eye. "Aidan tried spanking me as an adult, but I liked it too much."

"*Alistair!*"

The distant shout is proof that David was right to worry about people hearing us. We may have been successful at keeping quiet before, but Alistair has been his usual loud self, and obviously at least one person has been listening.

"Oops." Alistair doesn't sound at all remorseful.

"We may as well go down," David says with a big sigh. "I guess it was naïve to hope for a secret in this group."

I grab his hand and squeeze it, then lift it to my mouth and kiss it. "I will make it worth the sacrifice," I promise. David shivers, his gaze going hot, but then Alistair ruins it.

"That was *de*lightful, Caolan! Both sweet and sexy. Well done!" He walks out of the room, calling, "Did you all hear that? Wasn't it just the best? Caolan's got game!"

The translator spell stumbles. "What's 'game'?" I ask David, and he huffs a laugh.

"It means you're good at flirtation and seduction."

I straighten my shoulders and puff out my chest, then wink at him. "I have game."

His laugh this time is more natural and actually seems happy. It's a nice sound. "Yeah, you do. Come on;

there's no escaping this." He tugs on my hand, leading me toward the door.

"We could just go to your house now," I point out, really liking that idea. "We have finished talking about work, haven't we?"

"*Don't even think about it!*" someone shouts from downstairs—Elinor, I think.

"Better to get it over with now," David says, but he's smiling and much more relaxed than he was a few minutes ago. He also doesn't let go of my hand the whole way back to the dining room, which is nice.

All eyes turn to us as we enter the room. Alistair is standing behind his chair, but everyone else is still seated. Dustin's eyes are wide, and he's grinning from ear to ear.

"Elinor said you and David are 'hooking up,'" he announces. "That's slang for sex."

I nod. "Yes. David and I have decided to satisfy each other's carnal needs." Lucifer Percy chokes on his wine. I look at David. "Did I say it wrong?"

"Not exactly. Uh," he looks back at his friends and colleagues, "can we not make this a thing?"

"No," Noah says, then turns to me. "I have questions about how this would work."

"No, you don't," Sam says firmly, then looks at me. "He doesn't."

Noah's expression clearly shows disagreement, but he doesn't say anything more.

"Well, I have questions," Alistair declares. "I thought Caolan was in love with David. That's the reason I gave my approval to this whole courtship. I'm not sure I can approve of you slaking your lust on him and then tossing him aside."

Aidan groans, then meets David's gaze. "I'm so sorry."

"I'm used to it." David shrugs. "Alistair, this may come as a shock to you, but your approval is not needed for anything that happens in my life. *And*," he continues as Alistair opens his mouth, "Caolan is not 'slaking his lust' on me. If anything, it's the other way around."

Elinor gasps. "You're taking advantage of his feelings for you just to get your rocks off?"

"That's not nice!" Dustin snaps, glaring at David. "Caolan deserves better!"

It takes me a few moments to get over my surprise. "Nobody is taking advantage. David and I have mutually agreed to… hooking up. Hook up?" I glance over at Elinor, who nods. "I still love him, and I also love sex, so it's an excellent solution."

"Ohhhhh," Andrew says. "Nicely played."

There are nods and knowing smirks around the table, and David shakes his head. "I've changed my mind. We're leaving. I'd appreciate it if all of you could try really hard not to be unprofessional about this."

"How are we supposed to be professional about you fucking Caolan?" Alistair demands, sounding confused. "I don't think that's legal in this country."

"Just go," Sam says to us. "I'll take care of this. Have fun." He blushes bright red. "Uh, I mean——"

"They know what you mean," Gideon tells him.

I look at Dustin, then Garin. "Do you mind——"

He waves his hand. "I can manage one baby dragon on my own," he promises. "Go. As Sam said, have fun."

I follow David from the room as Dustin protests being called a "baby dragon" and declares that he doesn't need to be managed.

We stop in the entranceway. "Aidan told me you can open a portal to places you've never been," David says. "Is that right?"

I hesitate. "Yes, but I need a picture or a thorough description of a unique landmark. The picture is best. And I can't get through wards." Working with only a verbal description is something I've trained for extensively and done quite a few times, but the portal is never as secure as when I have an actual image or memory. I like the idea of flaunting my skills for David, but I also want him as safe as I can make him.

"I don't have a picture of my place," he says. "And it's definitely warded. Let's take the train."

The word is one that doesn't translate completely. Instead, the translator spell conjures an image of some kind of machine. I assume it's a form of transportation.

"Yes, let's," I agree. I'm eager to learn more about Earth.

DAVID UNLOCKS and opens the door to his home, and I follow him inside, feeling the now-familiar resistance of sorcery wards as I do. The wards created by sorcerers feel somewhat different from the protective shields we use. Theoretically, I should be able to replicate sorcery wards, but I would first have to teach myself not to use the life force in my spellcasting, and I'm not certain where to begin with that. Something to check in the living archive—I can't be the first elf in history to have thought about this.

The train journey was rather mundane, although I did find the method by which the train worked to be interesting. David answered as many questions as he could and promised to find the answers to the rest for me. His patience is one of the things I love about him.

His home is not.

It's not like him at all.

In fact, it seems as though nobody lives here. The rooms I can see from where I stand are all furnished, but it's impossibly tidy, and there are no obvious personal effects anywhere. Perhaps some of the trinkets or furniture have special meaning to him, but it's impossible to tell, because they all complement each other perfectly, as though they were designed to do so.

The overall effect is cold and neutral, whereas I know David to be a warm and caring person. Even if he is obsessed with timekeeping.

"Let me show you around," he says. "Living room, obviously, and the kitchen is through there. Help yourself to anything you want, although I don't think I have much at the moment. Down here is the bathroom"—I follow him down the hallway and look in the doorway he points to—"and this is the bedroom." It's also impossibly tidy, except for the desk in the corner, which has papers stacked on the surface and an assortment of pens and those lovely ink markers that Sam calls highlighters. That desk is the most David thing I've seen here so far.

"So..." He hovers beside me awkwardly. "That's it." He shifts from one foot to the other.

He's *nervous*! My beautiful David is nervous about us having sex.

Well, I can fix that.

I grab his hand and lift it to my mouth. He seemed to like that before, and if nothing else, it creates contact between us.

His lightly indrawn breath is a good sign.

I kiss the inside of his wrist, lingering over his pulse point. I can just feel his heartbeat, even with such light pressure. If my memory of sorcerer physiology is correct, that means his heartbeat has increased.

Good. Mine certainly has.

Laying his palm against my cheek, I move closer and bend to kiss him.

"Wait," he blurts, sounding delightfully breathless. "Can you— Do you mind undoing the glamor first? I want to see *you.*"

Lust rampages through me, but I choke it back. I don't trust myself to speak without telling him how much I adore him—which would probably make him uncomfortable and change his mind about sex—so I simply nod and release the spell that alters my appearance. There's no change to how I feel, but David smiles and slides his hand up my cheek to stroke his fingers over my brow.

Then he leans up and kisses me.

We've kissed before, but this is different. This time, it's a precursor to us being together. His lips are so warm and soft, his body hard against mine, and as I pull him closer, trying to meld us together, his hands slide into my hair and grip tightly. As though he doesn't want to take any chance of me moving away.

I love it.

I don't know how long we kiss, wrapped in each other's arms, breathing each other's air, but when he finally draws back—just a tiny bit, just enough so our lips aren't touching—we're both breathless and aroused.

"Strip," he whispers. "I want you naked."

There's a protest on the tip of my tongue—I don't

want to let him go for that long—but then what he wants sinks in, and I step back, yanking at my shirt. His belt buckle clinks.

I kick my shoes away.

His pants drop to the floor.

I toss my shirt behind me, uncaring where it lands.

Finally, after too long, we're both naked and I reach for him again.

He comes to me, but his gaze is fixed on my cock.

"What?" I ask, looking down. It all seems in order—hard enough to stand on its own, but that's to be expected with all David's beautiful skin on show.

I sneak a glance at his cock and blink. "Oh." This is another physical difference between us. I don't think I ever read anything in the living archive about this.

His dick is long and *smooth*, the head slightly bulbous and leaking precum.

"Wow," David murmurs. "Can I…?" He reaches out but leaves his hand hovering, waiting for permission to touch. I grab it and wrap it around me, and he slowly slides his grip up and down, drawing a moan from deep in my chest.

"I wasn't expecting this. Do the ridges serve a purpose?" He drops to his knees and leans in to inspect it, his hot breath fanning over my most sensitive skin.

"A… purpose?" I gasp as he traces a finger lightly over one of them.

"It's amazing," he whispers. "The ridges are so perfectly even the whole length. Like a washboard."

"David," I whine, and he looks up and grins, then leans forward again and licks the tip.

"You have a choice," he informs me. "Would you prefer to come in my mouth or my ass this first time?"

I didn't think it was possible for my cock to get harder, but it does, throbbing almost painfully.

"Nope, forget I said that. I'm choosing—I want you in me. There's plenty of time for blowjobs later." He gets to his feet in one graceful movement, his beautiful cock bobbing, and I grab for it. My hand slides easily along the length in one smooth motion.

"Yeah, not a lot like yours, is it? Although we're similar enough for this to be fun." He backs slowly toward the bed, leading me along via my grip on his dick. "Could you get the lube, Caolan? It's in that drawer." He nods to the nightstand as he sinks onto the mattress, and I reluctantly let him go so he can settle against the pillows. The lubricant is easy to find, the first thing I see when I open the drawer, and I hold it aloft triumphantly as I turn back to look at him.

And nearly swallow my tongue.

He's lying back, knees bent, legs spread, fingers teasing around the rim of his hole, his blue eyes heavy-lidded as he gazes at me. He's so beautiful.

When he sees me watching, he rolls onto his side and pats the bed beside him. "Hurry up, Caolan. I need you."

I throw the lube at him and scramble onto the mattress. He chuckles as he catches it, then sits up and pushes me down to lie on my back. "Just lie there and enjoy. I want to ride you."

Yesssssssss.

I prop another pillow behind my head so I can clearly see as he pours lube onto his fingers and then stretches himself, looking me in the eyes the whole time until I have to look away and think about dirt and trees and bugs just to keep from exploding.

And then he's straddling me, his hot skin sliding against mine, and I look at him again, watch him lower his beautiful body, feel the tight pucker against me.

"Caolan," he murmurs, and I nod.

"Anything." I mean it. He can ask anything of me right now and I'd do it.

He says nothing more, though, just bears down over me, and my eyes roll back as I breach him and he slides slowly down my length.

"Unnnnnngh," he moans. "Oh fuck, those ridges…" He's panting, and I focus back on his face to see it flushed with color, his pupils blown.

I did that to him. Being with me.

My hips twitch involuntarily beneath him, and he makes a sound that reverberates through me.

I'm all the way inside him now, and he rocks slightly, back and forth, adjusting, his breathing unsteady, and it honestly is all I can do not to grab his hips and shove so deep we can never be parted. Instead, I grab his cock again, and he jerks, making us both catch our breath.

He meets my gaze. "Ready?" I whisper, a breath of sound, and his lips curl.

In the next moment, his powerful thigh muscles are bunching and he's rising, then lowering again, even, measured movements that draw out the pleasure until it almost hurts. I squeeze his dick, then stroke, matching the rhythm to his movements, and sweat forms on his forehead, the back of my neck, our breathing speeding up, faster, faster—

Until everything explodes. I clench my teeth, my back arching, hips jerking up, and David shouts something I barely hear. Heat flashes over my hand, across my belly, and I'm aware enough to realize that he's come, but I'm blind to anything else.

And then it's over, and I collapse back onto the mattress, trembling and sweaty and gasping, David falling to the mattress beside me.

How is anything that amazing? I knew it would be wonderful—how could it not be wonderful to join with the man I love?—but that was…

"Wow," he gasps. "I really regret that we haven't been doing that for the past few days."

I snort. "So do I." Of course, if it had been up to me, we would have. I roll onto my side so I can look at him, all flushed and sweaty, so unlike his usual immaculate self. I like mussed David, and I'm about to tell him how attractive he is when the strident sound of a ringing phone cuts the silence.

"Fuck," he mutters. "That's mine." He rolls out of bed, all his lithe, toned muscles on display under his pale skin, and snatches up his pants from the floor. The phone has stopped ringing by the time he pulls it out, and he looks at the screen. "Sam," he mutters. "Fuck, it must be bad."

I get out of the bed, my mind leaping ahead as I pick up my clothes and begin to dress, swiping David's cum off my stomach with a corner of the sheet. He's right; Sam wouldn't call now, tonight, knowing what our plans were, unless something important had happened. I pull on my underwear, trying to ease the shaking in my limbs as David lifts his phone to his ear to return the call —and an odd chirping noise sings through the room.

I look around for the source.

"Is that your phone?" David asks, then, "Sam, hey."

I grab for my pants. My phone? Someone's calling

me? It must be bad. I yank it out of my pocket, press the green button, and lift it to my ear. "Yes? Hello?"

"Caolan, this is Garin. You need to come back. Use a portal."

"What happened?" I demand, trying to pull my pants on one-handed. A few feet away, David has turned his still-naked back and is talking quickly into his phone.

"There was a strike on the advance team at the hotel, and another here at the house. Dustin and I were leaving to walk back and they tried to take him."

"*What?*" Fury erupts inside me. "Is he—?"

"Secure and well," Garin interrupts. "The shifters heard the attack, and our new allies came out to help. Between us all, they didn't stand a chance."

The red veil across my vision clears somewhat. "And the advance team?"

"One fatality and some minor injuries," he reports grimly. "But I think something else has happened too. The lucifer received a call just a moment ago."

"I'm coming very soon," I say. "As soon as David has finished his call." And put clothes on. As much as I like looking at his naked ass, it would be a distraction in such a serious situation.

"If I'm not here, I'll be at the hotel, but I'm leaving Dustin here. The wards seem quite secure, and our allies have proven themselves trustworthy."

There's unlikely to be a large space of time between his departure and my arrival, so I agree, and we end the call.

David turns around, meeting my gaze as he speaks into the phone. "I'm coming now. Caolan can open a portal." He raises a brow at me, and I nod. "See you in a few minutes." He ends his call, then begins to dress. "Was that Garin?"

"Yes. He says there was an attack at the hotel as well as the house."

"And also at the place where we're keeping the lucifer's seal," he tells me, and my heart stops beating.

"Did they…?" My voice is too strangled to finish, but he must understand, because he shakes his head. I breathe again.

"No. Two enforcers are dead, but the wards held and alerted the others. They'll need to be fortified. Or we'll have to move it—maybe both." He shakes his head as he buttons his shirt. "Are you ready?"

I reach out mentally, checking that I'll be able to open a portal from within his wards. As I suspected, they're designed to keep people out, not in. In the next moment, I have a portal open to the entranceway of Sam and Gideon's house. "Let's go."

He's through before I even finish speaking, and I follow him.

On the other side, two demons wearing enforcer uniforms are standing guard. I close the portal as David rushes into the living room.

"The boy is in the kitchen," one of the enforcers tells me.

"Thank you." I'll check on him first, then find out what's going on.

In the kitchen, Dustin is pacing quickly, words falling from his mouth at a rapid rate. He seems to be more excited than anything else, which is a good sign. Noah is sitting at the table, his face ashen, looking as though he can barely keep himself upright while Andrew fusses beside him. There's a half-empty glass with a grayish liquid in it on the table.

Dustin looks to be fine, so I turn my attention to Noah, frowning. The life force is moving very sluggishly through him. I don't know a lot about humans, but that can't be a good thing for any living being.

"What did you do?" I ask him as he picks up the glass, takes a swallow, and grimaces.

"Overdid it," he mumbles. "I'm still not recovered from when I teleported."

"Did you hear that, Caolan?" Dustin demands excitedly. "He *teleported.* A human! From one dimension to another! I'm sure that shouldn't be possible. It shouldn't, right? I wish I'd paid more attention to my studies, but I'm *sure* it's not possible."

Andrew's hands twitch. Time for me to step in before our alliance becomes strained. "Dustin, do you want to be helpful?"

He sobers immediately and straightens. "Yes, of course. What can I do?"

"Use your phone to call Garin. I'd like a full report of the situation at the hotel, but I need to be here right now, so I'm depending on you to be intermediary."

Nodding, he whips out his phone. "I can do that."

As he paces to the other side of the kitchen, I focus back on Noah, who's drinking the last of the gray stuff.

"Thank you," Andrew mutters. "I like him, but right now I'm a bit on edge."

"I understand." I really, really do. "What did you do, exactly, Noah?"

"Threw some fireballs," he says. "I haven't been using the magic during my recovery because we thought this might happen, but I couldn't just stand there while those douches tried to take Dustin."

"Your assistance is very much appreciated," I tell him absently as I watch the flow of the life force. "I can't say for certain, but I don't think you've done major damage. It looks like you've drawn too much of the life force too quickly."

Andrew's head snaps up. "You can see that? What else can you see? Can you fix it?" He sounds desperately hopeful, so much so that it pains me to shake my head.

"I can't, I'm afraid. There's a medic with the advance team who might be able to help." I wave to get Dustin's attention, and then tell him to ask the medic to join us when she's free. I imagine she's dealing with other injuries at the moment, and Noah's not critically hurt.

"Can you explain what it is?" Noah asks. "We know so very little about how humans use magic. It's on my list of things to ask Eerika about, but other questions have had priority." He rests an elbow on the table and props his head on his hand.

"I can tell you how it works for us and how I think it would apply to humans," I say cautiously. "I don't know a lot about humans."

"Anything you can tell us would be helpful." Andrew lays a hand on Noah's arm.

"Well, if human use of the life force works as ours does, you would draw it through yourself and direct it—does that sound familiar?"

"Yeah," Noah says. "Sort of."

"When you first began, did you find even the smallest tasks difficult?"

"Yes!" Noah perks up a bit. "I had to build my magic muscles and work up to bigger things."

I nod. This is familiar ground. "And after what happened, you'll need to build those muscles again. If I can extend that metaphor, tonight you forced them to do something they are not truly strong enough for right now, and as a result, they've seized up."

Noah squints, but Andrew nods. "So he hasn't truly set his physical recovery back?"

"I do not think so, but the medic could tell you for certain. I believe he drew too much life force too fast through his energy meridians. They stretched further than they're accustomed to in order to accommodate it, but now they've collapsed in tight to recover. That limits the amount of life force that can circulate through you and is why you feel so bad." I shake my head. "This is one of the few things that can't be self-healed at all."

"You can self-heal?" Noah asks enviously.

"To some degree, although it is always faster and easier for a dedicated healer to do it." I hesitate, because this is something I've been cautious about discussing with him. "It is connected to the ability that allows us to determine the length of our lives."

"I suppose that makes sense," Andrew says thoughtfully, his gaze appraising Noah. "You'd be, what, self-healing the damage done by aging?"

"Something like that." I hesitate again.

"Can you not talk to us about it? That's fine, we understand," Noah tells me, but I know from Eerika's reports that he's constantly eager for knowledge.

"No, I can talk about it. I'm just not certain… I have been unsure about how much you know on this topic." I choose my words carefully. If Noah already has this knowledge and is deliberately not sharing it with Andrew, I do *not* want to be the one who tells his secret.

"The topic of self-healing and deciding how long you want to live? We know nothing about it. Well, I don't anyway. Andrew's been alive longer than some dirt, so he—"

"Did you just compare me to dirt?" Andrew sniffs. "What does that make you? A dirt lover?" He looks over at me. "No, I don't know anything about it either. I'm a little more familiar than Noah is with what we've been calling folklore about your people, but this doesn't feature." He pauses. "Although some of it does suggest immortality, which isn't too far off."

I decide to stick to the facts. "It is essentially a constant self-healing to keep the body youthful. When we reach a physical age we enjoy, we create a spell that maintains a steady flow of life force throughout our beings. That is what prevents further aging. Should we later choose to mature further, we are able to do so and then reinstate the spell."

"That's super cool," Noah says. "So if you decide down the track that you want to be a silver fox, you turn off the spell for a while and let nature progress?"

Silver fox? The translator spell shows me an image of an Earth animal. That can't be what he means.

"I think there is some confusion. Does 'silver fox' have multiple meanings?" I've been caught out on this before. Their language and slang can be most confusing.

Andrew laughs, and even Noah snorts. "Yeah, sorry. Didn't think that one through. Silver fox can also refer to an attractive older man."

It… can?

He must see my confusion, because he adds, "The

word fox can mean an attractive person—I don't know why. It's slang from before I was born and not really used much anymore. And silver is because older people often have silver hair. So if you have an attractive older person with silver hair, they're a silver fox."

I smile and nod because it does make sense, in a convoluted way. And the animal in the image the translator spell showed me wasn't hideous, but I still don't think I'd like to be compared to one.

Dustin ends his call and comes back over to the table. "The medic will be here soon," he declares. "She is nearly finished. Garin says the advance team is pissed as fuck but in good shape." He seems to take great relish in swearing in English. "For reasons that aren't obvious, the strike team was small and focused on one apartment only. Once the alarm went up, the others were able to come in from behind and grind them to bits." He lingers over that phrase, then looks at Noah. "Did I say that right?"

Grinning, Noah nods. "Yep."

I don't think I want to know. He's making friends, which is a good thing. And Noah struck me as sensible enough—certainly David wouldn't put so much trust in him if he wasn't.

Dustin turns to me. "We're going to grind all our enemies to bits."

"That would be ideal, if messy," I tell him. "The rest of the report?"

He obediently conveys the relevant information, including the name of the elf who died and his role within the team, a comprehensive rundown of injuries and who received them, and the details already determined about the strike team—who are all dead. My sadness over that fact should probably not be solely because they would have been a useful source of information, but it's hard to feel bad for people who support the destruction of one dimension and the enslavement of another.

I'm impressed by Dustin, though. He's told me exactly what I need to know without getting too side-tracked or needing to refer to notes. Yes, he received the information just a few minutes ago, but there were a lot of names and details to keep track of, and he's done it.

Perhaps we've been underestimating him after all. This could be a very good experience for him.

His phone rings, and a delighted grin spreads across his face as he answers it. I can't blame him for that—phones are *wonderful.*

"Okay," he says, then looks at me. "The medic is ready. Garin said to warn the guards that they're opening a portal to here."

I don't waste time answering, just turn and go into the living room. David looks up from where he's talking to Gideon and Percy as I approach.

"Our medic is coming to treat Noah," I report. "By portal."

Immediately, Gideon goes out to the entranceway.

"Thank you," Percy tells me. "We appreciate that. Do you know if he'll be okay?"

"I'm not an expert, but I think he's fine. He just overexerted himself." I want to put my arm around David's waist, but I'm not certain if it will be welcome. Does using each other for sex allow for public intimacies?

I'm still wondering when Gideon comes back in,

followed by Garin and Teresa, a very competent medic I've worked with in the past.

"Thank you for coming," David says to her, and she grins cheerfully.

"This will be my pleasure. Garin says the young human threw fireballs at the attackers. I like…" She pauses, clearly trying to find the right words. "…fiery attitude."

Percy chuckles, and David snorts, his pretty blue eyes sparkling. "You'll love Noah, then. It's this way." He gestures toward the kitchen, then says to Percy, "We're agreed, then?"

Percy nods. "As soon as Sam's off the phone, I'll tell him. Go."

I follow David and Teresa to the kitchen, wondering what they've decided. I still need to get a full report on what happened here.

I look around for Dustin. He's sitting at the table beside Noah, talking earnestly, but breaks off when he sees Teresa.

"Here she is! I was just telling Noah you'll take excellent care of him. This is Teresa, Noah."

Polite greetings are exchanged.

"And this is my annoying boyfriend, Andrew," Noah says resignedly. "He won't leave, but please feel free to completely ignore anything he says and does. He can be overprotective."

Teresa laughs. "Boyfriends are supposed to worry," she says. "But I am very good at ignoring worried boyfriends." She winks, then holds out her hand, palm up.

"Take her hand," Dustin explains. "She'll use her ability and the life force to heal you."

"Cool." Noah puts his hand in Teresa's. "So, Caolan didn't think I'd done anything permanent…?"

Teresa shakes her head. "Nothing like that. Just strain. I help things along, and then a big sleep and… protein?" She glances at me. My spell says that sounds right, so I nod. "That fixes the rest."

Andrew heaves a sigh. "Thank fuck," he mutters, and grinning, Teresa pats him on the shoulder with her free hand.

"You have not yet decided to stop aging?" she asks Noah, and I freeze.

Uh-oh.

"We can't do that like your people," he says, and before I can think of a way to discreetly signal her, she makes a pffft sound.

"Maybe not them," she jerks her head at Andrew and David, "but if you can use the life force to make fire, you can self-heal."

Well, so much for talking to Noah privately.

"What?" Andrew breathes.

"*What?*" Noah shouts.

"Really?" David asks. He pulls out his phone and makes a note.

Teresa looks at me. "Should I have not said that?"

Huffing a laugh, I shake my head. "It's fine. I was going to talk to Noah about it when the current situation was over. I thought it might be better to discuss privately at first."

"So it's true?" There's a raw edge of hope in Noah's voice that surprises me. He's made several remarks since I've known him about his life span, and I never got the impression that he was particularly distressed by it. Andrew, yes—his feelings about losing Noah in the not-too-distant future have been very clear—but Noah has always seemed unconcerned.

I nod. "Yes. This only uses life force, not any part of our personal power. You should be able to learn it."

He swallows, opens his mouth, closes it, and swallows again. I can see his energy meridians relaxing as Teresa works, allowing more of the life force to enter his system and improve his condition.

Finally, he clears his throat. "Would you show me? When all this is over and we have time."

"Of course."

Andrew sucks in a deep breath and buries his face in his hands. Noah lays his free hand on his boyfriend's arm.

Dustin gets up from the table and comes to stand beside me, frowning. "I don't understand," he whispers. "What's going on?"

I lead him out of the kitchen, not wanting to impinge on the very personal occasion.

"Noah is human, and humans don't live as long as the other species," I tell Dustin. "He and Andrew will now be able to spend longer together."

He still looks confused. "What do you mean, they don't live as long?"

"Species here have finite lives," I explain. "Humans have the shortest. They live for an approximately predetermined length of time, then die and go to the ether until they are reborn."

His jaw drops in shock. "They just… die? Whether they want to or not?"

There's a sound from behind us, and we turn to see David with an amused expression. "I'm afraid so," he says, and Dustin leaps forward and then hovers anxiously beside him.

"Should you be resting? Do you get any warning at all? You can't die now, Caolan just found you!"

Oh dear.

"I'm not dying anytime soon," David assures him. "I wonder, could I impose on you for a favor?"

"Of course!"

"Percy and Sam have some questions about ceremonies among your people—they're beginning to plan for when your grandfather and the king arrive. Could you advise them on that?"

"Absolutely. I have a lot of experience with ceremonies," Dustin says. "I'll go find them. Make sure you take care of yourself."

David waits until he's gone, then steps forward and kisses me. "Thank you for offering to help Noah."

I wrap my arms around him before he can move away, wondering if I can get him to write a list of things he'd be grateful for. There's a lot I'm willing to do to have him kiss me and look at me with that soft expression.

"If I had known how much it concerned him, I would have mentioned it earlier," I admit. "I thought it would be better to wait until there were no distractions… and to ensure it was something he wanted."

He kisses me again. "You're a good person."

Excitement rises in me—no, not that kind, although yes, my cock is stirring. With David pressed against me, how could it not? No, this excitement is because David is forming an emotional attachment to me. He thinks I'm a good person. He's touching me even though sex is not an option right now.

It's all I can do not to blurt out how much I love him.

Instead, I ask, "Is this okay?"

He draws back slightly, but I keep hold of him. "Is what okay? You being a good person? It's fine."

"No, I mean touching like this where someone could see us. Before, I wanted to touch you, but I wasn't sure if you would be okay with that."

He hesitates, thinking about it.

"Casual touching is okay," he concedes finally. "Maybe not like this in a room full of people, though."

I can handle that. Especially when he sighs and rests his forehead on my shoulder. "I thought you might like to be briefed on what happened here. I know you haven't had much chance to talk to Garin and Dustin since we got back."

"Yes, please." I'd much prefer to hear it from him while he's in my arms than go find Garin.

"They'd just left when it happened—were literally only in front of the house next door. Apparently a portal opened just feet away from them and four attackers came through fast. Dustin shouted, which Alistair heard, and they went out. Garin was doing a good job of fighting them off—one was down already—but two had grabbed Dustin and were dragging him to the portal. Gideon tells me he put up quite a fight—they both have serious burns on their hands and arms."

"Dragons can conduct heat through any part of their body," I inform him. "The attackers were sloppy. Untrained. They should have been prepared for that."

"Well, it's a good sign for us." He lifts his head. "Noah got overexcited and threw some fireballs, which I guess you already know, but I'm told it was fairly easy to thwart the attack. The guards at the vault report the same—the initial surprise allowed the invaders to get the upper hand, but as soon as our people began to fight back, it was over quickly. So whatever Tish and Éibhear have been plotting over the years, none of it included proper training for their soldiers."

I lean my head against his and rub our temples together, and he makes a sound that goes right to my cock.

"Do we know what the makeup of the attack teams was?"

He hmms. The sound rumbles through his body and mine. "Yes. Two elves, a hellhound, and a vampire at the vault. Here, two elves, a felid shifter, and a demon. And from what I heard, at the hotel it was mostly elves and one incubus?"

"That's what I've been told. None survived, I'm afraid. Our people were rather enraged when they realized one of their own had been killed."

"Completely understandable," he says gravely. "The demon Garin put down first and one of the elves are still alive, and the hellhound at the vault, so we have some prisoners to interrogate."

"I need to report to the king." It concerns me that these obviously coordinated attacks came so soon after our return. Obviously Éibhear has people watching us, to know which hotel was chosen and that Dustin was here at Sam and Gideon's house, but they moved fast to be able to attack within less than half a day—even if the attacks were poorly planned. "And I should go outside and see what the portal residue can tell me."

He pulls back sharply enough that I lose hold of

him. "You can do that? What kind of information can you get? Where they came from?"

"Yes. And only for a short time—a few hours at most."

He grabs my hand and pulls me down the hallway toward the front of the house. "Can you look at all three? Here, the hotel, and the vault? They probably all come from the same place, but if not, that's three potential locations we can pin down."

I smile fondly at his back. "I can look at all three, although one of the others at the hotel has already done so—he just needs help with the map."

David stops. "Didn't Noah show you the maps function on your phones?"

What a delightful tool that is! Except… "Yes, but we can't read the place names."

"Damn." He rubs his brow. "Do you think the king can assign someone to work on altering the translation spell? I can see this becoming a major issue very quickly."

"He already has. We discussed it today." I get a little quiver of satisfaction at being a step ahead of him, especially when he grins at me.

"I should have expected that. Come on."

We go past the guards in the entranceway and out onto the street, and I'm suddenly very aware of how exposed we are. The street is lined with buildings, all of them looking to be residential homes with lights in the windows. "Did any humans see?" I whisper to David. There was a portal in the middle of this street, in full view of many of these houses, and Noah threw fireballs. Could this one incident have undone millennia of secret keeping?

"We don't think so," he says, also keeping his voice low. "Garin said there was nobody on the street, and it was all over fairly quickly. Someone may have seen something through a window, but if so, they never came out of their house. Sam has the interns monitoring social media just in case, and public relations has a standard story about it being a publicity gimmick for an upcoming event that they can roll out if necessary."

"This has happened before?"

He stops in front of the house next door and looks around. This is the place—I can feel the portal residue very clearly. "Well, not this exactly. We've never had to think about portals before, and fireballs very rarely. But general situations that might expose us? Yes. Especially with young people."

"The young ones are the worst," I agree, thinking of all the chaos Dustin and his friends can cause. "Can you show me the map on your phone?"

He scrambles to pull it out of his pocket. "You know already? That's amazing. What else can you tell?"

"It was created by someone inexperienced," I begin as he taps the screen. "And from not too far away."

Frowning, he holds the phone out. "How can you know that? If all portals go through the void, I mean."

I shrug. "I just can." I look down at the screen, which shows an odd-shaped landmass surrounded by blue.

"I figured we'd start with the US and scroll around the globe if we needed to, but if it's close, it should be on that map anyway."

"It's there," I say, putting my finger on the screen. "But the map is so small, I can't pinpoint— Ohhhhh." I watch excitedly as David slides two fingers in opposite directions over the screen and the map enlarges. "That's very clever!"

"Noah didn't show you that. Although I guess there wasn't a need, since you can't read the map yet anyway. Use one finger to slide it in the direction you want," he instructs, demonstrating, and I eagerly pull it away from him and practice.

"Okay," I say finally, focusing on what I'm actually supposed to be doing instead of playing, "the origin point for the portal was here." I zoom in as far as I can, until the area I'm looking at is just a gray bar across the screen. David takes the phone back and zooms slowly out.

"When you said close, you weren't kidding." He turns around and points. "That house, maybe? Will you be able to sense it if we get closer?"

"Yes. Wait—they were across the street?" And wasted energy opening a portal and staging a frontal attack when they already had numbers on their side? They would have been better served using their power to create a distraction and then striking from behind.

It's embarrassing to know that such poorly trained insurgents have been two steps ahead of us for so long.

"Looks like," he confirms. We stroll over, trying to seem casual in case humans are watching. Which reminds me…

"Do we know who lives there? Are they human?"

"No idea. Sam might know. Let me call him real quick."

We stand right in front of the house, which has lights on in two windows, while David talks to Sam. "It's fine," he reports, ending the call. "Sam says the people who live here are on vacation right now. The lights are on a timer. They actually asked Sam to keep an eye on the house. He's freaking out now that there might have been a break-in and he somehow didn't notice."

That's not likely—one of the shifters in our group would have smelled unknown elves that close—but sure enough, the front door to Sam and Gideon's house opens and Sam comes rushing out, followed a moment later by Gideon—who I suspect is more worried about Sam racing into potential danger than about his neighbor's home.

"Well?" Sam demands, stopping beside us.

"We haven't checked yet. Let's go. Gideon, do you want the front or the back?"

"Front," he says grimly. "Although if there's anyone still there, they'll have seen you and be ready."

"I doubt there's anyone still there," David says, but I feel him drawing forth his power.

It's so sexy.

Pushing that thought aside, I ready my own power and follow him down the narrow alley between the houses. It doesn't take long before I can feel the tingle of the portal residue up ahead. I tap David's arm and gesture forward. He nods, and we proceed cautiously. About halfway down the alley, with the lights from the next street glowing up ahead, the house ends and a fence begins. I stop him and point to the gate... which is ajar, the lock broken.

A low whistle gets our attention, and we look back up the alley. Gideon and Sam are coming toward us. We step back from the gate and wait.

"Front locked," Gideon says so softly, I almost can't hear him.

David nods, points to the gate, then holds up three fingers... two... one...

We burst through. David and Gideon have clearly done this before, going in separate directions to check the small courtyard. I go directly to the back door and test it. It's securely locked.

David comes to stand beside me. "Are they in there?"

"I don't think so. The portal was created here in the courtyard, and the lock on the door is intact." I jiggle the handle again, just to be sure.

"Sam?" David asks, and I turn to see where the felid shifter has gone. He's walking around the courtyard, breathing deeply, and I remember that shifters possess a keen sense of smell.

"Only four," Sam reports. "I didn't smell any of them by the door, but they're all over the alley."

"I think it's safe to say one or more of them followed you to the house from the hotel, then went back for the others. They watched from the alley, then... what? Decided that was too exposed for a portal?" Gideon sounds doubtful.

"We can ask the prisoners," David suggests. "I think the priority is knowing this house is secure for now and stationing a guard here so it can't be used like this again."

"Agreed," Sam says. "And I'll get someone to repair the gate. They didn't happen to portal in as well as out, did they?"

I shake my head. "Just one portal, and it's an origin point."

"Wow, you can tell that? Awesome." He sniffs. "I'm

going to go smell where the portal opened and see if there's a difference."

"After that, can you see if you can track these guys back to where they came from? Or get Alistair to do it if you've got too much else on your plate. We're going to the vault," David says. "Hopefully they used a more direct portal to get there, and I want to check in with the team on guard anyway."

"Stay in touch," Gideon says. "We'll see you back soon?"

"An hour, max," David promises, and even though I already knew it would be the case, I mentally farewell any hope I had of crawling back into bed with him tonight.

That's okay. We have a lot of time for that.

CHAPTER SIX

David

"So there's nothing here?" I double-check with the incubus leading the CSG strike team. Caolan was able to track the portal used to get to the vault back to what we think is an advance staging base. Unfortunately, at least one person on the other side knows what they're doing, because even though we got the teams together fast, the base is abandoned—presumably they bugged out when their attack teams didn't return.

"No personnel," the team leader confirms. "They did leave fast enough that a lot of stuff got left behind, though. We haven't found a step-by-step description of their plans or anything, but there's a lot of other stuff."

It doesn't sound exciting, but it actually is. The everyday minutiae of life can give us an idea of how many people were there, what species they are, and some hints to where certain individuals are from. Any information is valuable. We just have to get an expert over here to begin the assessment.

I glance over at Caolan, who's talking to the dragon who headed up the king's strike team. Neither of them look particularly happy, so I'm guessing they won't have anything extra to add.

Turning back to the team leader, I begin, "Okay, could you—"

My phone rings. That's not new—it's been ringing or chiming with messages pretty much nonstop for the last few hours. But Caolan's phone is also ringing, and as our eyes meet, the memory of what that meant earlier has consternation crossing his face—and probably mine.

I answer. "Yeah?"

"Get back now." It's Sam, and his tone is grimmer than I've ever heard.

"What—"

"Now, David." He hangs up.

Fuck.

"Wrap things up here," I tell the strike team leader. "We'll send a team to relieve you, but it might be a while." Depending on what's gone down. "Hold the base until then."

"We've got it, sir."

Almost before he's finished speaking, I'm jogging toward Caolan. He says one more thing to the dragon, then turns and comes to meet me.

"Did they tell you…?" I trail off as he shakes his head.

"Just to go back. Ready?" He opens a portal, and I step through. I'm getting used to this form of travel.

Sam and Gideon's house is chaos, even more so than earlier. There are people shouting from all directions.

"Do you know what's going on?" I ask one of the enforcer guards in the entranceway.

"The lucifer's in the living room," he replies. I don't

wait for Caolan, just turn on my heel and stride into the living room.

It's bad. Even if I couldn't tell that from looking at Percy and the fact that there's an enforcer in the room, I'd know because Dustin is sitting on the couch, hands over his mouth and tears tracking down his cheeks. I haven't known him long, but I didn't think anything could quell his attitude.

There's an elf I don't know here also, talking to Garin in fast elvish, and I'm guessing he's the source of the drama.

Percy turns from where he and Sam are muttering to each other and sees me. "David," he calls, attracting attention from everyone else. "And Caolan, good," he adds as Caolan comes up beside me.

"What's happened?" I demand. I want answers, dammit.

"The attacks here weren't the only ones tonight," Percy says. Caolan's gaze goes to Garin and the elf, then to Dustin silently crying, and he pales.

"The king?" he asks hoarsely. "Brandt?"

Garin breaks off what he's saying and motions for the other elf to join us. "The king is safe," he says. "So is Brandt." He nods to Percy. "Thank you, Lucifer, for allowing us to converse in our own language. Birgir's translator spell is not well-tuned yet."

"Of course," Percy replies. "Could you repeat what you told us for David and Caolan's benefit?" He glances toward the couch. "Just… excuse me a moment." Turning to the guard, he asks, "Could you get Noah, please?"

The guard hesitates and looks at me, clearly not wanting to leave Percy unguarded. I nod, desperately impatient to find out what happened, and he ducks out of the room.

Percy smiles faintly at Garin. "Please proceed."

Garin looks Caolan in the eye. "They got inside the shield—still unsure how. Two full teams at the king's residence. Six dead, five elves and a dragon. And they got the spell."

For a moment, I don't understand what he means. They got the spell? What—

Oh. Oh *fuck*. The spell. *The* spell. The one needed to corporealize the magic. They got it? They stole it? *Fuck.*

"The seal," I say to Percy, trying not to panic. They can't get that too.

Sam answers, "I've already sent more enforcers to the vault. And I woke up some ward experts to beef those up too. I need you to check in on that, though, since I don't know what they're doing."

I pull out my phone and make a note, although there's no fucking way I'll forget that. I just need to do something to organize my mind. "No problem. I'll go there now."

"Wait," Garin says, and my gut drops to my feet. "There was another attack." He draws in a breath. "On civilians."

Noah comes in, interrupting the story yet again, and while I consider him a dear friend, right this second I would happily strangle him. Is this story *ever* going to get told?

"You wanted me?" he says to Percy, who inclines his head toward Dustin.

"Would you…?"

Noah nods. "Yes, of course. I should have thought."

He looks at me. "Gideon asked if you could join them in the kitchen when you're done here."

"Thank you." I'll check in quickly, and then borrow Gideon or another demon to take me to oversee the wards at the vault. It'll be faster that way.

Noah goes to sit beside Dustin and puts an arm around him, and Caolan says to Garin, "They struck the dragons, didn't they?"

Garin's face says it all. "They stole a dragonet."

Caolan actually staggers back, and I dart a hand out to steady him.

"What?" he gasps. I know the kidnapping of a child is horrendous, but given we're dealing with people who literally destroyed a dimension and want to upset the balance of existence, his reaction seems a little excessive.

My confusion must show on my face, because Garin explains. "The dragon reproductive process is very difficult. Young dragons are rare—so rare that the idea of harming a child didn't even exist in their consciousness until after they met elves. They didn't have a word for kidnapping."

Okay, so I really like dragons.

"How?" Caolan asks. "How did they get to a dragonet?"

"Numbers, the element of surprise, and some very dark spellcasting," Garin says. "One of the child's mothers is dead, and the other is heavily wounded and so enraged that Brandt had to have her sedated. The entire dragon community is screaming. If there had ever been any chance that one of them would join Éibhear, it's gone."

"There has been no ransom demand?" Caolan checks, and Garin hesitates. They both turn to the other elf—Birgir—who seems to be struggling to keep up with the conversation. Caolan asks him something in elvish, and he shakes his head. "They've definitely taken her for the spell, then," Caolan concludes.

I don't know why I didn't put that together—maybe because so much has happened tonight—but Éibhear and Tish need a dragon to enact the spell. And now they have one. A frightened child one.

"How old is the child?" I ask. *Please don't let them be very young.*

"She is toddler," the new elf says painstakingly. "Her name is Gytha."

"Thank you," I reply. "Has the king tried to retrieve her?"

The elf squints, nods, and looks at Garin. His translator spell must be struggling.

"The king and Brandt ordered a full assault on Éibhear's base as soon as they were told of the abduction, but it was empty," Garin reports. "We assume they were expecting a rescue-slash-retaliation mission. King Raðulfr was able to ascertain that there are no other energy shields on the planet, and given how ravaged and dangerous things have become, it would be impossible for anyone to survive there without one." His voice wavers a bit at the end. It can't be easy to acknowledge your home is falling apart.

"So they must have all moved here to Earth," Sam concludes.

I pinch the bridge of my nose. "Where they'll join Tish on all the hidden bases we're struggling to locate."

"We need more soldiers over here," Caolan tells Garin. "To start searching for the dragonet, if nothing else."

They start discussing the logistics of that, and I excuse myself and head to the kitchen, pausing on the way to squeeze Dustin's shoulder. First, talk to my team, then go make sure the wards around the seal are titanium lined with reinforced concrete lined with something else that's incredibly strong.

While I'm worried about the child and her well-being, I'm terrified that Éibhear and Tish now have three of the four components needed to enact their evil scheme. All that's missing is the seal.

We *cannot* let them get it.

I RUB my burning eyes and fondly remember the pleasure of a full night's sleep. I don't think I've had more than a few snatched hours at a time since the coordinated attacks last week.

In the past eight days, we've stepped up plans for the migration. The king sent a much larger contingent of soldiers over than we'd planned to have so early, partly to search for the stolen child, and partly to begin preparation for any confrontation. That means they're severely under-resourced in their enclave, so we're going to bring civilians over faster too. In fact, we've already started. Today's the third day of transfers.

On the positive side—if there can be one in a situation like this—once news of the missing child got around our community, all uncertainty about the migration and the situation with the CCA ceased. In fact, we've gotten a substantial number of defectors—townships similar to the one Alistair visited not long ago that have been set up as CCA strongholds but are so aghast by the idea of children being stolen that they no longer want to be associated. The other side wasn't thinking clearly when they did this—sure, they needed a dragon, but when you have a population with low fertility and a strong attachment to their children, showing that you'll use toddlers as tools is stupid. Aidan Byrne, the shifter species leader and Alistair's boyfriend, is heading up the team responsible for debriefing the defectors. The shifter ability to smell changes in body chemistry when people lie is proving useful there.

In just a few minutes, King Raðulfr and Brandt will arrive. The ceremony we'd discussed is largely redundant now, but we decided to proceed anyway. If nothing else, it will cement this alliance in the minds of all our people. And in times of trouble, things like this can be a touchstone—something to cling to.

Caolan comes up beside me where I'm trying to stay out of the way of the audio-visual team as they set up to livestream the event and hands me a protein bar and a bottle of water.

"Thank you." I lean in and kiss his cheek, and he beams.

Honestly, I think Caolan is the one thing that's kept me grounded this past week, and yes, I know how absurd that sounds. But having someone to fall into bed beside, even if it's just for a short time, has made me more willing to put work aside for sleep. Plus, during the day as I see how busy he is, how many people need his attention and how little time he has for himself, I find myself making time to ensure he eats and hydrates. My teammates think it's hilarious that I've never stopped for food breaks myself, but now I'm doing so to feed Caolan. Of course, as you've just seen, he does the same for me. Andrew (the asshole) calls it our interspecies mating ritual.

Which it's not. Really. I mean, sure, we "mate" in the sexual sense—after the drought I've been through, I can't imagine being too tired for that—but it's not a mating ritual in the relationship sense.

Or so I'll keep telling myself.

I don't want to worry about that now, anyway. There will be plenty of time to sort out what's going on between us after the crisis has passed. Our priorities need to be getting the elves and dragons to safety and stopping any and all attempts to take over the world and enslave our people.

"David!" I look over to where Rabhya, the head of our PR department, is waving. She taps her watch, which is her signal that we're ready to start.

I shove the last bite of my protein bar in, chew, and take a swig of water. "Ready?" I ask Caolan, and he nods.

"Do you want me to leave the portal open while I'm there?"

I shake my head. I know that's harder for him, and frankly, we don't know how long he'd have to keep it open for. The king is expecting him, but with the elven sense of time the way it is, the best indicator of "when" we could give him was "midafternoon." Even that seemed to confuse him somewhat. So he might not be ready, and it might be a while before they arrive.

Getting elves to understand the concept of time is going to be a real endeavor. Caolan has been trying, but the current situation isn't helping any. Most tasks are being categorized as "urgent, do it first/second/third" or "it can wait for later," which isn't conducive to maintaining a schedule.

And yes, that has been making me anxious. Very anxious. Lack of a schedule is the first step on the road descending into chaos and anarchy. What's next, the world runs out of coffee?

Caolan smiles at me one more time before opening a portal and stepping through. It closes behind him as I suppress a shiver, not wanting the whole room to know how sexy I find his casual demonstration of power—although the shifters can probably smell it. There are no biochemical secrets when shifters are around.

Sure enough, Alistair slips up beside me, a sly smile on his stupid face. I brace myself.

"Hey, I know you don't really like surprises, so I wanted to give you some warning."

Nothing good has ever been said after an introduction like that.

"Surprises are bad," I say firmly. "Very bad. No surprises, Alistair. I have enough to worry about right now."

He pastes on an injured expression, which is a good indication that he's going to say something ridiculous. Learning to decipher hellhound facial expressions is a survival tactic when you work with so many of them.

"That's why I'm *warning* you," he huffs. "So you're not surprised." He stops, and I get the impression he's waiting for... what? Praise? A treat?

I settle for gratitude, although I'm not sure yet if I'm actually grateful. "Thank you."

He smiles. "You're welcome. So, we're having a birthday party for you tonight."

What?

What?

No. Oh, no. *Fuck*, no.

"No."

He nods. "Yes. Happy birthday, by the way."

"Thanks," I say automatically. "No party."

"It's not up for debate, David. We're having a party. It's not every day a man turns… however old you're turning."

Do you see how ridiculous this is?

"Alistair—"

"It's all planned," he continues happily. "Sam was a bit of a party pooper, but Dustin got really excited about it all, so I managed to convince him karaoke and the smoke machine were a good idea."

Fuck. My. Life.

"Alistair—"

"And I know now is not the time for us to lose our inhibitions, so no alcohol, not even the human kind. We'll just have to get high on sugar instead! Andrew was in charge of the cake, so there are like six of them."

"Alis— Did you just say there are *six* cakes?"

He nods. "He got a bit excited at the bakery, apparently. Noah was supposed to keep him under control, but he just thought it was funny and recorded the whole thing. You can watch it later."

There's a familiar stabbing pain behind my eye.

"While I really appreciate all the thought you've put into this"—and I really do. It's nice to know your friends care—"we really don't have time for a party. Even one without alcohol."

"Mmm, I see where you're coming from, and sure, things are busy right now, but we all knew you'd say that, so I have a message for you from Percy." He reaches into his pocket and pulls out a folded Post-it.

Clearly not a long message.

Sighing, I take it, unfold it, and read:

It's an order.

Yep. This is my fucking life. One of my oldest friends just ordered me to have a birthday party.

Alistair cranes his neck, trying to see what's written, and I crumple the note and shove it in my pocket.

"Fine."

His grin is instant and spreads over his whole face. "Great! You won't regret this, David. And just think how good it will be for everyone to have a chance to relax and bond. Think of it like an interdimensional government mixer. Or a cultural event. Dustin has been asking a lot of questions about birthday parties, and now we can show him one."

That almost makes me feel better, until I remember that Dustin's questions have been mostly about children's birthday parties.

"There's not going to be any games or anything, is there?" I try to remember back to my childhood and the games played at parties then but come up blank. Things have probably changed since then, anyway.

"No," he assures me. "Just karaoke." He's half turned away when he says over his shoulder, "And the piñata."

Of course there's a piñata. Well, at least that means there will be a stick handy to beat people with.

Before I can call him back and demand to know what he filled the piñata with—you never know with hellhounds—a portal appears in the middle of the room.

Immediately, one of the elves standing near Rabhya opens what Caolan told me is a pinhole portal—about the size of my palm and apparently used for communication and transmitting spells over distances. That's how the ceremony will be shown to the elves and dragons who haven't yet migrated.

"Ready?" Rabhya shouts, and there's a chorus of replies from her team. Lights go on above cameras, indicating that they're filming, and at a bank of screens and computer equipment, two people tap furiously at keyboards. We planned this ahead of time, so Caolan knows to ask everyone on his side to wait before coming through. Rabhya assured us fifteen seconds would be long enough.

Of course, that meant we needed to demonstrate to Caolan how long fifteen seconds actually is.

"Streaming!" one of them calls, just as two elf guards step through the portal. Perfect timing.

They scan the room, see Garin, Dustin, and some of the other soldiers who are already here, and then step aside to flank the portal. Next comes Brandt, who smiles and waves… but unfortunately not at the cameras. He adds a flirty little wink. I look to see who he's winking at, and it appears that he's chosen the one section of wall in the room that doesn't have a person standing in front of it.

Never mind. People watching won't know that. Maybe we can start some gossip—he's very attractive, and everyone loves a good celebrity romance. It can only do this alliance good for people to think the dragon wing leader is getting it on with one of our own, right?

I make a mental note to talk to Rabhya about that.

King Raðulfr steps through the portal, a small, regal

smile on his face. He looks serious and intelligent, and he and Percy are going to blow this out of the water. Two distinguished, honorable leaders joining their people for the betterment of existence... it's a **PR** dream come true.

Two more guards follow, then Caolan comes through and closes the portal. As Percy steps forward, the species leaders ranked behind him—and don't even get me started on what a migraine it was to get them all here for this—Caolan slips out of camera range and comes back to my side.

Our leaders greet each other, and the simple ceremony begins. It's actually rather lovely, and definitely momentous, our peoples coming together in this way after nine thousand years with no contact. My chest tightens a little as the immensity of it all comes crashing down on me. I can't believe I'm right in the middle of such historic events.

As if he knows what I'm thinking, Caolan slips his hand into mine and squeezes. My rising anxiety vanishes.

Don't read anything into it. It means nothing more than me needing to know there are others in this situation with me.

Percy finishes his speech welcoming the elves and dragons to Earth. At Rabhya's suggestion, we avoided mentioning Tish, the CCA, and Éibhear during this ceremony. She thought it should be about unity and positivity rather than associating the migration with the horrific reality of its cause. Not that the elves and dragons won't already be thinking about that, but the goal is to showcase a glorious future. Or something.

The king begins his speech, and it's much the same

as Percy's, just with different words. I only half listen, leaning against Caolan and resting my head on his shoulder as I mentally rearrange my plans for the evening now that I have to attend this birthday party. Oh fuck, they're not going to expect the whole cake-cutting, candle-blowing, speech-giving part, are they?

What am I talking about? Alistair's involved. He'll probably want to light the candles using a flamethrower.

"…look forward to seeing connections form between our people. Connections in the workplace, friendships, and romantic relationships. It warms my heart to see that this has already begun, with two of our finest leading the way as always. Caolan, David, may your happiness glow like a beacon of hope for us all."

What?

One of the cameras swings toward us.

What?

I straighten and step away, but it's too late. The camera is already panning back, and fucking *applause* has broken out amongst the people who are supposedly our colleagues and friends, led by our treacherously sneaky leaders.

"Did you know he was going to say that?" I hiss at Caolan, but one glance at his stunned expression gives me the answer. "Never mind."

King Raðulfr wraps up his speech, Rabhya slashes her hand across her throat, and the cameras are switched off.

"That was…" Caolan shakes his head. "I wish he hadn't done that. Still, I'm sure there are many people called Caolan and David. Nobody will know it was us."

Oh, to be so clueless.

"Do you remember how we talked about

livestreaming and that visual images of all this would be available for people to watch?"

He nods. "Yes. Like the television. And they found a way to cast the images for everyone who hasn't crossed over yet to see too."

I point to the camera that caught us looking all couple-y. "See that? That's what captures the images. And it was pointed at us. Believe me, everyone saw."

He studies the camera, then me. "Are you a very recognizable public figure?"

"Are you?"

Looking back at the camera, he sighs. "We're doomed."

"David!" Rabhya races over, her face lit up with glee. "That was amazing! Did you know he was going to do that?"

"No. And I wish he hadn't."

"Don't be such a gloomy gus. This is fantastic. The comments section exploded after that, and the number of shares skyrocketed."

"Shares? Rabhya—"

She waves dismissively. "Please, this is not my first rodeo. As far as the humans know, this is some film student's final assignment."

It's still riskier than I'd like, but she's done stuff like this before, so I just have to trust her.

"Let me gauge the reaction over the next few hours, but if it continues like this, we're going to want to set up some interviews, okay?"

"Not okay," I say, but she's already walking away, calling to her assistant. "This is not good," I tell Caolan.

He puts an arm around me. "No."

So of course that's when Percy, the king, and Brandt come over. All three are smiling sheepishly.

"Your Majesty, I'm very unhappy right now," Caolan warns.

The king pouts. Actually pouts. "How better to show everyone that the way forward is through unity than with an example of it? People love a good romance."

I wince. That's scarily close to what I was thinking before. Only, I didn't think I'd be the example shoved into the spotlight.

"It would have been nice to be advised of your plan, Your Majesty. Especially since David and I are not actually in the midst of a romance, and your antics are unlikely to aid me in convincing him it would be a good idea."

Guilt slashes at me. Maybe it's wrong of me to lead Caolan on like this when clearly he's still hoping for something more between us.

Not that I'm completely against the idea. Just… not now. And not until I know a lot more about him.

The king turns to me, eyes wide.

Oh, no.

"David, please accept my most heartfelt apologies if this has made you in any way question Caolan's devotion to you! He is the best of men, truly."

His voice has risen, and we're attracting attention—not that we weren't already the focus of all eyes. If I could teleport, I would be gone so fast, they'd wonder if I was ever actually here at all.

"David understands that," Percy soothes, thankfully stepping in to save me. "It's done now, anyway, and we can only move forward. Let's get started on our talks so we can finish as much as possible before David and Caolan have to leave."

"Leave?" My surprise is obvious. "Where are we going?" These treaty talks are the most important item on my schedule. There's no way I'll leave before they're done.

"To your birthday party," Percy says patiently. "Hopefully we'll all be able to attend, but you need to be there for all of it."

I grit my teeth. "I'm sure the party can wait until I arrive. After we're finished."

He shakes his head. "No, I've been assured it can't. Anyway, it's your birthday. It won't hurt you to have a few hours off."

"We'll talk fast," Brandt assures me. "I am very excited to attend a birthday party. Dustin has been telling me about them. I think when it's my turn, I will have ponies and a clown." He frowns. "The clown is the one who performs tricks, correct?"

"That's a magician," Percy corrects, leading the way out of the room. "A clown wears face paint and tries to be funny."

I'm struck with debilitating horror at the thought that Alistair might have arranged for clowns or magicians—or fuck, maybe even ponies. He did say just karaoke and a piñata, right?

I pull out my phone and text Sam to check.

"What's wrong?" Caolan asks, as usual ridiculously attuned to my mood.

"Do you know if Alistair got a clown for the party?" I stop walking and look at him. "Did you know about this party?"

He nods. "Noah told me yesterday. I did not know it

was your birth day," he says it carefully, as if unfamiliar with the term, "until he suggested I might like to give you a gift."

So there are going to be presents, then.

I manage a weak smile. "I hope you didn't go to any trouble. I don't even celebrate my birthday anymore… this party is really more for the others. A distraction. They needed an excuse to have a party, and my birthday is a good excuse." Fuck, I'm babbling. I make myself stop and take a deep breath. I'm calm. I've been calm for a long time, and I'm going to keep it up. No chaos in the part of my life I control.

Caolan lifts a hand and lays it against my cheek. "It is never any trouble to do things for you."

Punch to the gut.

THANKFULLY, there are no clowns, magicians, or ponies at my birthday party. Sam assured me there wouldn't be, but when dealing with hellhounds, you need to expect some surprises.

Like the fact that it's not at Sam and Gideon's place as I expected it would be. Instead, we're at Andrew's— and I guess Noah's now, too—luxury penthouse. Karaoke is inside, but those of us who aren't interested in emulating Celine Dion and Mariah Carey are out on the rooftop terrace. Whoever was in charge of decorations put floating candles in the pool, and the mocktails are plentiful, thanks to the temporary bar and bartender set up in the corner.

It's actually a great party.

"This is nice," I tell Noah, relaxing into the deck chair I claimed.

"Thanks," he says, "but I can't claim credit. Sam did the food and drink, and the rest was Andrew and Alistair. Watch out for the piñata, though," he warns. "I'm not actually sure what's in it, but they were way too gleeful about it."

Fucking hellhounds. And Andrew… you'd think that at his age, he'd have settled down some. But noooo, that would be too much to ask. Instead, he's teaching Caolan the words to "I Wanna Dance With Somebody" so he can have a turn at karaoke. Caolan, to his credit, seems confused and apprehensive.

Dragging my attention away from a scene that would likely cause Whitney Houston to roll in her grave, I turn back to Noah. "How've you been?" I haven't seen as much of him in the past few days, and I've missed him. He's a smartass, but he's intelligent and focused, and I never had to tell him anything twice.

"I'm good," he declares, waving his hand dismissively. "Busy, you know? But those fireballs don't seem to have done any lasting damage, and I've started doing small exercises to rebuild my magic muscles. Don't tell Andrew," he adds quickly.

"Don't tell me what?" the vampire himself asks, joining us and sinking into an empty chair. Noah groans.

"If you heard that, you heard the rest," he mutters. "I swear, I'm fine. I'm not overdoing it."

Andrew presses his lips together, then sighs. "Okay. But just take it easy."

The smile that lights Noah's face is beautiful, and he leans over to kiss Andrew. "I will, I promise. I'm going to get some more of those mac-and-cheese balls. Anyone want anything?"

I demur, Andrew asks for the blood-infused crab cakes, and then Noah's gone.

"Thank you for my party," I say. "I know you hate having people over."

He nods. "I really, really do. But, as Alistair says, you're my bestest bestie. And fuck knows you deserve a party."

I say nothing. I don't trust myself to speak. It was Andrew who had the insight to see when I needed help and the power to follow through on that. It was Andrew who made sure I was never again forced to live in chaos. Andrew has been a dependable part of my life since before I was old enough to advocate for myself, and I can never repay him for what he's given me.

That he counts me a friend—much less one of his best friends—is an honor I cherish.

"Soooooo," he begins, and I just know I'm going to hate what comes next. Cherishing his friendship doesn't mean I think he's perfect. "Since it's just us here right now, let's talk about you and Caolan."

I look around desperately. There are nearly fifty people here, and not a single one of them will interrupt us.

"There's nothing to talk about. How are you and Noah doing?"

"Sure there is," he says, ignoring my attempt at deflection. "The two of you are practically living together."

"We are not!" The words burst from me before I have a chance to consider what Andrew's reaction to my vehemence will be.

Sure enough, he smirks. "Has he or has he not slept at your place, in your bed, with you, every night for the past week?"

"That's because we're using each other for sex," I protest, but even to me it sounds weak.

He scoffs. "Fuck buddies don't sleep over every night. They don't bring each other food and cuddle in public. They don't check in with each other several times a day."

There is literally nothing I can say to contradict that. Wait—

"They do if they're friends too."

"Wow, you're really going to be stubborn about this, aren't you? Okay, you and Caolan are friends. We're friends too, right? We've been friends for, oh, about four hundred and fifty years. You and Percy have been friends just about that long too. When was the last time you brought me or Percy coffee and a muffin and put your arm around us during a briefing?" His smirk turns into a full-fledged grin.

"I don't have time for a relationship right now," I say, giving up on trying to pretend he's wrong and just going for the blunt truth. "It can only be sex."

The grin fades. "This isn't a good time to be exploring new love," he concedes, "but Caolan knows that, David. He's just as much in the middle of this as you are. Has he been pushing you for a bigger commitment? No," he continues before I can reply. "He hasn't, because he knows you want to stay focused right now, and he respects the fact that you're not ready for more." He stops, looks at me for a long moment, then sighs.

"Don't," I warn, but of course he ignores me.

"I understand why you're wary. Caolan very impulsively declared feelings for you without ever having spoken to you. He doesn't believe in to-do lists and has spent his whole life ignoring the concept of time. All those things trigger bad memories for you. But you need to widen your view just a little."

The bastard stops there. I hold out as long as I can —which is not long—and then demand, "What do you mean?"

The smirk returns. I understand completely what Noah means when he says he sometimes wants to smack it off Andrew's face.

"I'm just saying, Caolan has also put in a lot of effort learning about you. He's a well-respected aide to the king, trusted to carry out important duties like making contact with us. And maybe he can't tell time yet, but he's trying to learn—for your sake. He values you and he's always attentive to what you need." Andrew shrugs. "It's only been a few weeks, so I'm definitely not saying you need to make a lifelong commitment, but I think you should consider that he's not like *them*. You already know that, though, don't you?"

I sigh, pinch the bridge of my nose, and nod. It's impossible to deny. And yeah, we're more than just fuck buddies—I know that too. I've begun factoring Caolan into my schedule and my daily decisions. I was just avoiding thinking about it, putting it off until after we've saved the world, because I'm chickenshit.

"I'm not disagreeing," I say preemptively. "I do have feelings for Caolan." Saying it out loud just makes it seem more real, but I can't deny the intrinsic *rightness* it makes me feel. "I'm just… I can't get past the fact that he leapt into this based on one look at me. It's exactly the sort of thing they used to do. Something would catch their attention and they'd pour all their focus into it for a few days, then abandon it when the next shiny thing came along." They being my parents. And one of those not-so-shiny-after-all things was me.

My parents were so dedicated to their life of parties and social climbing that they poured every cent into it. Some days, that meant I had to rely on myself to get fed while my parents ate at whatever social event they'd managed to wrangle an invitation to. We sometimes had a housemaid, if there was enough money left that month after they paid for their indulgences, and she was a sweet girl who would bring me bits and pieces from her mother's kitchen. On a few occasions, my parents hied off for a few days to visit someone, forgetting they'd left a young boy at home alone. I didn't know where they'd gone, how long for, or even if they were planning to come back at all.

Worse than that, though, was autumn—hunting season. House party season. They would rent our house out to make a little extra money for the next social season, then whisk me on a whirlwind of visits to strangers' houses, where I was always unexpected and unwelcome. I never knew where we were going or how long we would be there. Schooling was deemed unnecessary beyond reading and writing—after all, as long as I could read and reply to invitations to social events, what other need for learning could there be?

My childhood was chaotic and disorderly until I was eleven, and I hated every second of it.

Andrew's watching me with a pensive expression. "Sometimes I think about tracking your parents down and beating them to bloody pulp. It wouldn't change anything, but it would give me immense satisfaction."

"Me too," I agree, "but I always refrain, because it really wouldn't change anything, and they're not worth the time and effort it would take. They're out of my life now, and Jane's." My sister was born long after I reached adulthood and cut all ties with my parents, so I didn't learn of her existence until she was already four years old—and being neglected just as I had been. I brought her to live with me and raised her myself—which, to be honest, I'm not sure our parents noticed—and even though children are incredibly chaotic, she was and is one of the biggest joys in my life.

"I'm not going to tell you how to live," he says with an air of finality, "but I'm just saying, if you can see that your parents aren't worth your time anymore, maybe don't give them so much space in your head." He pauses. "Did Caolan tell you that I asked him what it was about you that attracted him?"

Mortification sweeps over me. "You didn't."

He laughs. "Of course I did. And that's nothing compared to the grilling Gideon gave him."

This is why some people prefer not to have friends.

"Anyway," he continues, "you should ask him about it."

It takes me a moment to realize that's all he's going to say.

"Wait, you're not going to tell me what he said?"

He smiles over my shoulder, and I turn to see Noah approaching. "Nope. I think you should ask Caolan. But only when you're sure you're willing to give things with him a chance." He tears his gaze away from Noah long enough to fix me with a serious look. "Don't lead him on, David. He's a good guy. You deserve a good guy."

Noah arrives before I can think of anything to say to that.

"You both look very serious. Should I come back?" he asks, hovering.

"No, we're done with serious." Andrew takes one of the plates he's holding and tosses a crab cake into his mouth.

"Good, because the karaoke tournament should be wrapping up soon, and you know what that means."

"I don't know what that means." Should I be worried? Don't I have enough to think about right now, what with Caolan being amazing and Andrew making me wonder if I'm being an ass?

"Alistair and I wrote a schedule for tonight," Andrew says between bites. "In honor of you. Because we know you love schedules, so it's part of your gift. Alistair had a copy framed for you."

I'm not letting myself get distracted by that. I'm really not.

"So what's scheduled for after the karaoke tournament?" I *really* want to see this schedule.

"Piñata," Andrew and Noah chorus.

"Are the contents of this piñata going to make me wish I'd never been born?" I ask Andrew.

He shrugs. "Anything's possible."

That does not make me feel better.

Aidan comes over to join us.

"David, cover your ears," he instructs, then faces Andrew squarely. "I haven't been able to get a straight answer out of Alistair, and that worries me. What's in the piñata?"

"What is with everyone asking me that? The whole point is to be delighted and surprised when it bursts and you discover what's inside." Andrew manages to sound offended even though he's grinning widely.

Aidan and Noah exchange glances. "Can you assure us that we will actually be delighted and surprised, not horrified and shocked?" Aidan persists.

Andrew tips his hand in a so-so gesture. "I would be delighted and surprised" is his answer, and I groan.

Before any of us who are sane can make the decision to go in search of the piñata and confiscate it, the music from inside—and the horrible singing—cuts out.

"It's piñata time!" someone—Alistair—shouts, and there's a rousing cheer. Mostly from the hellhounds in attendance and our interdimensional guests, who are excited about every aspect of "the birthday party."

"Too late now," Aidan murmurs, and Noah makes an agreeing noise.

"Maybe it won't be too bad," he suggests. "It could be chocolate or cookies. You know how hellhounds are about cookies."

I'm clinging to that hope and trying not to remember the time it was glitter. There was a light breeze that day, and that shit ended up *everywhere*. I found some in my underwear that night.

Or the time it was slime.

Alistair comes outside, carrying the piñata and followed by everyone who was inside, and one glance has me bursting out with laughter. They must have gotten it specially made, because I can't imagine there would be much call for old-fashioned alarm clock piñatas.

"We tried to make it personal," Andrew says dryly, and since nearly everyone there is acquainted with my obsession with schedules and timekeeping, there's a round of laughter. He gets up and goes over to Alistair, and they begin arguing over the best place to hang it.

Caolan comes over to sit in Andrew's chair.

"Did you have fun with the karaoke?" I ask him, and he shrugs.

"Singing is fun, but it's hard without knowing the song," he concedes. "Alistair and the other hellhounds take it very seriously. That makes it less fun." He takes my hand, sending warm tingles spiraling through me. Should I pull away? Is it wrong for me to encourage him like this?

Fuck it. It's my birthday. If ever there's a time to be selfish, it's today.

"Are you having fun?" he asks, and I smile at him.

"I am. I didn't think I would, given everything that's happening, but I really am."

He leans over and kisses me softly. "Happy birthday." He hesitates. "Did I say it right?"

Fuck fuck fuck fuck fuck fuck fuck.

I think I could fall in love with him.

"Yeah," I manage. "You said it right. Thank you."

"Okay!" Andrew calls, thankfully interrupting us before the moment becomes awkward. "The birthday boy gets three whacks, and if it hasn't burst by then, anyone else who wants a turn gets one." He hefts a—

"Andrew, for fuck's sake, we can't hit a piñata with a cucumber," Noah says exasperatedly.

"But it's a long one!" Alistair argues. Aidan groans. On the other side of the pool, Sam is laughing so hard, Gideon puts an arm around him to keep him from falling in.

"How are these people my best friends?" I ask nobody, and Caolan squeezes my hand.

"They balance you," he says, "and you give them balance."

I have to run that through my brain a few times. I have a funny feeling it's a direct translation that doesn't work as well in English as it does in elvish, but it kind of makes sense. And yeah, we do all balance each other out. Gideon used to be a lot scarier when he first joined the team, for instance.

Noah's gone over to the piñata and is going toe-to-toe with Andrew and Alistair over the cucumber. Aidan is backing him up. Sam is still laughing—possibly because he can hear every word of the argument—with Gideon almost smiling indulgently at him. Ellie's recording it all with her phone, because that's what we do when one or more of us makes an idiot of ourselves.

I twist around in my seat, searching for Percy. He's standing near the sliding door with King Raðulfr and Brandt (both of whom had a go at karaoke and neither of whom should ever be allowed to sing in public), smiling widely.

Like a stab through the heart, I suddenly miss Lily. Childhood friend to me and Percy, and one of our team members until Tish killed her, she would have loved this so much. She would have rolled her eyes at Andrew and Alistair's antics but then called me a stick in the mud and made me get up and use the cucumber.

And she would have loved Caolan. A guy who adores me unconditionally? It's what she always said I should hold out for. When the other kids at school teased me about my timekeeping obsession, she told me not to worry, that one day I'd find the person who thought it was adorable and fell in love with me because of it. She used to read a lot of the terrible heroic romances that were so popular back then, even sneaking them into the classroom and reading them in her lap during lessons.

When Tish murdered her, he killed the best person I've ever known.

Blinking away the sting of tears, I let go of Caolan's hand and stand up. "I guess I'd better move this along, or we'll never get to the cake." I march over to where the great debate has degenerated into threats to make people sleep on the couch and take the cucumber from Andrew. He immediately protests.

"Get out of the way, unless you want to get accidentally clobbered." I'm still not sure I can actually do this with a cucumber—although Alistair was right, it's a long one. It's highly likely that my hand is going to be smacking the piñata, though.

"Did someone spike your drink?" Andrew asks. "I thought we'd need to blackmail you."

I meet his gaze. "Lily would have made me do it."

His mouth quirks as sadness fills his gaze. I'm not the only one who misses her.

"She'd have made you wear the blindfold too."

Fucking Andrew. Always pushing his luck.

"For her, I would have worn it. For you, not so much."

He laughs. "One big whack for Lily, then." He raises his voice. "Stand back, everyone!"

"Oh my god, are you actually going to use the cucumber?" Noah asks. "What is even happening?"

"Hooray for the cucumber!" Sam yells, and we all turn to look at him.

"Is he drunk?" Aidan asks Gideon, who shrugs and shakes his head.

"I'm not drunk, just high on coffee and sugar," Sam

declares. "You all brought me coffee and a cookie or chocolate bar every time you asked for something today."

Considering how much we ask Sam for on a normal day, that's a terrifying amount of caffeine and sugar.

"You didn't have to eat it all," Gideon points out reasonably, and I cringe as Sam's face darkens.

"Let's get started!" I shout, desperately attempting to avoid having Sam push Gideon into the pool. All eyes focus on me… and the cucumber I'm brandishing.

This is going to do wonders for my professional reputation.

Biting back a hysterical giggle, I turn toward the piñata, adjust my grip on the cucumber, draw my arm back, and swing.

Thwack!

A cheer goes up.

That was kind of fun. I haven't done anything like this in a long time.

Thwack!

Thwack!

The damn thing hasn't burst yet. I'm not sure if that makes me happy or not. On the plus side, everyone else gets a turn now. On the downside, who knows what's going to fall on top of some poor unsuspecting innocent head when it does burst. At least I know I'm not going to sue Andrew and Alistair if I end up with confetti down the back of my shirt or in my eyes.

I hand the cucumber, which is starting to look a bit bruised, off to Alistair, who's shouting about forming a line. Chances are that cucumber is going to be pulp by the time the piñata bursts.

As if reading my mind, Sam sidles up beside me and

says, "Wanna bet on whether the cucumber lasts longer than the piñata?"

Brandt, who managed to score the first place in line, smacks the piñata enthusiastically.

"I'm in for fifty that the piñata wins."

We watch as a succession of people beat up a papier-mâché alarm clock. That thing is *strong*. I mean, I know a cucumber (that's rapidly becoming mushy) isn't the ideal tool to burst it, but still, after this many hits, there should be some weakness.

Caolan comes to stand beside me, and I automatically slide an arm around his waist. I like touching him. Maybe Andrew's right.

On the other hand, is it wise to take advice from a man who thinks beating a piñata with a cucumber is a good idea?

Finally, *finally*, a tiny rip appears. Shouts of excitement ensue, and the next few people aim carefully, causing the opening to widen. I lean forward, trying to catch a glimpse of the contents, but to no avail.

One last smack, and it bursts. The contents rain onto the terrace.

"Is that…?" Sam leans forward. "Oh, fuck my life."

I just stare.

Scattered over Andrew's terrace, with some having fallen into the pool, individually wrapped in clear plastic sleeves, are dozens of virulently colored silicone dildos.

There's a riot of laughter and shouts as some of the partygoers scramble to grab their favorite colors. Alistair is expounding on the specs of the damn things, talking about length-to-girth ratio and how there were sparkly ones, but they were slimmer, and he figured it was worth sacrificing the shimmer for "a cock that will fill you just right."

Aidan puts his hands over his face, shaking his head, but his shoulders are trembling with what I'm guessing is laughter.

Percy comes over with a neon blue dildo in his hand, still in the plastic. "I thought I should grab one for the birthday boy before they all get taken," he says solemnly, holding it out to me. His mouth quirks, but he ruthlessly suppresses the smile.

I take it from him just as solemnly. "Thank you. I wouldn't have wanted to miss out." Turning it over, I marvel at the ridiculous color, but have to admit it's a good size—not unrealistically big, but enough for a good stretch—and has a pretty comfortable grip. This isn't a cheap piece of crap. They must have spent a fortune on these.

The laugh bursts out of me unbidden, but it takes only seconds for everyone to join me.

My friends balance me.

I THOUGHT I was prepared for multiple cakes, but I really wasn't. My jaw is so far dropped that I'm pretty sure I resemble that clown game from carnivals—you know the one, where you have to put balls in the clown's open, moving mouth.

The cakes just keep coming.

Maybe I don't balance my friends as much as I should. I mean, I knew Andrew had a thing for cake, but I didn't think he was this out of control. And I thought Alistair said there were only six? I may not be an expert mathematician, but even I can count to six, and there are definitely more cakes than that. Thankfully, none of them is very large, but we'll still be eating leftover cake for days.

"Is it customary for there to be so much cake?" the king asks from beside me, his gaze fixed on the admittedly delicious-looking feast before us. If I'd known there would be this much, I probably wouldn't have had quite as much of the other food. "What is the tradition? One cake for each landmark span of time? Or one for every —" He glances around, then back at the table, frowning. "I was going to say one for every ten people, but there aren't that many people here."

"One cake is customary," I tell him. "But Andrew loves all flavors of cake, and I believe he had difficulty making the selection."

"Do you mean each one is different in more than appearance?"

Say what?

I turn slowly to face him and Caolan. "Don't you have something similar to this in your society?"

They both shake their heads. "Our sweet foods are smaller," Caolan says. "The texture is different too. I had my first cake only a few days ago, when the clearance came through that all Earth food is safe to eat. Aidan bought it for me, but it was only this big." He traces a circle on his palm, and I guess that Aidan took him to the coffee place down the street and got one of those individual-size cakes they have. I feel a slight pang that I missed sharing that experience with him. If I'd known, we could have had coffee and cake together, but I spent most of that day in meetings with the migration team and didn't even learn about the clearance until we got home that night and Caolan asked if we could try "the pizza Alistair told me about" for dinner.

"Cakes can have different textures," I tell them. "Though I'm not sure that we'll have that much variation tonight. I can see a carrot cake, though, and that one looks like mud cake, and—"

"What?" The startled exclamation comes from both of them.

"You make sweets from mud?" the king asks, and I grimace. I know better—I should be more careful.

"No, sorry. It's chocolate cake, but a very rich one with a high fat content. Ah, there's—"

Once again I'm interrupted, but this time by Alistair calling me forward. I sigh in resignation. "Did they tell you about the birthday song?"

Caolan nods. "Alistair taught Dustin the words, and he taught the rest of us. We've been practicing."

Great.

The candle-blowing and cake-cutting go surprisingly well, and I manage to dodge Alistair's suggestion of a speech by announcing that cake is new to elves and dragons. At first I think Andrew might faint, but he rallies and declares that they should try a piece of each type of cake. I snag myself a piece of cheesecake and one of lemon and coconut pound cake and then slip away to enjoy it by the pool. My moment of peace won't last long—there's a pile of presents stacked beside the cake table—but that's okay. This is one type of chaos I can handle.

Ten minutes later, Caolan comes to find me. "Mud cake is excellent, but only in small pieces," he informs me, planting himself in a deck chair. There's a smear of chocolate on the side of his mouth. "I think I like the lemon drizzling cake the best. It was sweet and sour."

"Lemon drizzle," I correct, because he's asked me more than once to help him get things right. "You have chocolate ganache on your mouth."

Rather than wiping it away himself, he picks up the napkin by my plate and hands it to me. "Please?"

I chuckle, but obediently clean him up. Then, unable to resist, I kiss his soft pink lips. "Mmm, delicious," I tease.

"Chocolate or lemon?" he asks, and I smile at him. "Neither."

Heat flares in his eyes, but he only smiles back. I love his smile, especially when he's not wearing his human disguise. Don't get me wrong, he's hot as a human, but his natural features suit him best.

"What other flavors did you try?" I ask.

"Raspberry and white chocolate—that was good, but very sweet. I liked the cheesecake, but it wasn't what I expected. It's not much like cheese."

"Different kind of cheese. We'll get some next time we go to the grocery store, now that we know they're all safe for you to eat. There are lots of different cheeses."

"That would be fun. I also liked the carrot cake. I didn't think I would, since carrots taste weird, but it didn't taste like carrot at all."

"It's got lots of other good stuff in it," I agree. "If you want, we can try cooking carrots in different ways, see if you like it better. How have you had it so far?" I try to remember if we've eaten carrots together, but I don't think we have.

"It was in my salad at lunch one day," he says. "In really thin strips."

"Raw, then. Yeah, that can be an acquired taste. It's sweeter when it's cooked."

He shrugs. "I liked it in the cake, so I might like it cooked other ways." He hesitates. "Is it customary for the piñata to contain sexual aids?"

I clear my throat in an attempt to hold back the laughter. There are still a few unclaimed dildos scattered around and some in the pool, which someone will need to fish out—I'm betting Andrew. Noah will probably watch and make snarky comments about diving for dick or something.

"No," I reply. "Chocolates or other candy or small toys are more customary, although you really can put anything you want in there, as long as it's not too large or heavy."

He's silent for a moment. "It's not possible to keep hellhounds and dragons apart, is it?"

I snort. "I've already considered that, and no. We might be able to manage it initially, but ultimately, the dragons will integrate more fully with our population. It's going to happen eventually, so we may as well ease in slowly. Surely it won't be that bad."

A shout from across the pool draws our attention. Two of the dragons appear to be playing tug of war with the plate containing the last piece of mud cake, with two more dragons and four hellhounds egging them on. As we watch, the hellhounds start chanting "fight, fight, fight."

The first piece of cake gets thrown.

"Or I could be wrong."

Fortunately, Andrew steps in then. He would have let them fight it out and just watched, but wasting cake is a cardinal sin in his book, so he breaks up the fight with fangs and claws out, hissing viciously when one bolshie dragon objects.

The dragon backs down. You don't want to go head-to-head with Andrew over cake.

There's a ripple of unease now, the happy party vibe wavering a little, so of course Alistair leaps into the breach and announces that I'll be opening presents while everyone enjoys their cake.

I go over to the pile and reach for a small one on top, but Alistair shouts, "Do mine first!"

"Which one is yours?"

He points to a brightly wrapped gift halfway down the stack. "That one. Do it first. Here, I'll help you get it." He rearranges the stack of gifts. From the corner of my eye, I notice Andrew nudging Noah, a broad grin on his face. Ellie has her phone out, holding it up to record.

Whatever this is, I may not like it.

"Here!" He thrusts the present into my hands. I look down at it, then squint. I missed it the first time around because the background is so garishly orange, but the print on the wrapping paper is tiny erect penises.

I snort. "Love the paper."

"Thanks," he says proudly. "It took ages to choose the right one. Aidan picked the card, though. I wanted the one in the shape of a dick."

I open the envelope and slide out the card, which is a nice generic happy birthday one. "Is there a reason you're so fixated on dick right now? Or is it something about me that prompted the theme for this party? Are you trying to tell me what you really think of me?"

A low laugh runs through the gathered guests as Alistair shrugs.

"Nah, you're the best. Now that I'm getting a good

dicking on the regular, it's hard to think about anything else." Aidan's groan rises above the jeers and heckles.

I put the card aside and rip open the paper.

"Look at him go!" someone shouts. "Not gonna save the paper, David?"

I'm too busy staring at what I've revealed to answer. A sound bursts from me—I'm not sure if it's a laugh, a groan, or both.

World Of Wangs is emblazoned on the box in my hands. I know what this is. After the first time Sam got teased about it, I looked it up. There is no way, absolutely no fucking way, I am opening this box here.

"What is it?" someone yells, and I hold it up. Those who recognize the name catcall, although I hear Sam cursing. The majority, though, seem confused.

"It's a set of interspecies dildos," I say calmly.

"Interspecies?" one of the elves asks.

"Most Earth species have different-shaped cocks," Brandt explains blandly, and I flashback to him telling us about his wild youth on Earth.

"Ooooohhhh," chorus the elves and dragons. Eyes widen, and the crowd edges closer.

How is this my life?

"Let David open all his presents first, and then I'm sure he'll let you play with his cocks," Alistair bargains, using what has to be the most unexpected sentence ever.

"Nobody plays with David's cock," Caolan growls.

"You must be doing something wrong, if Alistair thinks David needs a box of sex aids," someone—I want to say Hagen—jeers.

This is the weirdest birthday I've ever had. "Next present, please!" I say loudly, but can't resist adding, "And believe me, Caolan is doing *nothing* wrong. That box won't get opened." No need to tell them I've got a drawer full of dildos and other toys that Caolan and I are already making full use of. Sex without toys is like plain vanilla ice cream. Delicious, but monotonous if that's all you ever have.

Caolan flushes pink as the teasing picks up, but he's grinning now and winks at me.

Alistair passes me another gift, and we get into a present-opening rhythm. It's really sweet that people brought gifts at all—I wasn't expecting that. My close friends, sure, but not from everyone—even the elves and dragons. Although I'm surprised when I open one and find a laminated printout of a local bus timetable.

"Uh, thank you," I tell the elf it's from.

His smile is relieved. "Caolan said you like schedules. Alistair took me to the office supply store"—he says it carefully, as though testing the words out—"but all the schedules there were empty. So he suggested this."

Of course he did. I very carefully don't look at him.

"Well, I don't have this one, so it was an excellent choice," I assure the elf. I don't want to embarrass him in front of his colleagues, but I will definitely murder Alistair later.

"This one next," the cheeky hellhound says, pushing a small box toward me and studiously avoiding my gaze. I take it from him.

This one doesn't have a full-size card, just one of those little gift-tag ones taped to the pretty old-gold-colored paper. I flip it open and recognize Noah's hand-writing.

I wish I'd been able to show you more. Happy Birthday.

Underneath, in painstakingly printed letters, is Caolan's name.

My heart clutches, but I'm not sure why. I look at him, and he's smiling, but it's a tentative thing.

I tear off the paper and open the box.

And blink against the glow.

Nestled against black tissue paper is a leaf from the tréghel tree. It takes me a second to notice that it's been preserved somehow—there's a clear film over it. That likely explains why it's still glowing even though it's not attached to the tree. Threaded through a hole at one end is a chain with oddly geometric links made from a material I don't recognize.

My head spins.

He noticed how much I liked the tree. He remembered. And he went to the trouble of preserving a leaf for me.

A leaf from a tree that will soon be extinct. A relic from another dimension. A piece of his home.

As gifts go, you can't get more priceless than that.

Taking the box with me, I stride over to him and kiss him with all the confusing feelings I have in me. I ignore the shouts and catcalls. I ignore the laughter and suggestive comments from those standing beside us.

His arms come up to pull me against him, and we keep kissing, just us, mouth to mouth, and with that kiss, I show him all the things I'm so afraid to admit.

When I finally pull back, we're both panting, but smiling.

"Thank you," I tell him.

"Anything for you."

CHAPTER SEVEN

Caolan

Two weeks after David's birthday, things are going… as well as can be expected. The migration is progressing and should be complete within a few days. Officially, that's good news, but the knowledge that my homeland is soon going to be permanently sealed off as it decays into nothingness is… distressing. I'll never be able to go back there, and the closer we get to that day, the more painful I find it.

David has been wonderful. I've never mentioned how conflicted I am, but he knows. He knows when I need hugs and when I need to be distracted in other ways, and he's always there for me. He still maintains the fiction that we're just sexually satisfying each other, but in every way that counts, we're paired. I'm not sure what happened to him to make him so leery of what's between us, but I can wait until he's ready. He's worth it.

He wears the gift I gave him all the time. At first, he was taking it off to shower, but when I explained that the nature of the spell that preserves it makes it—and the chain it's on—impervious to water, he stopped taking it off at all. When we lie in bed at night, the soft glow of the leaf is a comfort to me. I may lose my homeland, but I'll have David.

In the meantime, the search for our stolen baby dragon is still underway. Éibhear and Tish have done an excellent job of hiding her, and without knowing where she is, we're loath to mount an assault on any of the compounds we've identified. The last thing we need is for them to move her—or worse, for her to be injured in the attack. We have agents working to find information, and they're slowly but surely trickling data back to us.

Today, David and I have a meeting with the teams that are managing the resettlement. Things have been going fairly smoothly, but there are some small issues that need to be resolved, so we're getting both sides together to talk through them. Technically, David and I don't need to be there, but it seems King Raðulfr's announcement of our relationship has turned a spotlight very brightly on us. Noah told me we're the latest hot celebrity couple and we're being shipped as Dalan. I'm not entirely sure what that means, but people have actually recognized me on the street. Even humans—this has spilled into their world, although they seem to think it's part of a fantasy. They get very excited about it, and some have asked me to sign things.

Ultimately, it means David and I are now required to attend a lot of meetings and events where we're not really needed. We're glad to do some of them, like the visits to the temporary settlements of my people. They were so happy and excited to see us together and talk to us. In that instance, the king and Rabhya were right about our relationship being a beacon of hope. But this meeting is a waste of our time.

My timekeeping is getting better, especially now that I understand how to use the reminder function on my phone. The king's senior spellcasters finally found a way to make the translator spell work on written words as well as spoken ones, and it's made a huge difference to us. We're still not good at hand-writing things, but there isn't much need for that anyway. We can use phones and computers, where each letter can be created with the touch of a button—or "key," as Sam told me they're called. I don't understand why it's a button on an elevator and a key on a computer, but as long as it works, I don't care that much.

Right now, I'm waiting outside the elevator for David. He went downstairs to get us coffee to fortify us during this meeting while I compared notes with Andrew, Gideon, and Garin on the latest intelligence reports.

"You know," Andrew says conversationally, leaning against the wall beside me, "you could wait for him in the office. Or even in the meeting room. Doesn't it make you feel weird to be staring at the elevator like this?"

"No more than you feel weird when you check the time every two minutes when Noah is in a different room," I reply. It took me a while to realize what he was doing, but once I noticed, it became impossible to ignore. "Why are you here, anyway?"

"I'm keeping you company," he says, sounding offended. "Don't you want my company?"

I'm saved from answering when the elevator doors open and David steps out. He has a cardboard tray with two paper cups and a paper bag on it. I hope it's cake, although knowing David as I do, it's probably toast or a healthy muffin. He's so adorably sensible.

He smiles when he sees me and starts in our direction.

"David?" Candice calls. "Do you have a sec?"

The smile turns rueful, and he goes over to her desk. I like Candice. She's the receptionist and is never too busy to answer questions or help with technology, even when it turns out to be a stupid thing. And she's been endlessly patient with the dragons. David said she's very atypical for a demon in that regard.

"We need to hire someone to help Candice," Andrew says. "The job needed two people even before all this happened."

I nod, because David has said the same thing—and so has Sam. "Percy doesn't want to bring anyone new in right now," I tell him. "David was going to see if some of the interns could help, but—"

"Davy!" The shout rings through the reception area, and I look back toward the elevators. A man and a woman, both sorcerers, are coming out of one. The woman has her arms outstretched toward… I follow her gaze.

David? Is Davy a derivative of David? It doesn't suit him at all.

Beside me, Andrew hisses. Startled, I glance over and see his fangs and claws are out and his face is drawn into a vicious mask. I draw up my power. If these people are a danger…

"Who are they?" I ask. Every muscle is tense, and I want to go to David, but while his face is pale, he doesn't seem to be guarding against possible attack. Candice looks uncertain, her gaze swinging between David, the newcomers, and Andrew and me.

"His parents," Andrew growls. "Come on." He strides off, and I rush to keep pace. We reach the desk and David just as the newcomers—David's parents—do, and I push aside my surprise. I didn't realize David had parents. Well, I knew he must—I know enough about the Earth species to understand that—but he never speaks of them, not even in passing as I do mine. I assumed they were dead. After all, he raised his sister, Jane.

"…can't be here," David is saying. Someone who doesn't know him would say he's calm, but there's a faint note of strain in his voice, and one of his fingers is twitching against the cardboard tray. He's on the verge of losing control.

"Get out," Andrew snarls, not bothering with calm or politeness. The two enforcement agents stationed in reception start toward us.

"But, David, we came to celebrate with you! You've finally found someone to share your life with," his mother protests. Her gaze skims uneasily over Andrew, who's hissing again, and lands on me. "Look, here he is! It's Caolan." She holds her arms out to me and steps forward, then hesitates. I'm not certain if it's the look on my face, which I'm sure is very unwelcoming, or the fact that she's afraid to get closer to Andrew.

David sighs. "You've seen the media coverage."

His father blusters. "It's the only way we hear anything about you. You never call us. Do you know how hurtful and embarrassing it is to learn from our friends that our only child has found love?"

Only child? But what about Jane?

He shakes his head. "I'm not your only child."

His mother blinks. "Of course you are. I think we'd remember if we had another one."

The father frowns. "Wait… wasn't there a girl at one point? We had to leave the Duke of Devonshire's black-and-white ball because you were giving birth."

The mother raises a hand to her mouth. "Oh, yes—and after all the effort to get an invitation! I was heartbroken."

I think I might be ill. These are David's parents?

Poor David. And poor Jane…. No wonder David raised her.

"That's all behind us now," the father says hastily, perhaps because none of us seem the least bit sympathetic about their past plight. In fact… I take hold of Andrew's arm, just in case he decides to attack. It's David's prerogative to land the first blow, and as many after that as he wants. "We've come because we want to host a celebration for you!"

David puts the cardboard tray on the reception desk and pinches the bridge of his nose. "You want to use me and Caolan to rack up some social credibility, you mean."

"Davy—" his mother begins, but David's had enough.

"No. Leave now. I'm giving you one minute to go before I have you thrown out. And if you so much as mention that you have any connection to me, I'll let Andrew hunt— No, you know what? I'll give an interview describing exactly what my childhood was like and why Andrew had to rescue me from it. You'll never be invited anywhere again."

"You had a wonderful childhood!" the mother

declares indignantly. "You never had to go to school or have a bedtime like all the other whiny children. Instead we took you to all those lovely parties!"

So much has just become clear. Do these people not know David at all?

"David's told you to leave," I say, letting go of Andrew and stepping closer to them. I channel a tiny bit of my power to give the illusion of being bigger and more menacing. It's a child's trick but seems to work on them. They shrink back. "And I believe your minute is up." I gesture to the hovering enforcers.

They swoop forward, grim-faced, take hold of the parents' arms, and hustle them toward the elevator. "Could you call someone to take over until we get back?" one of the enforcers asks. The reception is the only area in the offices that isn't warded and thus needs to be guarded at all times.

"We'll wait here," Andrew assures him, then hisses again at the parents. "Forget you even know who David is," he advises. "I'm not as nice as him and Caolan, and I've wanted to come after you for centuries."

They're both still sputtering when the elevator doors close on them.

Without turning around, Andrew raises his voice and commands, "There had better not be anyone standing around watching right now. And I don't *ever* want to hear gossip about this."

I look over my shoulder to see who he's talking to. There's a small cluster of people on the other side of the security gate, but they scatter before he's finished speaking.

Even without looking at David, I can feel the humiliation and pain radiating from him. I make a snap decision. "Andrew, can you give our apologies to the migration teams, please? David and I have a last-minute issue to deal with." I don't wait for him to answer, just grab David's hand and the cardboard tray with our coffee and pull him along to the hallway with all the meeting rooms. One of them has to be empty. I'd take him home instead, but there's no way he'd agree to that—I'm surprised he hasn't argued about missing the meeting.

Finally I find an empty room. I let go of David's hand to flip on the lights and close the door. He goes over to the small table and slumps into one of the chairs, putting his head in his hands.

Joining him, I pull the coffee cups out of the tray and place his beside him, making sure to nudge it against his arm so he knows it's there. He sighs and lifts his head. His face is still pale, and his eyes are glassy.

"I'm sorry you had to see that," he mumbles, avoiding my gaze and picking up his cup.

"I'm sorry you had to go through it. And that those people have any connection to you."

He huffs. "Yeah. I'm sorry about that too." We sit there in silence for a few moments, sipping our almost-too-cool-now coffee.

"I guess I should explain," he says at last.

"No. Only if you want to. There's no obligation between us." I hope he understands that. This is obviously a difficult subject for him, and I'm not going to force him to talk about it merely to satisfy my own curiosity.

A tiny smile curves his mouth, and some color comes back to his cheeks. Or at least, he loses the pasty pallor.

"There's an obligation between us," he murmurs. "You're not… like them."

For a moment, I'm confused, and then the bottom drops out of my world and I barely stop myself from jerking back. He thought I was like *them*? He thought I was the kind of person who would neglect my own child? Is that why he's been so reluctant to accept our connection?

Why would he think that of me?

I realize he's still talking and force myself to listen.

"… people think I'm the way I am because of my childhood, that it's a post-traumatic reaction, but I've always liked structure. That's what made it so difficult. You saw how they forgot Jane even existed. If someone had taken me from them when I was a toddler, they would have forgotten me, too. They still did forget me sometimes, until they came home and I was there." He sucks in a breath. "It was chaos, and I hated it."

I don't say anything. My whole being stings with the knowledge that he thought I could be like that, someone who would cause him pain and force him to live a life he hates.

He didn't know you.

The voice is insistent as David speaks haltingly about his childhood. *He only knew that you had no schedule, couldn't keep time, and declared your feelings within seconds of meeting him.*

The sting eases a little but isn't completely washed away. I can see how these things would add up in David's mind to me being unreliable like his parents—after all, at that time, he knew nothing about elves or how we function. But it still hurts that it took until now for him to let go of those fears. He knows me now, surely. We've been almost inseparable for weeks.

His voice fades into silence, and I meet his gaze. There's an edge of fear there—of what, I'm not sure.

"You said before that Andrew rescued you." I'm not ready to talk about the rest.

That little smile comes back. "Yes. When I was eleven, they dragged me to a house party. There were never any other children there, unless the hosts had some, and these didn't. Sometimes I liked that better, because it meant I was free to explore the estate and the library, if there was one. But it usually also meant that nobody knew what to do with me. I had no nanny or tutor to make sure I was fed, and of course I wasn't allowed to attend meals with the adults, so…" He trails off, his gaze becoming distant, then shakes his head. "Anyway, this particular estate had an excellent library, and I was spending all my time there, researching and practicing weaves I really shouldn't have known anything about at that age. Andrew was one of the guests, and he came into the library one morning— looking for a book, I guess. I don't think I ever asked him why he was there. He was surprised to see me, but you know Andrew. Once he realized what I was doing, he asked who was supposed to be watching me, and I said nobody, and then he asked some more questions. Somehow the whole story came out." He grimaces. "I knew from meeting other children that my life was not the same as theirs, but I didn't realize how different it was. Andrew got angry—you saw him today. That's nothing compared to how he was then. He was swearing and kicking furniture and ranting about how, with fertility in the community being so poor, you'd think people would treasure their children if they were lucky enough to have them. Then he asked me what *I* wanted."

He falls silent and stares down at his cup.

"That was the first time anyone had ever asked me that—what I wanted. Not just what I wanted in life, but ever. I'd never even been asked what I wanted for lunch. It was… terrifying. And so wonderful." Sighing again, he pinches the bridge of his nose. "I didn't know how to answer—didn't even know what options were available to me."

The hurt begins to seep away, and a strong desire to go after his parents replaces it.

"He saw that I was struggling and explained that if I wanted, he would find someone else for me to live with, someone who would take better care of me. Or he could get me a place at a good boarding school." He laughs, just a little one, but my heart sings to hear it. "As soon as he mentioned school, I knew what I wanted. I'd been so envious of other people being able to learn things. So he went and found my parents, told them—and I wasn't there for this part, but some people who were have since told me about it—he told them that they would sign over guardianship of me to him or he would rip out their intestines and make them eat them, and then he packed me up and we left. We went to London for a few days while he made inquiries about good schools, and then he took me on a tour of several and let me pick the one I wanted."

I already liked Andrew, but now I'm ready to declare him my brother.

"How did you choose?" I ask. My voice is just a little bit hoarse, and I clear my throat.

David grins. "They were all fairly similar, but at one, I saw a succubus girl about my age arguing with a shifter boy. I didn't hear much of the argument, but at the end she said, 'You have to come with me, because if you don't, you're going to get so boring you'll turn into a stick, and then you'll only be good for playing fetch with hellhounds.' The boy and I both laughed—Andrew did too—and she turned around and saw us and said, 'Who knew going swimming was such a burden. Do you want to come?' That made up my mind. And they were my first friends."

"Do you still talk to them?" David is not the kind of person to let friendships fade away easily.

He nods. "The boy was Percy." His mouth presses into a firm line. "The girl was Lily. She… she died last year."

I reach over and take his hand. I've heard a little bit about Lily from Alistair and Noah. They were giving me background information on Dr. Tish, and Sam's kidnapping was mentioned. Noah never met her, and Alistair barely knew her, but they both emphasized how difficult her death was for the team.

"I'm so sorry."

His eyes go glassy again, and he makes a sound that might be a sob. "She would have liked you so much. And been so angry with me for the way I've treated you." His hand tightens around mine.

"The way you've treated me?" I echo, confused.

He nods. "Having sex with you but not committing to more. Don't misunderstand, Lily wasn't a prude, but she was always upfront. This thing we've got, where you're honest about how you feel and I'm insisting it's just sex… she would have hated that." He hesitates. "I wish she were still here to lecture me about being an idiot."

It's my turn to sigh. "I wish she were here too. I would have loved to meet her. But you're not an idiot. I… I know it's not always easy to let go of past traumas. And I understand how me meeting you and instantly declaring my feelings might have reminded you of how impulsive and reckless your parents are." I wince. "And then you found out about how elves keep time, and that would have scared you too. My point is, I always knew I couldn't expect you to return my feelings right away. I don't mind being patient and letting things develop between us. Especially now that we're having sex. Sex is good."

A laugh bursts from him, which was my goal.

"Sex is good," he agrees. "Between us, it's fucking awesome. But, hey, uh… Andrew said something. At my birthday. That he asked you what it was that attracted you to me." He stops abruptly. I can see where this is going, but I'm not going to rush him there.

He swallows. "He said I should ask you. So… what attracted you to me?"

My heart begins to beat faster.

"I didn't know what to expect when I walked into that room," I admit. "Alistair and Aidan had been courteous and welcoming, and I knew I had information that could help you all, but I was still a stranger in a new place, and none of you were entirely sure you could trust me yet. I was… angry. So angry and sad about what was happening to us. And part of me was angry that I had to be here instead of spending every moment I could at home with my loved ones." I take a deep breath as remembering those emotions causes them to rise within me.

"And then I saw you. You're handsome, David—a very good-looking man. But that was inconsequential at first. It was your soul. It glows from you, so pure and beautiful. Yours is the soul of a truly good person who cares so deeply for others, and I could not look away." I shake my head. "Elves don't have the ability to see souls like that. I considered the fact that yours shines at me so clearly to be a sign. And the more I have gotten to know you, the more strongly I believe that. I am willing to change and grow because I know it will be in the same direction you have already taken and bring me closer to you."

He blinks slowly. Then he gets up, goes over to the door, and flips the lock. Turning back to me, he says, "Undo your pants."

"What?" Is he…? What is he doing?

"It's official," he declares. "We're boyfriends. I'm halfway in love with you, and I want to celebrate this moment with a blowjob."

He loves me! Joy explodes in me, and my hands move to my belt buckle before my brain catches up. "Are you sure?" I ask. This is not like David.

"Yes. Sucking someone off at the office in the middle of a workday while there's a crisis going on is the most impulsive and irresponsible thing I've ever done, and it's going to be with you." He drops to his knees.

I'm not going to argue with that.

I reach for my belt, but David pushes my hands aside. "Nope. Your job is to sit there and enjoy it. I'll handle everything else."

I make a sound of excitement that causes him to

grin as he opens my pants and pulls me out of my underwear. I'm more than half hard already, just the thought of a blowjob from David enough to get my cock's attention.

"Mmm," David murmurs. "You look delicious." He gives me a few firm strokes, bringing me to fully erect, then leans down and licks the head.

My breath catches, and I put a hand on his head. His thick, silky black hair slides between my fingers, and he looks up at me and smiles, then licks me from root to tip.

I clench my hand.

"Wanna push my head down?" he whispers. "Just shove into my throat and thrust until you come?"

I try to swallow, but my mouth is too dry.

In the next moment, his hot, wet mouth is sliding over me, taking me deep. I don't know how he can do that, take all of me, but he's never gagged, not once, and the feeling of him enveloping me is beyond anything I could ever describe. He takes me all the way, until the head is in his throat, then swallows, and a moan bursts out of me, loud in the silence. I cast a quick glance at the door, hoping nobody heard.

Who am I kidding? Of course someone heard.

David slowly pulls off, using his tongue to explore every inch of me as he does. I know he's fascinated by the ridges on my dick, because he's spent a lot of time examining them up close. He's learned where I'm most sensitive and the best way to handle me to maximize both our pleasure. And now he uses all that knowledge to his advantage.

I'm not going to last long.

It only takes three more of those tortuously slow

thrusts to have me whimpering, and on the fourth retreat, David seals his lips just below the head and *sucks*.

When my vision clears, David is back in his chair, calmly ripping open the paper bag that came with our coffee. I blink a few times, trying to regain clarity.

"You got cake?" I croak. This really is a day for surprises.

He smiles at me, and it's so warm and tender and indulgent that I lean over and kiss him before he can answer. I can taste myself in his mouth, and the intimacy of it warms me. One kiss leads to another, slow, loving, sweet kisses—then I remember that I came, but he didn't.

"Would you like me to—" What's that word he used the other night? "—jerk you?" I ask against his mouth. I feel it curl into a smile before he pulls back.

"No, I think I want to build the anticipation. Besides, we're not going to have too much more time before someone comes to check on us, and if they catch us in the middle of a handjob, we'll hear about it until the end of time."

I nod, my mind skipping ahead to tonight, when the anticipation will be satisfied, and all the things I can do to show him how amazing and worthy and loved he is.

"Wait, is someone coming to check on us?" I take the chunk of cake he passes me and put it in my mouth. Mmmm… lemon. My favorite. He always spoils me like this.

"Count on it. Andrew will have gone back to the office in a pissy mood, maybe ranting a bit. We're all nosy, so whoever's there will demand to know what his problem is. He'll tell them my parents were here and they upset me so much that you and I didn't go to the meeting, and now they're all sitting there wondering if I'm having a breakdown. Eventually, one of them will crack—I'd put money on it being Sam first—and insist that someone come and find us to make sure I'm okay." He calmly sips his coffee, then pulls a face. "Cold. What a waste."

"I'll go get you another one," I offer. That will also give me a chance to duck into the office and tell everyone he's fine.

He shakes his head. "Don't bother. Let's just enjoy this break before we have to get back to work." He slides his hand over and wraps it around mine. "Are we okay? I mean… this has all been about my feelings. What about you?"

I lift his hand to press it against my cheek. I love the sensation of his skin on mine. "I won't ever lie to you. It hurt me that you ever thought I could be like them." He tenses, and I hurry on. "But I understand why. We're still getting to know each other, and you didn't have the certainty of having seen how perfect my soul is for yours."

He raises a brow. "We have paired souls? I thought you couldn't see that for yourself."

"I can't." I shake my head. "But others can. The king was the first person to reassure me."

David laughs suddenly. "Is that why he was being all strange when I met him the first time? Gideon was worried you were all plotting to kill us."

The sound that comes out of my mouth is a snort-cough-laugh. "No. King Raðulfr was ready to throw a party in your honor—and he probably would have bonded us right then if we wanted." I pause. "So… did you mean what you said? About us being…

boyfriends?" I stumble somewhat on the unfamiliar word.

David slides his hand free of mine and turns it to cup my cheek, then leans over and kisses me, his mouth warm and soft against mine. "Yes. If you're happy with that. I know I'm not the easiest person to live with, and I'm sorry, more sorry than I can ever say, that I ever believed you were anything like them. I'm sorry I let old fears control me. And I'm sorry I didn't tell you sooner that I have feelings for you. What's between us is not just sex." He kisses me again.

Someone knocks on the door, and a second later, it opens. I pull back from David's kiss just as Sam pokes his head around the door.

"Sorry to interr— Oh! Oh man, I'm really sorry to interrupt," he says, cheeks going slightly pink. I'm not sure if that's because we were obviously kissing or because it smells like sex in here.

David chuckles, and my heart sings. I love hearing such happy sounds from him. "I told you Sam would crack first. Come in, Sammy."

Sam enters and closes the door behind him. His gaze tracks over the remnants of cake on the table and the way we're huddled close together. It drops, jerks away, and his face flames. "Uh, you might want to..." He gestures to my crotch and studies the ceiling.

Oops. I never tucked myself in after David sucked my brains out through my cock. I attend to it now and refasten my pants while David snickers.

"It's safe to look," I say, and Sam cautiously lowers his gaze.

"Are you okay?" he asks David. "Andrew said your parents stopped by and were douchenuggets."

The translator spell fails completely on that word, and I interrupt before David can reply. "Douchenuggets?"

"Uh…" David and Sam exchange glances. "I can't remember what other slang we've talked about. Assholes?"

"Ah." I nod. "Yes. Assholes are detestable people. A douchenugget is like an asshole?"

Sam wobbles his hand back and forth. "Somewhat. On my personal scale, a douchenugget is worse than an asshole. After all, assholes at least serve a purpose."

"Let's not get into this now," David says before I can ask more questions. "You should ask Noah," he suggests to me. "He has an incredible vocabulary of slang slurs."

I make a mental note to do so as David turns back to Sam. "And yeah, my parents were here, and they brought their full arsenal of douchebaggery."

I note that word to ask Noah about too.

"But I'm okay."

Sam narrows his eyes. "Are you sure?"

David sighs. "Well, I wasn't. But my boyfriend here took care of me, and I know those people can't screw with my life anymore, so…" He shrugs.

Sam looks from him to me and then back again. A grin spreads slowly across his face. "Boyfriend?"

"I pulled my head out of my ass." David takes my hand and kisses it.

"YES!" Sam pumps his fist. "Yes!" He tackles David in a hug, then reaches an arm out and pulls me into it too. "I'm so happy," he says, his voice muffled against my shoulder.

I pat him on the back. "I will give you anything you want if you wait a few hours before telling Alistair or

Dustin," I promise him. I want some time to bask in this, and that won't happen with either of them following me around crowing and asking intrusive questions.

"Deal," Sam says promptly, breaking the hug. "But then I get to tell everyone. You can't preempt me."

"Fuck my life," David mutters as he begins clearing away the remains of our snack.

"We won't say a word," I affirm, sticking out my hand for Sam to shake and seal the deal. That's an Earth mannerism I quite enjoy.

<hr>

CHAPTER EIGHT

David

<hr>

As the final day of the migration comes and goes, Caolan becomes more and more tense. King Raðulfr and Percy agreed to allow a five-day buffer from when the last civilians arrived on Earth to when travel between dimensions was cut off permanently. During those five days, a hundred soldiers went back and did one final sweep of the planet for anyone who might possibly have been living outside the protective shield and survived. It's a dangerous mission, and it was volunteer-only.

Today is day five. The last of the soldiers returned this afternoon—and nine of them were killed; it's *that* dangerous without a shield as time slowly collapses. These were highly trained and skilled warriors, watching each other's backs. There was never any chance that civilians had survived, but we had to check.

Tomorrow morning, King Raðulfr will permanently seal off their dimension from this one. It wasn't originally our intention—the king was just going to implement a travel ban, this time without any exceptions. It sounds like the same thing, but it isn't. The way I understand it, the permanent seal will apply to all beings and species and dimensions in existence, whereas the king's travel ban is specific to the elves and their portals. This seal really will be permanent and eternal. Apparently, the magic conveyed the need for this step to the king, Percy, Brandt, and all our species leaders—just so there could be no confusion.

Caolan's a mess.

Not outwardly. On the surface, he's been his usual self, stepping up to speak for the king and getting the job done. But whenever he gets a free moment, time that's not taken up with urgent tasks or people asking for his input, he gets quiet, his face becomes grim, and that warm energy I've always felt from him shrinks back. He's not sleeping—oh, he's always careful not to wake me, but more than once these past few weeks, I've woken to find him staring at the ceiling, his beautiful pale hair spread across the pillows every which way.

I can't even begin to imagine what he and all of them are going through. For thousands of years, they've been watching their homeland crumble around them, forced to take shelter in a relatively small shielded area to survive. And now they have to say goodbye forever, knowing they can never return. It's all well and good to say that at least they have their lives, but this kind of trauma isn't something you can just let go of. It's going to haunt most of them for a long time.

I have an idea for how to distract Caolan tonight, but first I have to get through this meeting with Rabhya. We were both supposed to be here, but Caolan is debriefing the returned soldiers, so I've been left alone to face the PR machine.

"You want me to what?" I ask, sure I've misheard her. I've worked with Rabhya for years. She can't possibly think I would agree to this.

"You and Caolan need an Instagram account," she repeats. "Our spin for the humans on the livestream was that you are a real couple who helped out a friend by appearing in his film assignment for a special effects course. That means all the follow-up from community members—and the elves and dragons who are already mastering social media—can be explained away easily."

"We are a real couple," I say dryly, although to be fair, we weren't officially at the time of the livestream.

"I know." The heavy patience in her voice is kind of funny. "That's why I think you should do this. You've seen from your visits to the resettlement camps how strongly the refugees have seized the idea of you and Caolan together as a symbol of hope. We're getting the same kind of response from within the community. People are nervous and afraid, and they see you two as their knights who will protect them."

I squirm. "That's not—"

"David, relax. We both know that taking down the bad guys is going to involve a lot of people and effort. But you and Caolan are symbolic as a couple—one from each culture, both strong and highly regarded. You stand as representatives of all the people who are fighting to restore the status quo—or make things better—and of a future where the community and the newcomers will meld together."

Fucking fuckbunnies. She must see the horror on my face, because she bursts out laughing.

"It's not that bad, I swear. I'm not asking you to wield a flaming sword or anything. Just post the occasional picture of you and Caolan together looking normal and happy."

"I'm not really good at that," I warn, wavering. How can I refuse if she genuinely thinks it will be helpful? Especially remembering some of the elves we met at the resettlement camp. They were so hopeful and excited to see us together.

"Well, someone here at CSG can manage the account, if you want. You'd just have to send us the pictures. Or you could ask Caolan if he wants to give it a shot?"

I don't love the idea of giving up control of something with my name on it to some random person in the PR department, so that's probably not going to happen. The taking pictures part is what I'm terrible at, anyway, so it wouldn't make a big difference if someone else is posting them. But asking Caolan… that's not a bad idea. He loves his phone—I mean really *loves*. And he already takes photos of stuff all the time, although he's yet to learn about selfies. I've been grateful for that, but maybe I need to introduce him to the concept. Or get someone else to. And learning to use Instagram would be a good distraction for him right now.

"Let me talk to Caolan," I concede. "No promises, though."

We wrap the meeting with her extorting promises that Caolan and I will do another round of visits to resettlement camps and an interview with an online community magazine—I'm not sure how she got me to agree to that one. I was definitely saying no, but somehow ended up with her emailing me a list of questions to answer. These PR people are super sneaky.

I head back to our office. Chances are the people I

need to speak to will be there—or if not, Sam will know where they are. I'm in luck, though, because we have a full house. I pause in the doorway to absorb it. It's not often we're all at our desks at the same time, especially not these days.

"…only takes about three days before your body digests itself," Alistair finishes. From the looks of horror on everyone else's face, it's a good thing I didn't hear more of that story.

"I swear you wait until you know I'm here to say this shit," I declare, and Alistair blinks innocently.

"What shit?"

"Never mind." I shake my head and deposit my organizer on my desk. "I'm glad you're all here. I need some help."

"What's wrong?" Sam demands. He grabs his phone. "What do you need?"

I am so, so glad we found him.

"Two things, actually. I might need someone to show Caolan how to take selfies—"

"Me! Me! I can do that!" Alistair leaps out of his chair and looks around wildly, as though to take down anyone who might try to prevent him from doing this.

"—and use Instagram."

"Oh." He flops back down, dejection crossing his face. "I don't do social media."

"For which we are all so, so, so grateful," Ellie says dryly. "You can still teach him how to take selfies, though. I'm surprised you didn't cover that when you showed him how to use the phone."

"I can show him Insta," Noah volunteers as Alistair brightens. "And the reason Alistair didn't show the elves how to take selfies when he was demonstrating how to use the phones is because he'd already spent too long showing them Candy Crush and all its spinoffs." He rolls his eyes. "I don't know how your phone can even function, you've got that many crappy apps on it."

"Why does Caolan need to use Instagram?" Sam asks, a voice of sanity.

"I don't know yet if he'll want to," I caution, "but Rabhya wants an account for us both. Pictures that show how happy we are. She says people will find it comforting." I shrug awkwardly.

Alistair sucks in a breath.

Fuck. I should have kept my mouth shut.

"You're gonna be Insta-famous! Oh oh oh, it's going to be the best—your romance will span the globe and multiple civilizations, a beacon of hope and peace and multiculturalism—"

Andrew puts a hand over Alistair's mouth, thankfully ending his rambling. "It's a good idea," he says, jabbing Alistair in the ribs as he struggles, then adjusting his grip to cover his nose as well. Hah. As if oxygen deprivation would stop Alistair. "There's been a lot of positive feedback about you two." He levels me with a steady look as Alistair finally stops wriggling. "Are you okay with being such a public figure?"

"He's already a public figure," Ellie points out. "There's a website called IwannahaveDavidsbabies.com, remember? It gets updated all the time with news about what he's doing, and there's a page where people can comment with what they'd be willing to do for a night with David."

I close my eyes. I'd forgotten about that site. Or rather, I deliberately pushed it out of my mind.

"That site's been chaos since Caolan came on the

scene," Sam says chattily. "Nobody's sure if they want to be happy that David's happy or rip Caolan apart for daring to touch him."

My eyes snap open. Before I can say anything, though, Sam holds up a hand. "Metaphorically rip him apart. There have been no actual threats of violence." He grins. "I showed it to Caolan the other week. He was chuffed to have won you when you have so many admirers."

"You showed it to… Never mind." I'll deal with that thought another time. "And to answer your question," I turn back to Andrew, "I'm not thrilled about it, but since I'm already kind of a public figure anyway, I figure I should do what's needed to make people more comfortable in this environment. But if Caolan hates the idea, it's not happening."

There's a round of nods, and Andrew says to Alistair, "If I let go, are you going to be a normal person?"

Alistair glares but nods, then sucks in air as Andrew moves his hand.

"What was the other thing you need?" Gideon asks.

"A distraction for Caolan," I say bluntly. "Tomorrow—"

"Say no more." Alistair holds up a hand. "I'm on it."

Oh no. Oh fucking no.

"A *low-key* distraction," I rush to add. "No glitter. Or dildos."

"You're leaving too much off that list, David," Sam admonishes, turning to Alistair. "No smoke, bubble, or laser light machines. No flash mobs. No fireworks or explosives of any kind."

Sniffing, Alistair gives us an injured look. "I'm not a child, you know. I do know what's appropriate in these circumstances." The doubtful silence lasts a second too long, and he throws up his hands. "Fine! How about a movie night? Something engaging. Uhhh… *The Rocky Horror Picture Show*."

"No throwing things," Sam, Gideon, and I say at the same time.

"Why would he throw things?" Noah asks, and Andrew turns on him with wide eyes.

"You haven't seen *Rocky Horror* in a theater?"

Noah shrugs. "I haven't seen it ever."

Andrew sits down. "Oh no."

Alistair rubs his hands together. "This must be rectified. We can't possibly neglect a virgin."

"Oh no," Sam echoes faintly.

Noah squints. "Yeah, I don't know what you're talking about, but I'm not doing anything that involves Alistair de-virgining me. Not that he could. That ship sailed a long time ago."

"Movie night," Alistair declares. "I'll see if it's showing anywhere so we can see it in all its glory, but if not, I can refrain from throwing things at Gideon's stupid big TV."

I really want to tell him no, but *Rocky Horror* would definitely do the trick distracting Caolan—and he'll probably love it, whether it's the full experience or not.

"Why my TV?" Gideon demands. "You have a TV."

"My place won't fit us all," Alistair replies reasonably. "I promise I won't throw anything. I'll organize dinner and snacks and even clean up after." He looks around the group and sees all our doubtful faces. "Come on, it'll be fun. And it's a super tame distraction."

He's right, and we do all need a break from work and worry.

"No machines of any kind? Or party favors?" I check, and he crosses his heart.

"Just the movie and food," he promises.

"Okay," I concede. "If Sam and Gideon don't mind."

Sam agrees slowly, his brow furrowed as if he's trying to remember something, and Gideon grunts his assent.

Alistair claps. "Great! I'll get the costumes organized."

"Damn it!" Sam shouts. "I knew I forgot to ban something."

Laughing, Ellie shakes her head. "I can't believe you didn't remember the costumes."

"Costumes?" Noah asks. "Are we watching it or performing it?"

"Do we really need costumes to watch it at home?" I ask reasonably.

"Not *full* costumes," Alistair says solemnly. "We don't have time to get a good makeup artist. But everyone has to wear one costume item."

"I feel like I should be googling this," Noah mutters, turning to his keyboard.

Please don't let me regret this.

I don't regret it.

How can I? Caolan's face is alight with laughter. He's been animated since we arrived and Alistair presented him with a Frank-N-Furter wig to wear. Alistair took over the job of explaining the movie to him, Noah, and Dustin, who tagged along, and they're having a blast.

As the final credits roll, Alistair flips on the light and asks, "What did you think?"

Noah grabs a slice of now-cold pizza. "I think people were on a lot of drugs in the seventies. But it was fun."

"That was wonderful!" Dustin declares. "I want to see it in a theater!" Alistair has been busy explaining the etiquette for group viewings.

"Are all movies like this?" Caolan wants to know. "What a wonderful type of entertainment."

I mentally kick myself for not making more time to just chill out with him. We've watched random TV shows when we get some time free, but never a whole movie. "Nothing's quite like *Rocky Horror*, but there are some great movies."

"We'll have more movie nights," Alistair promises. "If Aidan's still not back tomorrow, we can have another one tomorrow night. *Lord of the Rings*, maybe. Or the original *Star Wars* trilogy. Something epic and amazing."

"You'd need a whole fucking weekend for those," Andrew points out. "What about *Spaceballs*? That's funny like *Rocky Horror* and not too long."

"Why are all the movies you're choosing made over a decade ago?" Noah asks, which begins an argument about whether there have been any classic-level movies made recently.

I snuggle beside Caolan and pass him my half-empty bucket of popcorn. Alistair went all out in planning for tonight, and seeing the delight on Caolan's and Dustin's faces when they tried popcorn for the first time was worth it. Of course, being Alistair, he provided an assortment of flavored popcorns and made us all do a tasting first. Mint chocolate chip popcorn is just wrong.

"This is delicious," Caolan asserts, digging in. "Caramel makes everything better."

"Can't argue with that. Did you have fun tonight?" I sneak a few pieces of popcorn, and he smacks my hand away. "Hey! That's mine—I'm sharing with you."

"It stopped being yours when you gave it to me." He crams more in his mouth.

"What happened to your love for me being so powerful it knows no bounds?"

Shaking his head, he finishes chewing. "I didn't know about popcorn then." He leans over to kiss my cheek as I laugh. "Really, this is the same food as the vegetable I had the other day?"

"Not exactly the same. They're both varieties of corn, but the one you had with dinner doesn't pop like this."

"What do you mean, 'pop'?"

I reach for the bucket, but he yanks it away. "Relax, I'm not going to eat any. I just want to show you something." I dig to the bottom and manage to find a kernel that's only partially popped. "Okay, see this hard part? That's a corn kernel, what popcorn starts out as. When heat is applied, it pops open and this fluffy part develops. Or something like that, anyway."

Caolan takes the kernel from me and stares at it, fascinated. "Really?"

"Yes, really." I make a split-second decision to stop at the store on the way home. "I'll show you later." We'll probably be up half the night while he masters the art of popping popcorn, but hey, I wanted a distraction for him, right?

He grins at me, and my heart melts. How was I ever able to resist him?

Alistair plants himself on the other side of Caolan. Dustin is with him. "Hey! So, this is probably a good time to practice selfies."

Caolan blinks. "Practice what?"

Oh crap. With all the chaos of leaving work and rushing over here before Alistair's "screening time," I forgot to mention my meeting with Rabhya. I give him a quick rundown.

He nods slowly. "So people put pictures of themselves on this Instant Gram—"

"Instagram," Dustin corrects. "I have two hundred followers already!"

"—and other people look at them?"

"That's basically it, although I think it's a bit more complicated. If you want to try it, Noah will show you how."

"We can do it together!" Alistair announces. "It's really remiss of me not to be on social media. I'm depriving the world of all my awesomeness."

"Uh-oh," Ellie mutters.

"If I don't like it, can I turn it off?" Caolan asks.

"Yes," Noah calls across the room. "We can delete your account. Or you can just stop using it."

"And Rabhya thinks this will be good for people?"

I nod.

"It really will," Dustin says earnestly. "People ask me about you and David all the time." He's gone above and beyond in his role as civilian liaison, to the point that the king and Brandt have begun making noises about giving him more responsibilities. His self-esteem, which was pretty robust to begin with, has bloomed too.

"I'll try," Caolan says. "I very much want to learn selfies, and I'll try Insta-gram."

"You're saying it wrong," Dustin corrects with the arrogant impatience of youth. "It's all one word. Instagram."

"Oh my god," Noah mutters.

Caolan produces his phone, and Alistair shows him how to flip the camera function and take selfies while I sneak some more popcorn. Caolan practices a few times, his face solemn, then tries a cheesy grin, followed by a scary glare. He's having way too much fun with it. I may have created a monster.

Then Noah takes over. They download Instagram and set up a profile in both our names.

"You're now officially known as DavidandCaolan," Noah says.

"I still think you should have gone with Dalan," Alistair insists, pouting.

Noah ignores him. "You need a profile pic. Caolan, why don't you take a selfie of you and David?"

Instantly, Caolan leans in and snuggles up beside me, holding his phone out in front of him.

"Smile, David," Noah prompts sadistically. I flip him the bird and make myself smile. This was so a mistake.

But Caolan exclaims happily over the picture, excited by all the filter-choosing and other stuff Noah is showing him, so I guess it's worth it.

"And... profile is done. I linked the video from the livestream in too, so people will make the connection."

"So I just take pictures and put them in there?" Caolan asks.

Noah shrugs. "Basically. Here, I'll follow a few people to get you started and you can see what they post. And you should post your first picture."

"The selfie?" He seems to love that word.

"No!" Alistair waves his hands. "I have a better idea." He grabs Caolan's phone and gets off the couch. "Snuggle up, you two. Put that popcorn bucket back in your lap, David. Now smile." He snaps a few shots. "Okay, now feed Caolan some popcorn. Let's get a playful romantic vibe."

"Or I could feed you your teeth," I suggest. "I know a weave that will yank them right out of your gums."

"Oooh, touchy," Noah taunts. "C'mon, David. Alistair's right. People will love it."

I glare at him, and he laughs and goes to take the phone from Alistair.

"Who even are you?" Sam asks him. "Since when are you a social media expert? You don't like people."

"I like people more when they're on a screen and not in my face," Noah replies absently as he flips through the photos. "Okay, I've deleted the crap ones. Pick one you like, Caolan, and we'll post it." They bend their heads together over the phone, Dustin putting in his two cents, while I finish the popcorn and get up to help with the clearing up. Sure, Alistair said he'd do it, but since he arranged all of this as a favor to me, the least I can do is throw away a few empty pizza boxes.

"What exactly do these hashtags do?" I hear Caolan asking as I come back from the kitchen.

"They help other people find your pictures," Dustin explains importantly. "See, Noah put #MovieNight and #DateNight. So all the people looking at those hashtags will find your photo."

"And they are," Noah says, frowning at the screen. "I guess Rabhya was right about you being popular, because you're already getting likes and follows."

"Let me see." Caolan takes the device. "These people will see my pictures?"

"Yep."

"How extraordinary!"

"DAVID! DAVID!"

Fuck. I abandon the oatmeal I'm pouring from a sachet into a bowl and race into the bedroom. Has he hurt himself? I didn't hear a thud or anything.

He's sitting up in bed, all tousled and sexy, just like I left him, but now there's an excited grin on his face as he studies his phone.

"Come and see!" he demands. "This photo I posted last night has *thousands* of likes!"

Thousands? I don't know much—or anything—about social media, but thousands of likes on a profile that's less than twelve hours old seems weird.

"The photo of us with the popcorn?" I ask, sitting on the bed beside him. He kisses my bare shoulder.

"No, the one I posted when we got home." He tips the phone so I can see, and I freeze.

Fuck my life.

I clear my throat. "You posted a picture of me without my shirt on? When did you even take this?" And oh crap, does that first comment really say what I think it says?

"When you were getting ready for bed." He must pick up on my lack of enthusiasm. "Should I not have?"

"It would have been nice if you'd asked me," I say honestly. "I'm not sure I love the idea of thousands of strangers seeing my naked torso." The picture shows my body in quarter-profile and my face in profile and has been carefully cropped so not much of the bedroom can be seen. I figure he took it right after I took my shirt off but before I went to the bathroom and took off my pants. I take the phone and look at the full post, which includes Caolan's comment about how beautiful I am and how lucky he is and about a dozen hashtags… and then more comments than I want to think about. Some of them are actually nice, saying how sweet his feelings are and how cute we are together. Some of them… well, let's just say they're not sweet.

"I'm sorry," he says immediately. "I wanted to show everyone how beautiful you are. I should have asked you first. I'll delete it—Noah showed me how." He takes the phone back, contrition written all over his face.

"Leave it," I tell him. "Deleting it now would be pretty pointless. And hey, it got a lot of attention, right? People are finding us. That's what we wanted." Although I really have to remind myself why.

Caolan's frowning, and boy, is he hot when he frowns. All broody-looking. "I don't like some of these comments," he says. "This one is very mean. How do I get rid of it?"

I shrug and get off the bed. "You're asking the wrong person. Noah will know, or Dustin. Do you want oatmeal for breakfast or eggs?"

"Oatmeal," he says absently, still scowling at the comments. "With fruit and maple syrup, please." My elf boyfriend has a sweet tooth. "If these people can't be properly appreciative, I won't show them any more pictures of you." He looks up. "But no more with your shirt off, no matter what."

How could I have ever thought he wasn't right for me?

"I love you," I blurt, then slap my hand over my mouth. Fuck. I didn't plan…

His whole face lights up.

…but I can't regret it.

Leaping out of bed, phone abandoned, he grabs me in a hug so tight, I can't breathe. That's okay. I don't need to breathe when I can be wrapped up in him.

"I love you," he declares, pulling back to look at me. "I love you."

I yank his face down to mine and kiss him. Neither of us has brushed our teeth yet, but I don't care. Right now, there's nothing I want more than this kiss, this moment, with him.

Of course, when two mostly naked men in love are kissing, things don't stay innocent. I'm backing him toward the bed, his hands cupping my ass inside my underwear, when my phone rings.

Caolan groans, and I make a split-second decision.

"Ignore it," I whisper, and the illicit thrill of ignoring a phone call that might be important shivers through me. Whoever it is can leave a message. Based on how I'm feeling, we're probably not going to be long anyway.

Caolan kisses me harder, seemingly as turned on as I am by the idea of playing hooky for a few minutes, and the ringing stops.

Then immediately starts again.

This time, I'm the one who groans as I break our kiss. "I'm sorry," I say. "So, so sorry."

He drops a kiss on my nose. "It's probably urgent. You should get it." He smiles. "We have time."

It's a lovely thought that warms my heart as I grab my phone and answer it. My cock, on the other hand, is not impressed.

I KEEP an eye and an ear on Caolan where Noah's showing him how to delete comments as I confer with Percy and King Raðulfr. We're in Percy's office, and in just a few moments, the king—with the help of the magic—is going to seal off dimensional travel once and for all. He looks incredibly haggard. So does Brandt. I imagine thoughts of today kept them from getting any sleep last night, and I thank all the forces that created the universe for Alistair's movie night and Rabhya's social media demands. Caolan didn't sleep amazingly, but at least he got *some* sleep… and his mind hasn't been focused solely on what's about to happen.

"Please forgive me for asking," I say to the king, "but just so I can officially record it, you're absolutely certain that nobody opened a portal back to your world since the soldiers returned yesterday?" He and Caolan explained to me that it would be impossible for that to have happened without his knowledge. Éibhear might have found a way to circumvent the travel ban, but the whole reason King Raðulfr discovered what Éibhear was planning for Earth was because he could feel it when the interdimensional portals were opened. Knowing that most elves didn't have the knowledge or power to get around the ban, he narrowed down the possible culprit and sent out agents like Caolan to gather intelligence.

"Absolutely certain," the king affirms. "Nobody has opened an interdimensional portal since the soldiers returned. In the past five days, the only portals opened have been the ones the soldiers used."

"Thank you." I nod to Percy. He turns to the king.

"Do you need anything from us? Can we assist you in any way?" he asks solemnly.

The king sighs, his usually ageless face suddenly seeming older. "I'm not entirely certain. The travel ban itself was a highly complex spell and required a great deal of energy. To make it permanent and unbreachable by even me will require the aid of the life force." He grimaces. "I've been somewhat remiss in my duties by not investigating what's required before this."

"Of course you haven't," Percy says, the warmth of his personality a soothing balm. "This is a difficult time, and you've been busy with so many other duties."

I step back and leave them to it. Percy will sort this out and let me know if I'm needed.

Someone knocks on the door, causing a momentary surprised silence. All of us who should be here are here, and enough of the senior staff knows what's happening this morning that they'd ensure we wouldn't be disturbed. I like to think we've managed to keep the information from the community at large but highly doubt it.

Waving everyone back to what they're doing, I head for the door. I'm the only one who can open it right now anyway, due to the heavy-duty wards I've woven. We didn't want to chance interruptions at an inopportune moment. Those same wards are advising me that whoever's on the other side of the door has good intentions.

Although, if someone with bad intentions had gotten this far into CSG headquarters, I'd expect to have received a warning phone call, for the outer wards to have alerted Percy, and/or for everyone else in the building to be dead.

There's a cheery thought.

As if reading my mind, Gideon detaches himself from his conversation with Garin and Andrew and joins me on the way to the door.

"It's fine," I tell him. He just shrugs.

Overprotective demon. I don't know how Sam tolerates it.

I unweave a gap in the ward and then flip the lock and open the door. Kirsch, our head of Security, is on the other side, and I don't like the expression on his face. Without having to confer, Gideon and I slip out and close the office door behind us.

"What is it?" Gideon asks. The anteroom where Percy's assistant usually sits is empty. Percy, at my request, loaned her to the migration team for the day. They need extra hands as they work out how and when to move people from the resettlement camps to more permanent housing.

"Nothing yet," he says. "The word has gotten out what you're doing here today. I'm getting reports that the mood in the camps is very low."

I exchange a glance with Gideon. "That's not unexpected."

Kirsch shrugs uneasily. "I don't know what it is, David. I have a very bad feeling. Things have gone too quiet."

A niggle of concern rises in me. Kirsch is very good at his job. If he's worried, I should be too.

Behind us, the office door opens, and we turn to watch Andrew come out. There's a grim set to his mouth. "What's happened?" he asks.

"Nothing. Kirsch is uneasy."

Andrew nods. "Something's going to happen."

"You have a feeling?" Fuck. Fuck fuck fuck. I miss the old days, when Andrew's premonitions of disaster were few and far between. "Can you give us a hint?"

"It's not connected to what the king needs to do this morning," he says immediately. "The itchiness ramps up when I think about Tish and Éibhear, so something they're planning, presumably."

Because that's helpful. The bad guys are going to do something bad. Gee, thanks.

Leashing my inner sarcasm, I turn back to Kirsch. "No reports of movement?"

"None." He shakes his head. "All our agents are reporting quiet and calm. It's the first time since this all started that every encampment we know about has had such little activity."

"Yeah, that's not good." Gideon narrows his eyes. "They're doing something and trying to lull us into a false sense of security."

Pinching the bridge of my nose, I ask, "What are their most likely targets? The resettlement camps?"

"No," Andrew says immediately. "That doesn't feel right."

"Us?" Gideon presses. "Here at the office?"

Pulling a face, Andrew says, "I don't know. That feels a bit murky. Maybe us but not the office? Or the office but not us. Or another CSG office?"

"I'll put out an alert to all offices," Kirsch says. "Could you let me know if you get any clarification?"

"Of course." We all know it's unlikely, but hey, we live in hope. If we're lucky, the heightened security will be all we need.

Kirsch goes to arrange it, and the three of us go back into the office. I reweave the ward securely closed and make sure it's at full activation before turning my attention to the rest of the room. It's mostly silent now. The king and Percy are still standing together, but now they have their hands linked and eyes closed.

Sam comes up to us. "The magic made it clear that Percy needed to be involved. Something about energies from both dimensions being needed for a permanent seal," he murmurs.

King Raðulfr begins to speak, his voice low and sonorous. The words are elvish, so I don't understand them, but the cadence is… chilling. This is not a spell to be invoked lightly. This is a last-ditch, no-other-options kind of spell. I know this because it's the first time ever that I've been able to *feel* elven spellcasting. Every time before, I've been able to see the resulting weaves, but not feel them being created. This, I feel in every atom of my body.

From the way everyone else in the room is reacting, I'm not the only one. I guess permanently sealing off a dimension is a serious undertaking and needs major mojo.

The king's voice rises, and the usual ebb and flow of the magic begins to speed up around me.

And then something slams into me.

I blink, sure we must have been hit by a bomb or

grenade, but there's nothing. I'm still standing. The room is the same.

But everything is different.

The king drops to his knees, releasing Percy's hands, but Percy kneels with him and places an arm around him as he sobs. Brandt, face pale and drawn, joins them on unsteady feet.

The magic continues to flow as it always has, but there's something sad about it right now.

Reminding myself how to put one foot in front of the other, I go to Caolan. He's shaking, and Noah's got an arm around his waist, basically holding him up. I take over, and Noah goes to help Ellie with Garin.

Wrapping Caolan in my arms, I squeeze, letting him know he's not alone. If the creation of the barrier affected me like this, I can't imagine how he's feeling.

He clings to me, burying his face in the side of my neck, and we just hold each other.

I'm not sure how many minutes pass before Sam says, "David?" I blink my vision clear, not aware until that moment that I'm crying, and meet his gaze. His eyes are rimmed in red, his features drawn. "The wards. Can you…? Someone should check…"

Fuck. He's right. We're probably not the only ones who felt this. Billions of beings across Earth could be wondering what the fuck happened. Only a tiny fraction might suspect the truth.

I undo the wards so Sam can leave. Gideon, Alistair, and Elinor follow him out. Noah stays with Garin, and Andrew is helping Percy get the king and Brandt off the floor and into chairs.

In my arms, Caolan takes a deep, shaky breath.

"The life force is everywhere, in everything," he

murmurs, drawing back. "It mourns the loss of a limb today."

That's a much better analogy than "barrier." There is no barrier between that dimension and the rest of existence—it's been excised completely.

The leaf against my chest weighs heavy, and tears sting my eyes again.

"How are you?" I ask, and it comes out in a hoarse whisper. I don't want to leave him, don't want to push him, but as much as I want to make him my priority right now, I can't. There's a whole world that needs me.

He draws another deep breath. "I live."

I lift a hand and press it against his cheek. "Will you be okay here? I need to go help the others. The impact of this…"

He nods. "Go."

From the couch Andrew's settled him on, the king says, "It was worst here, David, because this is where the spell was concentrated. All beings will have felt something, but none as badly as here."

Well, that's something, at least. "I'm so sorry for your loss, Your Majesty." It's an awkward, trite phrase, but what else is there to say?

The door bangs open behind me, and I whirl, pulling power up from within me.

It's Sam.

He's wild-eyed and breathless.

Andrew comes forward, and I *know*.

"The lucifer's seal is gone."

CHAPTER NINE

Caolan

I DIDN'T THINK I could feel worse, but Sam's words send panic and dread rushing through my veins.

"What?" The word explodes from Lucifer Percy. "How?"

"Blunt force. They took advantage of our—and everyone's—distraction and rushed the vault room with dozens of assailants. Just now—not fifteen minutes ago."

"The wards," David says. "How did they get through the wards to the actual vault?"

"With a dozen dead elves. Kirsch didn't have the full explanation, but that's apparently what the elf sergeant on site said. They came through a portal, overwhelmed the guards on duty, then held their ground against the reinforcements for long enough for some of the elves to do something that had them literally drop dead before they grabbed the seal and left through the portal. They were there for no more than ten minutes."

Nausea swirls in my gut. Is there no end to Éibhear's evil?

"This changes everything," David is saying. "We

assumed the wards gave us some protection, especially now that we've been able to reinforce them with elven magic. But if they can just… just cut through them—"

"They can't," Brandt says, his voice croaky. For the first time in my recollection, he seems old and frail. "They won't be doing that again. They don't have the numbers to sacrifice them thus."

"I don't understand," Lucifer Percy says, and the king shakes his head.

"Blunt force. Sam said it before. But blunt force is not just physical. If you throw enough power at any ward, it will break, yes?"

"Yes," Percy concedes. "But no one person has that much power, to punch through so quickly. That's why we weave alarms into our wards—by the time the intruder can break through the ward, backup has arrived. And while a dozen people could all throw all their power at a ward, the way wards are woven means they respond to each energy individually. Eventually, that kind of assault would bring a ward down, but not as fast as this."

This time, the king nods. "What Éibhear has done is use an old and long-forbidden spell. It allows a single elf to draw power from a group of others and use it as their own. The wards would react as though it was a single energy, but the force would be that of many."

The horror I'm feeling is suddenly reflected on the faces of my Earth friends. But the king isn't finished.

"The problem with the spell is that once initiated, it cannot be ended until those it draws energy from have none left to give, not even that generated by the pumping of their heart. The only survivor is the channeler. This is why the spell was forbidden so long ago. Most don't even know it exists."

"So… would the elves involved have known what it did? That it was a suicide mission?" Noah's voice is shaky.

The king spreads his hands. "I don't know the finer details of the spell. It requires each elf to speak a line and link in, but whether they must first know the outcome…" He trails off.

Noah nods. "Excuse me." He walks out of the office, brushing past Sam, and a moment later, we hear a clatter and the sound of retching.

Andrew strides toward the door, muttering, "I'll just…"

Lucifer Percy draws in a deep breath, then wrinkles his nose and gives a little cough. Oh—he can probably smell Noah's vomit. A negative of the shifter enhanced sense of smell. "We can't do anything for those elves now, except hope their souls have passed to the spiritual plane. Our focus has to be on getting the seal back—or at the very least, stopping Éibhear and Tish from using it."

"Gideon's gone to the vault to talk to the survivors. Are there any elves there who can do the portal-tracing thing?" Sam asks, and I force my fractured mind to come together and think.

"There is someone with the ability to create portals on every shift," I affirm. We made sure of that. "They should be working on it already."

"Negative," Elinor says, coming to stand beside Sam. "The portal elf was one of the ones killed in the first rush."

I start toward them. "I'll go. Warn Gideon I'm

coming." The last thing we all need is for someone to see a portal opening and get jumpy.

"Will do." Sam lifts his phone.

As I pass through the antechamber, where the smell of vomit permeates the air, I hear Elinor say, "Andrew wanted Noah to go home and rest, but he nixed that. They're going to coordinate intelligence reports with Kirsch. Alistair's prepping a strike team and has put a full assault force on standby."

I break into a jog, heading for the unwarded reception so I can open a portal. There aren't many people in the halls, but the few I pass are edgy and moving quickly. In reception, Candice is talking on the phone while the sound of another line ringing fills the air. She looks shocked and flustered, and it takes only a few seconds of listening for me to realize she's being inundated with calls about the effect of the king's spell. So strange—it's been only a few minutes, but with the new problem, I'd almost forgotten about that.

I take the time to pull out my phone and call David.

"Are you there?" he asks in greeting, and from the rush of sound in the background, I can tell he's moving.

"No—still in reception. Candice needs help with the phones."

He swears. "We need the interns here. Uh… tell her she has my permission to route most of the lines to the finance department. I'll call the manager and let her know."

I barely have time to make a sound of agreement before he ends the call.

"Candice?" I cross to her in two long strides. She looks up but keeps talking, her expression a mute plea for help. I gently remove her earpiece/microphone combination and hold it up to my ear. The woman on the other end is shrieking about the world ending.

"Madam, the world is fine. Please relax. Have a nice day." I pull the earpiece away and look at it as the woman squawks. "How do I end the call?" I ask Candice. Mutely, she pushes a button on the panel in front of her, which has four flashing lights on it. The ringing continues. "David said to route most of the lines to the finance department."

Relief crosses her face. "Really? Because I can handle one call at a time. Even two."

I nod, and she immediately taps some buttons on her panel. Two of the flashing lights stop. "Thanks, Caolan."

I want to ask if she's okay, but I've already delayed too long. "Take care of yourself," I say as a compromise, then turn away and open a portal.

When I step through into the antechamber outside the vault room, I get only a few glances.

"Sir." The sergeant in charge of the elf unit on guard here steps forward but doesn't waste my time. "Their portal was here." He gestures to an area in the middle of the room blocked off from passing traffic by random paraphernalia—two chairs, an umbrella, and a few shoes. A quick glance around shows me which guards volunteered their footwear for crime scene duty.

I would have known where it was even without the help, the tingle of residual energy brushing up against me. This portal was a work of art, but something about it makes me want to back away from the residue. I'm fairly certain it was created by Éibhear. There aren't many old enough and with so much practice at opening portals to create something this beautifully detailed—

and the basic evil of him would account for the creepy feeling.

Making myself concentrate, I pull out my phone and open the maps app. It takes me only a few moments to narrow down the location of origin. Gideon comes out of the vault room to join me.

"Anything?" he asks, and I nod.

"I can't give you a town name, though. There isn't anything." I zoom the map out again slightly, trying to find a landmark. Gideon peers at the screen.

"Wait," he says, then slides the map over a bit. "Okay, that's Argentina. Somewhere in the Patagonia National Park." He taps a contact on his own phone and puts it on speaker.

"Yeah?" Sam answers. "Anything?"

"South America," Gideon says. "In the middle of nowhere. I can give you coordinates."

"Wait," David says, and I realize Sam must have his phone on speaker too. "Is it Argentina? In the national park?"

"Yeah. Significant?" Gideon and I exchange glances.

"There was a large community settlement there that was wiped out by humans during the species wars. It's considered one of the biggest atrocities that was committed—the settlement dated back about six thousand years and was, according to history, a center of learning and culture. We abandoned it after that."

"That's where they are," I murmur. I can feel the truth of it.

Gideon slides the map around a bit more. "Are you sure? It seems a bit remote for a settlement. Especially given the lack of transport back then."

"Says the demon who can teleport," David points

out. He rattles off some coordinates. "I just looked it up. Is that it?"

Grimly, Gideon says, "To within half a mile."

"Was this place in any of our intelligence briefings?" I ask, trying to remember. I'm sure someone would have mentioned a historic abandoned settlement.

"Nope," Sam says. "This is an entirely new site for us. I'm pulling satellite pics now. It looks like there are some recent ones for that area, so we might be able to get some solid intel."

"We'll start prepping," David says. "Are you nearly finished there?"

"I need to see the dead attackers, then we'll be back," I promise. "Is Garin there? Remind him that the dragons may be of use for this kind of assault." A remote area with no allies or civilians nearby? Dragons are perfect for this situation. If worse comes to worst, they can just raze the whole settlement with their flame, leaving behind only barbequed enemies.

"He's already asked us how many dead are acceptable to prevent Tish and Éibhear from using the seal," Sam says dryly. "I'm sure he'll love it when I tell him about this. Talk soon."

Gideon ends the call without saying goodbye, which… isn't a surprise, and we head into the vault room.

It's a mess. The walls, which I've been advised are fire-retardant and bombproof, bear scorch marks. Bodies lie where they fell. The vault door is half-gone, and what remains hangs from a single hinge. The wards, woven with a mixture of sorcerer and elven spellwork, are tattered, a huge, gaping hole rendering them useless. The energy of the spell that punched through lingers in the fibers around the edge of the hole, and it gives me the same creepy feeling the portal in the antechamber did.

"Sergeant," I call over my shoulder, studying the remnants of the spell. A moment later, I hear the scuff of his steps.

"Yes, sir?"

"Did you or anyone see the elf who cast the spell to break through the wards?" It's not that important, but I'd feel better knowing for sure.

"I didn't, sir, but one of the others might have caught a glimpse. We were trying to break through from out there, and they were already in here. Let me ask."

As he retreats, I go over to one of the bodies and begin to examine it. It's not hard to tell which elves were involved in the spell—their bodies are almost mummified, dried up and desiccated from having the energy sucked out of every cell.

"Problem?" Gideon asks, and I shake my head.

"More curiosity than anything. I think it might have been Éibhear himself who channeled the spell."

Gideon raises a brow. "Do you really think he risked coming himself, put himself in the hot zone?"

I shrug. "He's arrogant enough to do it. And if he's the only one who knows the forbidden spell, he'd be the only one who could."

"Let's hope it was him, then," Gideon says. "I'd really rather not have too many people know that spell. One is more than enough."

I'm not going to disagree with that.

The bodies tell me very little. The ones involved in the forbidden spell were all elves, which was expected, but the others are a mix of elves, a dragon, and Earth species. Some are our people, who were killed in the initial surprise attack. The rest are the enemy, taken down by our forces trying to get back into the room.

The sergeant returns with a young elf. "Tell Captain Caolan what you saw," he prods. The young one straightens.

"Sir. I only saw him for a moment, just a flash, and I was distracted, but he looked like Éibhear."

"Thank you. That's good to know. I'll be back to talk to all of you later." After. First, we need to stop Éibhear and Tish from using that spell to corporealize the life force.

"ARE WE READY?" Lucifer Percy asks with his usual calm. If an outsider was to judge by him, we could be preparing to go out for a leisurely lunch.

Instead, we're armed to the teeth, backed by ranks of enforcers and soldiers, and ready to end this battle once and for all.

"You won't stay behind?" David asks Percy again. I know exactly how he feels—King Raðulfr and Brandt stand right there with the lucifer, ready to storm the enemy settlement with us. We'd all be much happier if they were locked in a secure, guarded bunker somewhere. But apparently the life force made it very clear that they had to accompany us.

Please don't let it be because they're fated to die.

The lucifer shakes his head. "I can't."

David draws in a breath through his nose and sets his jaw. "And the timing?"

"Still no urgency," the king says. "Don't stop, but we

have some time left." The life force, now fully attuned to what's happening, has been able to give us some small hints. It meant being able to take an extra hour to prepare and formulate a plan rather than just racing through portals and hoping for the best outcome. Once we had the location coordinates, Gideon and Alistair had some demon intelligence agents teleport into the area and reconnoiter. Despite their seeming victory this morning, things are not going well for Éibhear and Tish.

Their first mistake (today) was indeed that none of the elves who volunteered to assist Éibhear with the forbidden spell was told it would be a suicide mission. When the survivors returned to the settlement and the word got around, dissension began in the ranks. Settling that down prevented them from beginning the ceremony immediately. It also gave our agents the chance to mingle in during the confusion and take pictures, allowing us to have landmarks to fix on when creating portals.

Then, the dragonet they stole refused to shift into her dragon form. The spell must be "sealed by dragon flame," which is not entirely clear but seems to mean that dragon flame must be present as the last word is spoken. But dragons cannot flame while in their biped form, and as long as that terrified child remains biped, the spell cannot begin.

I don't know why she prefers to remain in her more vulnerable form, but it gave us some much-needed extra time. And now we're going to rescue her and bring her back to her mother, finally.

Alistair, Garin, and David bend their heads together, confirming readiness, and then David gives the order: "Let's go."

Noah, whose job is to maintain contact with the forces staging simultaneous raids on the other enemy compounds we'd identified, relays the order into his headset.

I open a portal, aware of others around me doing the same and the whole rank of demons teleporting out. The first groups through the portals are elves and sorcerers, given the task of establishing a ward barrier to give the others shelter as they arrive and provide reinforcement for the demons. David is one of the first to cross, and my gut tightens as he goes. But he needs to be there —we made the decision that while our leaders couldn't stay behind, they would wait for the initial assault to ease and a safe area to be created. That means that David and Garin need to be on the ground to oversee and give direction.

He can look after himself. I know this. People keep telling me.

But I hate having to stay back while he's in danger.

The last of the troops allocated to my portal are through, and I turn to call to Sam. "Clear! Any news?"

He has a wireless earpiece in one ear, a line open to David, who's using a "satellite phone." I'm not entirely sure how that's different from a normal phone. Sam explained a little bit about what satellites are, but there's still so much I don't know.

"They've nearly got a bunker set up," Sam says. He's the coordinator for our battle site. "Just another minute. They're sending anyone who's not fighting back away from the settlement into the trees to deal with later."

I hope that doesn't come back to bite us.

"We've got visual contact with the baby, but nobody's been able to get near her yet. One of our demons tried teleporting to her, but they've warded against that."

The king swears.

"And they're ready for us. Let's go."

Following the plan, two enforcers go through first, followed by Noah and Sam—who the life force insisted had to be present, despite Gideon's and Andrew's vociferous protests. Then the lucifer, the king, Brandt, and finally me, closing the portal behind me. I considered keeping it open in case our leaders needed to stage a hasty retreat, but it only takes a second for me to open one. If I'm killed, there's also a chance that an open portal would become unstable before closing, potentially harming or killing anyone in the vicinity. Or worse— sucking them into the void.

Once my portal is safely closed, I take a moment to ensure our leaders are actually sheltered and not in any immediate danger. I should have trusted more in my beautiful David—there's one tough ward around us right now. It even dilutes the sound from the battle, making it possible for us to talk at a normal level. This is no quick creation—he must have been weaving the components for this for a while, and with elf magic intertwined, it's all but infallible.

Speaking of David… where is he? Definitely not within the wards.

"Where's David?" I demand, and Sam sighs.

Noah points. "As soon as we got here, he went out there. The others are with him." From the not-quite-tremor in his voice, I'm guessing Andrew is one of "the others." "He's pretty badass. I didn't know he could do half this stuff."

Bracing myself, I scan in the direction he's looking

and soon spot my love. He is, indeed, badass, as Noah puts it. Right at this second, he's got an invisible band of force wrapped around about a dozen of the enemy, tightening it and drawing them closer and closer together, until they're squashed into a mass of bodies, unable to move or fight back. Prisoners for us to deal with later. It's impressive.

Especially when he follows that up by blasting a furrow into the ground beneath the next onslaught of attackers, sending them tumbling in all directions.

Reluctantly, I pull my gaze from him. My primary task is to protect and support our leaders right now.

Brandt has his gaze fixed across the expanse before us, locked on to the stolen dragonet. We seem to be in a mostly cleared, flat… field? The area is not considered optimal for growing crops, but there was likely *some* agriculture here in the past, and it almost certainly would have been revived when people began using the settlement again. On the other side of the field, I see stone buildings—they appear crude, but that could just be from time and a poor effort to rebuild recently. There is also a plethora of tent canvas.

Before there, though, is the spot where Éibhear and Tish have clearly begun preparations for the spell. They huddle behind a ward, a small table bearing a scroll and what I assume is the lucifer's seal with them. Their side of the battle is being directed by a small group not far from the ward—two elves, a sorcerer, and a hellhound. Ten feet away, behind another ward, the dragonet is in the arms of an elf. The dragonet's not paying any attention to the terrifying battle raging before her, though; instead, her focus is on us. Or more specifically, on Brandt. Her wing leader. His presence would sing in her veins, and the hope visible on her tiny face even at this distance tears me apart.

Leaning in, I ask Sam if David and the others are aware of where the commanders are.

"Yes," he reports, "but they say they haven't had a moment free to do anything about it. Every time they try, they get rushed."

I narrow my eyes and study the scene anew. It does seem oddly coincidental that despite the many clusters of troops we have and the way they're slowly but surely overtaking the enemy, every time any of them turns attention to the commanders, they find themselves swamped by insurgents.

"This ward is only one-way, correct? I can cast a spell outward?"

Sam nods. "Yes."

Slowly, gradually, I build and cast a spy spell, letting it creep out unnoticed onto the field of battle. It slithers amongst the chaos, searching, searching…

There! A similar spell, one designed to warn the maker when negative attention is cast in their direction. Sneaky.

I check on my charges. Brandt is still utterly focused on the dragonet, and I can feel energy building around him. I don't know what he's planning, but if I'm going to support him, I'll need to get this done quickly. The king and the lucifer are intent on watching the ebb and flow of battle, occasionally pointing things out to Sam and Noah, who relay them through their headsets to our people on the field.

Okay. Now. How to attack without seeming to?

Keeping my gaze and my thoughts pinned on a group of insurgents grappling with one of our teams, I build an explosive spell. Then I open a tiny gateway into the void, angling my body to shield it from sight and hoping nobody will feel it with all the chaos. I wait for the perfect moment, mentally reciting the alphabet over and over to block out any thoughts…

…and open another gateway out of the void, shoving the spell through just as one of the elf commanders jerks his head toward me.

The last thing he sees is me twiddling my fingers in a little fuck-you wave Alistair taught me.

And the best part? Body parts and gore have no intention to harm. They pose no danger, unlike a bullet or blade. So they rain right through Éibhear and Tish's ward. Watching blood and gray matter splash across Éibhear's face certainly improves my day.

A cheer goes up amongst those of our people who noticed. A moment later, Sam turns to me with a huge grin on his face. "David says you can name whatever sexual favors you want for the rest of the year."

"If you like, I'll have it written into his employment contract," Lucifer Percy says nonchalantly. "Seeing that was worth having HR lecture me on appropriate behavior."

"I think we can work it out between us," I reply, fairly certain he's joking. I turn my attention away from the battle, which, with the military leadership of the other side gone, is breaking down into routs, and focus on Brandt. More and more energy is building around him, and I'm sure the air temperature has gone up slightly in this area. "What do you need?" I murmur to him. We can't snatch the dragonet back while that ward around her stands, but an assault on the ward might cause her guard to harm her—or might cause harm directly if there's any backlash.

"Another distraction. She nearly had it that time. And a demon to teleport her to us."

"Gideon will do it," Sam says, then murmurs into his headset.

I have no idea what Brandt meant by "she nearly had it," but if he needs a distraction, I can give him one. I pick a group of insurgents who've broken away from our troops and prepare a spell that tosses their bodies high in the air—adding some wholly unnecessary sound effects. That part is just a childish trick, but it will definitely create a distraction.

"Ready?" I ask. Brandt nods.

"Ready," Sam relays.

I sling the spell.

There's no blood or gore splatter this time, as the spell is designed differently, but the screams from those being thrown about paired with the sound of nonexistent explosions certainly grab attention.

And the dragonet strikes. The energy Brandt has been building is sucked away so sharply, the air seems too thin to breathe. The power bursts from her, decimating the ward from the inside and incinerating her guard. Some of it smashes against the ward protecting Éibhear and Tish, and a few of their people who are close enough and unprotected shriek as the wave of hot energy envelops them.

Gideon is already by the dragonet's side, snatching her up and flashing away. He appears beside us a moment later, and the toddler lunges out of his arms toward Brandt.

"Thank you," Brandt says, his voice breaking. "Hello, sweetheart. I have you now."

Gideon smiles, and I do a double take. I don't think I've ever seen that expression on his face. It's gone a second later as he turns and jogs back out through the ward and into the fray.

"Is she unhurt?" the king is asking, and Brandt nods.

"Physically, yes. Noah?"

"Five of the eight compounds are ours. No sign of counterattacks."

"Caolan?"

I know what he wants—we talked about this. I open a portal to the settlement camp where the dragonet's surviving mother is. She was slowly weaned from sedation, but since then she has been under guard to prevent her from literally burning the world down in search of her baby.

"Leave it open," he orders. "I'll be back in a moment." He steps through, and I turn half my attention back to the battle. Anyone with strategic experience would have known that the tide was always in our favor, but even a civilian would be able to see that now. The fighting is all but done, with clusters of the enemy now surrendering, while the diehards fall back to form a living barrier in front of Éibhear and Tish's ward.

It's over. With the dragonet gone and all the adult dragons here under strict instructions not to shift and flame, they cannot complete the spell. Most of their forces here are decimated, and if Noah's reports are right, so are most of their forces elsewhere. Their advantage was always that we didn't know where they were and where they were keeping their hostage. That's gone now.

David comes back to the ward, stepping through. He's more disheveled than I've ever seen him, his face streaked with grime and blood.

"Is any of that blood yours?" I demand, casting a spell to assess his physical condition. He shakes his head even as the spell reports that he's got a sprained wrist and some minor lacerations to his torso, but no head injury that might be the source of the blood.

"I'm fine. Bumps and bruises that can wait." The steady look he aims at me dares me to contradict him.

We'll finish this discussion later.

"With your permission," he says to the lucifer and the king, "we're going to move you and this ward forward so you can demand their surrender."

"Permission granted," the king says, and the lucifer nods. As David, two other sorcerers, and three elves prepare to move the ward, the king turns to me. "Are you ready?"

Éibhear has been tried and sentenced. The life force assisted the king with the spell that would ensure his soul death—his soul will not travel to the ether and eventually be reborn any longer. His next death will be his last.

And King Raðulfr offered that death to me, in honor of my service. Vengeance could be mine if I so choose.

Despite everything, it was not an easy decision. I believe in the rule of law that says his life is forfeit for his crimes. My people do not sentence to death lightly or often. In all memory, living and dead, there are only three instances, including Éibhear.

He does not decry his innocence.

He does not express remorse.

When offered the opportunity to cease his crimes, he

instead found a different world to wreak them upon. And plotted to destroy the order of the universe.

Living existence is not safe as long as he lives.

"I'm ready."

Beside me, I feel a rush of energy in my portal, and Brandt steps through. Following him are the Earth species leaders. Aidan, I know, but the others are strangers—a vampire, a succubus, a demon, and a sorcerer.

The ward is moved across the field, over bodies strewn about like dolls—broken, bloody dolls with sightless eyes.

More stains upon Éibhear's soul.

When we're within fifteen feet of the last enemy line, a hulking demon near the front shouts, "Stop right there!"

We stop, and the king turns to the lucifer. "After you."

Percy smiles, then raises his voice. "Please stand aside. You have erred, and you will face consequences, but you need not die."

The remaining ranks of the enemy, perhaps fifty or so, falter. There are a few amongst them who sneer and stand firm, but the rest...

David told me about this. About the young ones who were never taught the truth of the life force. Who don't understand that leaders are selected by it, not by themselves. I can see it now as they feel the full effect of the lucifer's presence. Those who are here through deceit and not choice suddenly find themselves conflicted. Truthfully, we could take them. There are so few of them left that they would pose no challenge. But we would all prefer the healing begin now.

Percy looks to his species leaders.

Aidan steps forward. "Shifters, please stand aside. I ask in the name of the magic that created us all. That guides us all. Please come back to us."

Toward one end of the rank, a young hellhound, his face a picture of confusion and misery, steps forward. Instantly, an older hellhound snarls and lashes out, knocking him to the ground.

It's a mistake.

Those who were unsure are now certain—where the lucifer and Aidan offered peace, their own struck them down. A fight breaks out and quickly takes over, dragging in all the Earth species and the remaining elves.

David shakes his head. "May I?" he asks, and the king and the lucifer reluctantly grant permission.

The percussive shock of whatever David does rings through the valley, knocking the enemy to the ground. Interestingly, many among them remain standing, looking about in confusion before quickly making their way over to where a group of enforcers waits to take them into custody.

"How did you make it so it didn't affect our side?" Noah asks curiously.

"Now is not the time," Andrew says dryly, taking his hand.

"How do we take down that ward?" I ask, eyeing it. I can't see all of it, only the parts intertwined with elven magic, and I know most of the others can see even less, just hints of the energy being emitted. A properly woven, functioning ward is invisible—unless designed otherwise.

Before anyone can offer a suggestion, there's a surge.

The life force whips around us all, an etheric wind, and the ward wavers and comes down.

The shock on Éibhear's face will live in my memory forever.

I cast my spell in that moment of confusion, a solid boulder of force that whistles through the space between us, almost unnoticed, and punches through Éibhear's torso, leaving a gaping hole the size of a fist as he collapses soundlessly to the ground. Dead.

Eternally.

I've been so conflicted over this for so many weeks that I thought for certain I'd feel remorse. Regret.

I don't. He doesn't get to take anything more from me or anyone.

CHAPTER TEN

David

I FEEL the surge of energy from Caolan, the rush of *something* racing through space, and then Éibhear collapses, a hole in his chest.

It's done. This has been itching at Caolan since the king asked him to handle it—death for elves is a big deal, since they choose when they want to finish their lives, and soul death is a concept for the worst horror stories. To be the one to mete it out…

But all I feel from him now is calm. I want to take his hand, pull him aside and ask him how he is, but the middle of this battlefield with Tish standing mere yards away is not the place.

Speaking of…

"Murderer!" Tish bellows. He looks wildly around for supporters, but those who haven't already defected are still lying prone from my attack weave. Which is just as well, because I don't have any juice left—that took it all out of me. It's sheer will that's even keeping me upright right now. "Do you see how they maliciously strike down—"

"Give it up," Noah says scornfully. "That's not how it is, and you know it."

Tish's gaze fixes on him, and he sneers. "You! How did you escape me? How are you *here*?"

Noah smirks, manifests a fireball, tosses it in the air, and catches it. "Did you really think you could keep me prisoner?"

I choke down a laugh. Noah's clearly watched too many B-grade movies. Still, the look on Tish's face is worth it.

"This is over," Percy says calmly, walking forward into the space between us and Tish, beyond the safety of our ward. I frown. "You know it is. You're done. You're alone. We've taken your other compounds. There's nothing left of this foolhardy plan."

Tish moves so fast, I can't even shout a warning as he hurls a weave at Percy. I can't see exactly what it is, but it has the distinctive pattern of a genetic modification, and that's not a good thing.

Time ticks forward in slow motion, muffled and blurry, as though I'm underwater. My mouth opens. I reach desperately for any last shred of power I might have. Gideon flashes out of existence beside me. Alistair and Elinor leap forward.

We're going to be too late.

And Percy shifts, dropping under the weave, then lunges up and rips out Tish's throat.

Reality crashes back like a boulder, sound exploding into my ears as Tish's lifeless body drops to the ground.

Gideon blinks, now only inches from where Percy was standing a moment ago, his arm outstretched to yank our lucifer out of danger.

Alistair and Elinor skid to a halt, whining in confusion.

Sam bends at the waist and puts his hands on his knees.

"You know," Andrew says into the silence. "I think we may have underestimated Percy."

The cat that is Percy makes a snarl-hiss sound, his mouth stretching in what might be a smile. He shifts back, and yep, he's smiling as he opens his mouth—

The world changes.

I clutch Caolan's arm for balance—emotional balance. I know this feeling. This has happened before in my lifetime, more than once. The last time—

Looking back at Percy, I see the shock on his face— shock and relief and sorrow.

His time as lucifer is done.

Before I can go to him, a startled sound grabs my attention. Even as I turn, I become aware that the feeling of being near the lucifer is still strong, and so it's no surprise to see Sam sitting on his ass in the dirt, shock and awe and fear written all over his expression.

"Sam?" Gideon chokes out, stumbling over to him. Sam tips his head back and gazes up at him dazedly.

"I think our life's going to change," he murmurs. "I need to make a to-do list."

I huff out a laugh and let go of Caolan's arm, only to sway. Wow. Maybe it wasn't just emotional balance I needed.

He grabs for me and slides an arm around my waist as the adrenaline high begins to drain away and I become aware of awful pain in my wrist—the same wrist that was broken not that long ago. *Please don't let it be broken again.*

"You need to sit," Caolan says, but I shake my head.

"I'm okay. Percy," I manage, and my wonderful, handsome, heroic elf sighs and helps me over toward my childhood friend.

"Hey," he says in his typical unruffled manner, and even though the aura of the lucifer is gone, he still projects that sense of calm and serenity he always has.

"Hey," I reply. "Busy day."

He chuckles. "You could say that." Glancing around, he adds, "It's going to be a busy night too."

That's putting it mildly. The truth is, it's going to be a busy few weeks getting what's left of Tish and Éibhear's plot unraveled, their people questioned and charged, and their bases dismantled. Then months more going through all the data.

Not to mention the ongoing task of resettling all the elves and dragons and helping them assimilate to Earth.

Cold panic strikes me at the thought of Percy not being there to help.

"You're not leaving CSG, are you?" I blurt, a little louder than I had intended.

There's a muffled shriek behind me, and we all turn to see Sam scrambling to get up. "No! No, I need you!" He races over, Gideon following. "Percy, you can't leave. I don't know anything about being in charge."

"I don't know," Alistair says thoughtfully, joining us. "You're pretty bossy."

Sam glares at him. "Don't you have a boyfriend to annoy?"

"My *lover* is currently seeing to his people."

As always when Alistair calls Aidan that, I force myself not to cringe.

"Come on," Percy says to Sam, gesturing with a

hand that's spattered with gore. "We should be doing that too."

"You won't leave, will you?" Sam asks again, and Percy shrugs.

"Not right away. I'll help you get settled into the job."

For a moment, I think Sam's going to argue, but then he heaves a sigh. "I guess you've earned a break. And a life that's not devoted to others."

Gideon groans, his face pained. "Our life is going to be at the mercy of the masses," he complains. Sam grabs his hand and pulls him toward where our troops are checking bodies to see who needs medical attention and who's beyond that point.

"Let's start now," he says. "This will be good for you."

Alistair trails after them, heckling Gideon, and Percy watches them fondly.

"This may be the only time I've ever second-guessed the magic," I begin, "but I really wonder if it knows what it's doing, pulling Gideon so close to the spotlight." He barely tolerates the attention he gets as a member of our team.

Percy chuckles. "The magic hasn't completely deserted me, and I get a strong feeling that Sam's not going to be in the limelight for too long—just long enough to handle these transition years. In a decade or so, they'll be able to get back to their life."

I study his face. "And are you going to get back to your life?" Beside me, Caolan shifts his weight, then carefully lets go of me, hovers for a second to make sure I stay upright, and walks away.

I love him so.

Percy gazes after him. "You've got a good one there. Even if you were too stubborn to realize it at first."

"He's amazing," I agree, mentally kicking myself for those days we could have been together but weren't. "But you're dodging the question. Are you okay?" I know what it's like to have your whole life change in a single second, and while it was for the best for me, I don't know how Percy's going to handle this upheaval for a second time.

He sighs. "I don't know. But I will be. I just… need to get used to things again."

"Helping Sam settle in will be a good way of easing yourself out," I point out. "You can slowly move away from… this." It hits me hard that I won't be seeing him and working with him every day. The last fifty years have been an incredible journey.

Pushing past the sudden lump in my throat, I add, "Maybe you can try dating again. I bet Alistair would happily show you everything there is to know about hookup apps." Officially, Percy's been single since before he became lucifer. Unofficially, he and Lily were on-again-off-again for about twenty years before she died. That's not widely known—in fact, I may be the only one aside from them who knew, although I think Andrew suspected. They were always so careful to hide it, especially from shifters with their keen sense of smell.

He makes a slight face. "I'm not sure I'm ready for anything Alistair has to teach in that area," he says dryly. "Did you hear about the time—"

"Percy."

He stops, then concedes, "Maybe. I don't know yet. Things changed rather suddenly." He gestures to the battlefield around us. Not far away, medical teams are coming through portals to assess and transport the injured. King Raðulfr and Brandt have joined Sam and Gideon and the others in checking on our people. "And you know my father is going to have some opinions to shove down my throat. If we weren't in the middle of nowhere with no cell reception, my phone would be ringing nonstop."

This is true.

"I just want you to be okay. Promise you'll call me if you need me. No matter what."

A faint smile crosses his face, and he claps me on the shoulder. "David, I'm going to call you even when I don't need you. Now stay here, and I'll send someone over to check you out."

He jogs away before I can protest that I'm perfectly fine, thanks… which is just as well, since we've known each other too long for me to be able to successfully lie to him. You'd think after so many years and so much training, I'd know better than to use every scrap of my own power like that… but on the other hand, if you can't do it during an apocalyptic battle to save the universe, when can you?

An arm slides around my waist, and I turn my head to look at the man who's changed my whole perspective on life.

"You need a medic," he says grimly, but I shake my head.

"Not as much as others," I assure him. "My wrist is sore, but I can still move my fingers. Other than that, I just need protein, water, and sleep." The only things that will help me recharge my inner power well. "But there'll be time for that later. There's too much to do now."

Two minutes later, I'm sitting on a folding chair that

the triage team brought with them and being examined by a paramedic. My man is stubborn and not above hauling me bodily around when I don't have the strength to stop him.

We'll fight about that later.

The sorcerer paramedic hands me a protein bar and a bottle of water. "Get started with these while I bandage your wrist. It's definitely not broken, but it's going to be painful for a few days, so ice and rest."

"Sure," I agree, ripping the bar open with my teeth.

The paramedic pauses. "You're not going to do any of that, are you?"

I swallow my first bite. "Ice and rest? Of course I am." As soon as things are under control at the office. Maybe tomorrow sometime.

She sighs. "I'll get you a sling."

Caolan comes back just then. "The king, Sam, and Percy are going back to headquarters, and you're going with them," he says in this bossy, overbearing tone that for some reason completely cranks my engine. If I weren't so drained that thinking is an effort, my cock would be standing at full attention.

"There are still things—"

He holds up a hand. Yep, I apparently have a fetish for dominating men. Or dominating Caolan, anyway. "Garin, Andrew, and Noah are staying here to oversee what's necessary. I'm assigning an elf with portal capabilities to assist them. Alistair and Gideon are going to visit the other compounds and ensure things are being managed correctly there. Elinor is going to coordinate from the office. And Sam said he needs your assistance."

Part of me is miffed that they managed to organize everything without me, but I push it aside and nod.

"Okay, then." The paramedic brings me a sling, and I shove the last of my protein bar into my mouth and slip it over my head. Once it's adjusted to her satisfaction, she waves me off.

I'm feeling a little stronger already and manage to walk under my own power to where Sam and Percy are standing with the king and Brandt.

"Okay?" Sam asks, his concerned gaze searching my face. It's so disconcerting to feel the soothing power of the lucifer radiating from him. Really, though, I already know he's going to be great at this job.

"All good," I assure him. "Caolan's just a worrywart."

Caolan makes an offended sound, then sniffs. "You'll take that back when you need my help later, Mr. One-Arm," he promises, and I choke back a groan of irritation as I remember how fucking hard it is to navigate life when you can't use both hands. Buttons in particular suck.

"You're so handsome," I tell him, and the whole group bursts out laughing. Caolan rolls his eyes as he turns away and opens the portal, but he's smiling.

Time to get to work.

EPILOGUE

David

THREE MONTHS LATER

PERCY LIFTS HIS GLASS. "It's been a year but feels like a minute. You'd kick my ass if I got maudlin, but I have to say, I miss you, Lily. I hope you're getting some rest in the spiritual plane and preparing to come back and kick ass in your next life."

"Kick ass, Lily," we echo, and drink.

It's just the six of us here right now, in the private dining room of Lily's favorite restaurant, taking a few moments to remember her before the others join us for dinner. Funnily enough, tonight was Alistair's idea—he booked the restaurant, then told us all what he'd planned and that he and the others who never really knew Lily would arrive an hour later. He's so irreverent and offbeat most of the time that most people don't realize how perceptive and empathetic he can be.

And here we are, a year to the day after Sam was kidnapped and Lily murdered. A year after we met

Noah. A year after we realized the depraved depths Tish had sunk to.

So much has happened since then.

Sam clears his throat. "I didn't know Lily for as long as any of you, but in just a few short months, she became one of my best friends. And I really wish she'd been here for the past year, because we laid bets on whether David would ever find love, and she owes me money." A startled laugh bursts from me as he raises his glass. "To Lily!"

We all drink, and then I ask, "She didn't think I'd ever find love?" That doesn't sound like Lily. She was always after me to date more, determined that I *would* find love.

Sam shakes his head. "No, she did. We both agreed on that. But she bet you'd end up with someone who was just as addicted to scheduling as you are. I said you'd be corrupted by a wild child."

"Caolan's not all that wild," Andrew points out, sounding amused. "Spontaneous, maybe. But he's got the same dependability that David does."

I purse my lips and consider. "No, I think Sam won. Caolan might be dependable, and he might be addicted to his phone—and Instagram—but he still doesn't like keeping track of time." There's no anxiety in me at the thought, because even though he's consistently late *or* early to everything, never on time no matter how many reminders and alarms he sets, I know with everything in me that he'll never let me down. Caolan is always there when I need him.

Things have been chaotic since The Showdown In Patagonia—and yes, that's what it's officially being referred to as. Andrew said it as a joke (at least, I hope it was a joke) the day after, not knowing that at that precise moment, Rabhya and a group of journalists were behind him, walking through reception on their way to the boardroom for a press conference. We've given up trying to convince people to call it anything else. It's going down in history as The Showdown In Patagonia.

In addition to dismantling Tish and Éibhear's cults and processing the people they'd roped in, many of whom had basically been brainwashed from childhood, there was the legal issue of Percy killing Tish to deal with. Since Tish had not yet officially been convicted, some of his lingering supporters—the ones we'd never actually managed to connect to the CCA, but who were part of it nonetheless—declared it to be murder. A few hundred witnesses saw Tish attack first, but to make sure there could be no question, Percy submitted to charisma and interrogation by a vampire judge. His name was cleared—and another judge, who'd been running the inquiry into the CCA and Tish, ruled that there could be no doubt of Tish's guilt even without the over-whelming new evidence we were uncovering. So that door was firmly closed.

Then, of course, there's been the transition from Percy's leadership to Sam's. There's no question of whether he's legitimately the lucifer, because we can all *feel* it, but he's young and very new to the community, so some people still want to grumble about it. Sam, thank-fully, is proving them all to be whiners without cause. And today was officially Percy's last day at CSG.

It's going to be weird without him.

If the new lucifer had been a stranger, someone we didn't know, the team would probably have moved on. That's what's always happened in the past. The idea is that this team is made up of people with whom the lucifer is comfortable, which is why it usually becomes a game of recruiting friends—Percy reached out to me and Lily and Andrew, and then I suggested Gideon, who I'd worked with before, and he brought Elinor into the group. Lily introduced us all to Nadege, who was our admin before Sam. We're all eminently qualified for our jobs, but they're not ever jobs that are advertised.

But since the new lucifer is Sam, things are different this time. He'd probably hunt us all down with the pencil he used to stab Alistair if we even thought of leaving. The first thing he did was recruit Noah to be our new admin (and boy, that's an experience. Sam could get cranky, but usually only if we asked stupid questions. Noah, on the other hand, is just cranky all the time. He's giving Gideon a run for his money. Andrew loves it).

The second thing Sam did? Try to find a way to convince Percy to stay in a consultative capacity. We all knew it wasn't going to happen, but Sam's clingy when it comes to his chosen family, so we let him have a shot. He's finally accepted that Percy needs to move on and live his own life.

"I can't believe this is the eeeeeeeeeeeeend!" he wails suddenly, putting his glass down and burying his face in his hands.

Well… he's mostly accepted it.

Gideon pats his back gingerly with one hand and eyes Sam's glass with the other. We've been toasting Lily for a while, and Sam's always more emotional when he's been drinking.

"It's not the end," Percy assures him, smiling wryly. "I'll be back to visit a lot. And you can call me anytime."

He's decided that he doesn't want to stay here, where his continued presence might be viewed as a crutch for Sam, but he definitely doesn't want to go back to England—he came to the States so long ago to put some distance between himself and his father, and nothing's changed in that regard. So instead, he's going to travel for a while, see if he finds somewhere that feels homey to settle in. First stop: Argentina. Apparently he liked the scenery and fresh air the day of the showdown.

While Percy mollifies Sam, Andrew leans over and asks, "Have you told him yet about your vacation?"

My eyes go wide and dart toward Sam, who fortunately didn't hear. "Not here," I hiss, and Andrew chuckles.

"That's a no, then."

I shrug. "It's not for another eight months. I thought I'd give him time to get past Percy going and then ease him into the idea." Caolan and I decided we need some time for just us: no CSG, no king, no constant demands on us. We both love our jobs, but since taking on the additional duties as official intermediaries between our respective governments, we haven't had any time to enjoy each other. We come home every night completely exhausted, and the only time we see each other during the day is when we're sitting across a table negotiating the latest fracas between our people.

If we want things to last between us, we need "us" time. Three months. Part of it, we'll be traveling—he wants to see the world, and I want to show him. But we'll also spend some of it at home, deciding what we want our future to look like and watching dumb movies from the twentieth century. We might even finally decide if we want to stay where we are or find a bigger house.

Three months isn't a lot of time for all that, but it's as long as either of us is comfortable taking off work, and even for that, we had to first agree that we'd wait for things to settle back into normality—or as close to it as it would get.

"Don't let him guilt you out of it," Andrew warns. "You need this."

I look over at Sam, barely forty years old and suddenly responsible for the well-being of so many. "He won't guilt me," I say confidently. He might be flustered at first, but he's been hinting that I need a vacation since he first joined the team and found out how long ago the last one was (hint: never).

Sam stands, his chest rising with a deep breath. "You all are the *best*, and I'm so lucky to know you. Now let's get the rest of the family in here!"

It's going to be a looooong night.

But a good one.

"No, I really want to try it," Caolan insists, following me into the apartment and closing the door behind us. I drop the keys in their designated bowl and turn to face him.

"You're not going to like it," I warn for what must be the fiftieth time since we first started talking about this a week ago.

"Alistair says I will. He says it's a guilty miracle."

I sigh. I knew he'd insist, so I prepared for this moment, but… "I haven't done this for about fifty years," I warn. "It becomes addictive, even though you know it's wrong. It took me a long time to stop."

"I want to try," he insists stubbornly.

How can I refuse? "Okay. Let's go into the kitchen. I cleaned in here this morning and don't want to make a mess so soon."

He follows me, anticipation lighting his face. His hair is slightly mussed from the breeze outside, and that, combined with the alcohol earlier, is making me horny.

Of course, I'm usually horny for Caolan. It doesn't take much. I guess that's part of the reason I'm so willing to help him with this.

In the kitchen, I get what we need and put it on the counter. He looks at it.

"So I just…?"

I nod. "Yes."

"It doesn't need any preparation?"

"Nope. Just unwrap and shove it in."

He takes a deep breath and does just that.

"So what do you think?"

Slowly chewing, he shrugs, then swallows the bite of Twinkie. "I'm not sure. It… it doesn't taste *good*, exactly, not like other cake. But it still mostly tastes like cake. But not the cream. That doesn't taste like cream?" He licks the remnants of it from his lips, frowning. "I'm not sure if I like it, but I want more. Is this magic? Does the Twinkie have a spell in it?"

I succumb to temptation, grab another one from the box, and rip open the packaging. "No spell, no magic. Just chemicals and sugar." I lift the evil little cake to my mouth, but Caolan rips it from my hand before I can take a bite. "Hey!"

"No," he scolds. "You said it took a long time to stop before. I don't want to be responsible for that happening again." He looks at the half still in his other hand. "I want more, but it's best I don't have it. We should have a real cake instead."

"Technically, this is a real cake," I counter, wondering if it would be bad for me to use a weave to immobilize him so I can get my snack back. It probably wouldn't do much for the trust in our relationship.

"Maybe." He eyes it doubtfully. "I don't like it as much as other cakes, though, and that makes it very strange that I want to keep eating it. I think you should investigate whether there's magic in it."

"Sure," I agree. "I'll start right now." I grab my Twinkie while he's distracted and take a big bite. Oh sweet chemical bliss.

I grimace. He's right. It's not as good as fresh cake with real cream or buttercream, but the urge to take another bite is almost instant. I look at the package, which has eight more of these evil temptations in it.

"Tape the box shut," I tell him. "I'll take it to the office tomorrow and give it to Alistair." Or any other shifter. They burn calories just by breathing. I take the remnant of his Twinkie from him and throw it and mine into the trash as he opens the junk drawer and pulls out a roll of packing tape.

"You were right," he concedes, wrapping the tape around the box. "This was a mistake."

"You had to experience it to understand." I pat his shoulder consolingly. "We'll probably both relapse sometime in the future. It happens."

"It might happen now," he mutters, staring at the tape-covered box. "Quick, distract me."

"Wanna fuck?"

His head whips around, attention completely diverted from the evil snack cakes. "Why didn't you suggest that before? We could have avoided all this. Come on." He grabs my hand, but instead of leading the way to the bedroom, he tugs me closer and uses his other hand to swipe the box of Twinkies off the counter. "Climb up."

Oooh, kitchen sex. "We need lube," I remind him. Sure, we're surrounded by food products that could substitute, but I had enough of that before K-Y was invented, thank you very much.

"Later," he says. "First I get to suck you. I want to replace the taste of that cream with yours."

I open my pants, shove them down and off, then hoist myself onto the counter, legs spread. Caolan drops to his knees, and we both do a wiggle/shimmy to get into place. Once we realized the kitchen counter was the perfect height for blowjobs, it became a favorite of ours.

Caolan leans forward and kisses the tip of my already hard cock. "Hello, precious," he murmurs. "I've missed you."

I snort. "We had sex this morning," I remind him. It was hot—in the shower. I may need to get a new loofah, though.

"That was hours ago," he counters, then leans back and purses his lips. "Move your hips forward. I want your balls."

"I'll fall," I protest, but do it anyway. If I lean back and prop myself up on my hands…

"Perfect," Caolan announces, then closes his mouth over my cock.

I yelp, but before I can lose myself in the sensation of his hot, wet mouth around me, he takes my sac in a firm grip.

I'm not ashamed to say I beg.

With his hands and mouth, he works me over so beautifully, bringing me to the very edge and then backing off, switching tactics until I'm not sure which way is up anymore. He's stroking my dick, his mouth on my taint, when I feel the tingle begin in the soles of my feet.

"Caolan," I gasp in warning, and in a flash his mouth is on my cock again, and that's all it takes to make me spurt.

I slump back, my jellylike arms barely able to hold me up as I gasp for air. Caolan gets to his feet, licking his lips and looking very proud of himself. He leans in, and I gather the energy to meet him halfway for a kiss.

"I love you," he murmurs, and like always, those words make everything inside me click into place.

"Love you too."

Time is a social construct. Schedules? Invented to manage time. But love? Love transcends societies. It spans cultures and dimensions. It took me a long time to find someone I could love unreservedly, who'd love me the same way. I thought I needed someone who shared my habits.

I was wrong. I was looking in the wrong places. But thanks to two genocidal supervillains, he found me anyway.

"Caolan?" I ask against his mouth.

"Mmmm."

"Let's call in sick tomorrow, turn off our phones, and spend the day in bed."

Thanks so much for reading *Sorcerers Always Satisfy*! If you'd like to find out what happened at the singles party David said he'd organize, don't miss the bonus scene! Subscribe to my monthly newsletter: bit.ly/LouisaMBonus and download it now.

If you're in the mood to talk spoilers, head over to my Facebook Reader Group, RoMMance With Becca & Louisa and join the conversation.

Want a HEA for Percy? *Dragon Ever After* is book one in my spin-off series, Here Be Dragons.

If you're an "extras" kind of person, check out my Patreon (patreon.com/louisamasters) for early access to chapters, artwork, and other bonus material!

ALSO BY LOUISA MASTERS

Saddles & Suits

Alistair's Extraordinaries

Grave Situation

Elemental Men: The Complete Series

Style Me

Rebrand

Couture

Elf Magic

Wooing the Wiccan

Enticing the Elf

The Collective

Higher Demon

Demon Hunter

Demons-In-Law

Asher

Micah

Zachary

Franklin U

Mr. Romance

The Holigay Hookup *related novella

Batting Style

Ghostly Guardians

Spirited Situation

Vortex Conundrum

Conduit Crisis

Gateway Catastrophe

Here Be Dragons

Dragon Ever After

The Professor's Dragon

The Dragon Experiment

Conspiracy of Dragons

Hidden Species

Demons Do It Better

One Bite With A Vampire

Hijinks With A Hellhound

Sorcerers Always Satisfy

Hidden Species Box Set

Met His Match

Charming Him

Offside Rules

A Christmas Chance (novella)

Between the Covers (M/F)

Joy Universe

I've Got This

Follow My Lead

In Your Hands

ABOUT THE AUTHOR

Louisa Masters started reading romance much earlier than her mother thought she should. As an adult, she feeds her addiction in every spare second. She spent years trying to build a "sensible" career, working in bookstores, recruitment, resource management, administration, and as a travel agent before finally conceding defeat and devoting herself to the world of romance novels.

Louisa has a long list of places first discovered in books that she wants to visit, and every so often she overcomes her loathing of jet lag and takes a trip that charges her imagination. She lives in Melbourne, Australia, where she whines about the weather for most of the year while secretly admitting she'll probably never move.

http://www.louisamasters.com

www.ingramcontent.com/pod-product-compliance
Lightning Source LLC
Chambersburg PA
CBHW021244060726
47590CB00005B/1888